On Edge

Gin Price

The Poisoned Pencil
An imprint of Poisoned Pen Press

First Edition 2015

10 9 8 7 6 5 4 3 2 1

Library of Congress Catalog Card Number: 2015946476

ISBN: 9781929345205 Trade Paperback
9781929345212 E-book

The Poisoned Pencil
An imprint of Poisoned Pen Press
6962 E. First Ave., Ste. 103
Scottsdale, AZ 85251
www.thepoisonedpencil.com
info@thepoisonedpencil.com

Printed in the United States of America

To those who create and those who explore, seeing possibilities where most see only limitations—you inspire me.

To my family, whose support was all that kept me going at times. Specifically, my mom, Debra; my sister, Rachel; and my children, Shyla and Hayes.

To my agent, Andrea, who fought to find an editor who would understand that freerunning is a subject worthy of attention and *never* gave up. Thank you!

To my editor Ellen, who simply gets me. You bring out the best in me. It's a pleasure!

To the few who have touched me deeply by performing simple acts of kindness without reason. Sharon and Randy—two people who deserve recognition.

And lastly, a special dedication to my best friend from school gone way too soon: April. You are sorely, sorely missed.

Acknowledgments

I would like to thank all of the graffiti artists, and all of the traceurs, pro and amateur alike, who have braved criticism and snark from the Internet and posted their videos anyway. It doesn't matter how swank you are. It doesn't matter how up. I have enjoyed every vid from the fantastically bad, to the incredibly good, and I will never stop watching. You are appreciated. Not every watcher is a h8r. Keep 'em coming.

I must thank Mr. Dan who had spent many hours listening to me spout off ideas for this book, and who, with one suggestion, changed the course of my novel. I should've thought of it, considering my fondness, but sometimes we can't see what's right in front of us. Thanks for being my glasses.

I also have to thank David for being there for me when times were tough. When pain kept me down and threatened to change me, you gave me the ambition I needed to get up and find my adventurous side again. Thank you for supplying me with the perfect personality for my Brennen. I look forward to many more adventures.

One

I wasn't going to make it.

I had a stitch in my side as widespread as the distance between the Pizza Pie Pagoda and the apartment roof we ran across, so the chances I'd screw up and smack my head against the concrete waiting below were pretty good. The waist of my yoga pants began to unroll, the fabric sliding down with every pump of my aching legs and I had to waste precious energy to pull them up. But if I didn't, and I stepped on a hem, I'd stumble.

Stumbling would be bad—like lose-a-tooth-on-the-balance-beam-the-day-before-prom bad. Already I could feel the quiver of fatigue in my knees signaling my eventual burnout.

"He's going to catch me, he's going to catch me," I chanted between panted breaths.

I spoke more to myself than my companion, but he answered anyway. "Nah, baby-girl, you got this. Forearm, shoulder, booty, then knee up and walk away. Daily cake."

I grunted. Easy for him to say. This fiasco made it five consecutive hours of balls-out athletics for me while he was on hour two, and only slightly less out of breath than I.

"Get back here!" The voice behind bellowed, growing closer.

I threw off my rhythm a fraction to look behind me. "Damn, he's on us. How'd he get up here so fast?"

"You realize I had you this time, right?"

Appalled at my friend Surge's attempt to claim a victory when the game had clearly been called due to weather conditions—it was raining cops—I ran faster, pushing myself beyond my limits toward the roof's edge. I didn't care if my pants fell around my ankles mid-flight; I was going to win our little game today—and moon the state of Michigan doing it.

But first, I had to stay out of jail.

"Whoa! Come back." The cop yelled. He sounded more concerned now than angry.

Too late. There was no coming back once we'd made the decision to run.

"Boosh!" Surge yelled as we both hopped the lip of the roof and leapt across the expanse between the buildings, sprawled out and reaching through the air like action heroes.

Unlike the movies, nothing happened slow enough for me to process the danger of a jump. I committed to the plunge and depended on ingrained knowledge to take over.

The Pizza Pie Pagoda building came up fast. I bent my legs to absorb the shock and let my exhausted body fall forward and to the side. The remaining energy of the landing pushed me over in a Side-Roll, taking the impact from thigh to shoulder until the momentum brought me up to my feet again. Hurray, incoming bruise.

Surge's Roll was swankier than mine, but for once he didn't gloat. Probably because we didn't have time.

"You kids all right?" The cop called from the building over.

We didn't take the time to answer him verbally. We just waved off his concern and continued to ignore his command to give ourselves up. Surge grabbed my elbow and helped me to the side of the pizza place where we were able to hang off the side of the roof and drop down into the alley.

"How you doing?" Surge asked me, once we were making distance between us and the cop.

"Well, I worked my butt off in gymnastics practice, ran around the mall only to get kicked out because of your food court tabletop trick—"

"You've got to admit that was swank," he interrupted. "How was I supposed to know they were going to call in the real blue?"

"And now I've spent the last ten minutes upgrading from a trespassing ticket to an arrest."

"Only if we got caught, which we didn't. So you owe me five bucks." He grinned at me and I couldn't help but return it.

"We aren't off main, yet." I slapped his extended palm away. "When I'm home and couching, you'll get your five."

I tugged off my black hoodie as we walked, stuffing it behind a dumpster to come back for later. We knew the drill. You didn't walk around wearing the same colored clothes after a cop was running you down. The next corner you turned would probably have you stuffed in a squad car before the first lie left your mouth. Changing shirts wasn't much, but it was better than nothing. Besides, with my hoodie on, most cops mistakenly took me for a guy. I guess they thought girls had better things to do than monkey around the cityscape.

"Damn, there's the cop," Surge said.

I looked down the block and frowned. He didn't seem to notice us any more than the other pedestrians, but to be safe, I tugged Surge into the Slow Drip.

The few tables inside the coffee shop were up front with a window view, while racks and racks of tee-shirts and other gift items created an aisle to the registers in the back. Outside, a few more two-seater tables were full of the loitering public, making blending in a little easier.

"I guess we take a time-out for refreshments," I said.

Surge paced, looking out the storefront with his lips pursed. "He's going to keep circling and look in here eventually. Not sure stopping was a good idea this time."

"Hey Surge," a girl called out from behind us.

I turned and nodded a greeting at Ramona as she chatted up Surge. Dressed in her coffee-pot-shaped apron and tear-drop visor-hat, she was clearly working the counter.

Wenda, her best friend and my gymnastics nemesis, walked up and stood next to her. We were all on the same team but no one would know it the way they acted—except Wenda and I were both wearing our Kennedy Gymnastics Team tee-shirts.

"Hey guys," I said, trying to be a beacon of polite through the thick fog of seething hatred. Ramona tried to smile but settled on a grimace. Wenda didn't even try to hide her nostril-flare face.

"Ramona-girl, you think you could get us out the back of this place?" Surge asked.

Standing on her tiptoes, Wenda leaned up to whisper something in Ramona's ear while staring at me.

Subtle.

"I can take one of you through," Ramona started to say.

Surge snorted. "Forget it."

"No, no." I knew this was a good opportunity to draw less attention to ourselves. "Surge, you go out the back and I'll go out the front." I smiled my second-best smile at Wenda, while talking to him. "We'll meet up at the library and finish what we started earlier."

His glare at the two girls melted when he turned to me, and I suspected he did that on purpose to show anti-bitchery support. "Ooo. I accept your challenge! I'll even beat you there." He winked and then turned to Ramona. "Lead the way, mama."

With Ramona taking Surge out the back door, Wenda and I were left standing there. "Guess I'll see you next practice." I said.

"Oh, didn't you hear? We're going to do individual practices until coach returns from her vacation."

Odd. I hadn't heard, but I wasn't exactly surprised. Since Regionals, I'd suspected that some of the girls were mad at me. Now my suspicions had been confirmed.

"Well, then. See ya at school."

"Whatever." She did the hand brush-off and turned her back on me, cutting me down without saying another word.

Shaking my head, I turned and left the coffee shop.

No one had ever looked at me with such hatred before, and I couldn't figure out where it came from. I knew gymnastics competition pitted us against each other a lot—and I'd definitely ridden the group hard at Regionals at the end of last season—but it seemed like there was more to her attitude than just rivalry, but whatever. I couldn't puzzle through her bullshit when I still needed to get a few blocks away to avoid a tour of the city jail.

Losing my concern for Wenda was easy once I was freerunning again on my way to the library. No troubles or stressful thoughts stood a chance against the heart-pumping adrenaline rush of parkour.

I raced down streets using the objects in my way to increase my pace instead of slow me down. I swung under a metal railing and leaped over its parallel twin. I jumped over a fire hydrant and the three bikes locked on the rack right next to it, all without choking up.

My seamless movements cancelled out Surge's head start, and as I rounded the corner on the last block to the library, I caught sight of my friend a block to my right.

At the same time, he noticed me.

I heard his laugh across the distance and the challenge within it spurred me on. "Oh, you are so getting *shown*," I promised quietly, forcing my legs into motion.

So close, so close! If I could get to the lion statue first, I'd get the prize, but Surge wasn't going to make it easy on me. We both ran full speed, coming closer to each other and to our destination.

I vaulted over one wide stone railing, Kong-style, with my feet straight out in front, ready to catch me for my landing.

I didn't expect anyone to be standing there.

Two

"Oh my Gawd! You stupid skank!"

My feet landed briefly on the edge of the step in front of the girl running her mouth. Without interrupting my flow, I leapt up onto the flat surface of the stone rail and looked over my shoulder in time to see Surge launch over the chick's backside as she bent to pick up her books. He sailed through the air with one leg extended and the other bent forming a perfect L.

Classic! But I held my applause. I wasn't about to be outdone.

I didn't bother answering the girl's "skank" comment. No point, really. I was probably the only girl in school that could still be called a virgin, but neither title could be considered flattering, so why quibble?—as my mom used to say.

Calling me stupid felt a little harsh. In my opinion, she had no one to blame but herself for our near-collision. Anyone who was anyone knew these streets were more "ours" than "theirs" now. Even according to the Balls-In-A-Bunch Mayor Daemen: "Our streets have been taken over by these freerunners and graffiti painters."

I liked to think of that as an admission of ownership.

Besides, if she'd been looking up, instead of texting while waddling down the grand staircase, she'd be in possession of all her papers instead of chasing them around.

I jumped onto the back of a lion statue and ran up his spine until I teetered on the very top of his wavy mane.

Hold up.

Surge should've been on me by now, talking some smack to try and throw off my game.

The arches of my feet gripped the lion's ears as I paused to look for him.

Figures. I'd been about to do something exceptionally freak, and Surge wasn't even watching. He was bent over picking up the blonde's scattered papers as she stood there being completely unhelpful. Kinda like me, but I had distance as an excuse. When she started babbling incoherently about pickpockets and diversionary tactics while clutching her purse, I felt the urge to slap her down a bit. So what? We like to live free so that means we're criminals?

"Sorry about your unfortunate grip. My fault," I apologized-ish.

The girl turned her nose up at me and busied herself accepting the papers Surge held out to her, and though I couldn't hear what she said, her smile told a story of flirtation I'd read on plenty of faces before hers.

My boy's dark skin glistened with sweat earned from our one-upping game, so his white wife-beater stuck to his chest like skin, accentuating muscles all the girls drooled over. Who wouldn't flirt with him?

Other than me, of course.

Surge was...well Surge. I think there are laws against ogling my brother's friends. But if I were going to ogle any of them, he'd be my pick. It either had something to do with the fact

Surge and I got on well, or because the rest of my brother's friends were exactly like my brother: a bunch of jackasses with questionable morals.

"Surge." I complained. Okay, maybe I whined a little, but after the last few hours I deserved a minor meltdown or two.

Chased by the cops, ditching my favorite hoodie, and playing hide-and-seek in the Slow Drip so I didn't get arrested made me a little cranky. And so did distractions in the form of name-calling cookie-cutter chicks.

Nothing should disrupt the groove while freerunning, since the whole idea behind the expression is to get from point A to point B without pause. Fluid movement at all times was key.

Surge was obviously thinking about a different type of fluid and where he wanted to move it to.

"Are you *really* trying to get laid mid-game?" I swung in front of the lion's face and hooked my foot into his perpetually roaring mouth. Pushing off, I performed a backflip with my feet extended and landed effortlessly on the rail. Not the move I'd planned a few minutes ago, but Surge's grin said it all.

"You and your acrobatics." He shook his head at me and waved an absent farewell to the girl.

Like all females in Surge's life, she failed to hold his interest, though this dismissal could be a new speed record. Of course, her calling me skank could've been a factor. Surge was nothing if not loyal to my family.

Blowing her off like crumbs on a shirt, he hopped up a few stairs until he stood even with me. Holding his arms out to his sides, he bowed. "I do concede to thee, Lady of The Ledge."

He read a *Best of Shakespeare* book last year. The experience made him talk funny sometimes, but I liked it because he dubbed me Lady Ledge, LL for short. The name caught on and thankfully replaced the dopey street name my brother gave me. I couldn't live with being called Pigeon all the time, and the jury was still out on my real name, Emanuella.

"Sweet!" I flexed at Surge's praise and caught the reward he threw at me. Toffifay! The caramel, hazelnut, and chocolate candy goodness—my only addiction. My mom loved them when she was alive, and always kept a pack at the house. You couldn't find 'em at regular stores sometimes, so they were worth showing off for.

He looked at his watch as I shoveled a few pieces in my mouth—a slob move I never would've done in front of anyone else.

"We better get going. Your pops is going to have my beautiful black buttocks if you don't show up for the we're-going-to-screw-you-over fest tonight."

My dad insisted that I go to the school board meeting in case a student's perspective was needed to keep Kennedy High from closing. What a big waste of time. It'd cost too much to bus us all across town to Branfort, so our school was safe, in my opinion, but my father was paranoid.

"I don't trust those sons of bitches," he'd said over breakfast. "You're going to meet me there tonight and look forlorn and pathetic. Tell Surge I said hi and he better have you at the meeting."

I'd relayed the message to Surge when we first hooked up, hence why he looked slightly panicked now. My pops is a big, white boy trucker, who told whatever guy came 'round the house that he knew places to hide bodies all over the U.S. Maybe I should've been embarrassed by his violent imagery, but he probably felt threats were his only way of protecting me from my brother's friends while he was away delivering car parts and whatnot cross-country.

In truth, he didn't have to worry. Between Surge and my brothers, no one dared ask me out. I guess most little sisters would hate that kind of blockage, but I could honestly say a boy didn't exist in my territory I wanted to date. Not that I looked. A boyfriend wasn't a priority. I had dreams of going to college on a gymnastics scholarship, and after coming in first at Regionals, I was getting closer to that goal.

I figured my win, and the huge deal the media made out of the school I came from, was proof that Pops had nothing to worry about. Still, Surge was right, we had to go. We could run from the cops, but my dad was another story. "Alright, motor on."

I walked back up the spine of the lion ready to start the freerun flow again, only to hear Surge cluck his tongue in the code we used for incoming security. We'd used it so much lately I was surprised we didn't have blisters on the roofs of our mouths.

I dismounted from the statue and waved at the sharply dressed library guard who came storming down the steps toward me.

"You almost got close this time, Carl!"

"Quit antagonizing him, LL. Come on."

Surge grabbed my hand and practically dragged me all the way to City Hall.

We stayed grounded, which made the travel time longer, but Surge refused to freerun so close to police headquarters after our earlier encounter. I couldn't blame him. I faced a ticket or an arrest for disorderly conduct. Surge was on probation, thanks to the trespassing tickets he'd accumulated over the past two years. If he got busted now, he'd not only be in violation, but they'd probably add every charge they could: malicious destruction of property, failure to yield to pedestrians—breathing. That's what happens when freedom of expression collides with boundaries.

We arrived downtown with a few minutes to spare, but no time to catch our breath as we hurried to the front door.

City Hall is a three-story building, if you included the basement where all the financial offices were. That's where you went to pay your "idiot tickets," as Pops called them.

The outside looked like someone had painted the building with mortar and thrown pebbles at it. Most of the pebbles had either lost their shine or fallen off during the years since the building's birth, which was in 1954, according to the plaque above the main entrance.

Once, City Hall had been a modern and well cared-for establishment. Now, years of neglect and angry, destructive criminals had brought it down. An ongoing theme in the good ole city of Three Rivers.

A couple of cops held the front door open for us. Surge tensed as we passed as if he expected a net to come down on his head.

"Stop looking so shifty," I scolded as we walked down the corridor. "Cops within a mile radius will home in on that look of guilt."

"Don't need a mile when their jail is attached to this building, LL."

"It's been an hour and he didn't get a good look at us. Paranoid much?"

I opened the double doors to the conference room and blinked. The proceedings seemed to be on hold, as the board members talked amongst themselves. The lull made our entrance center-stage. Yippee.

The walls were lined with the general public. Police officers stood at attention at ten-foot intervals to protect and serve—the board members. They eyed us suspiciously as we entered.

"See? I just got mentally written four tickets by those cops for SWB."

The officers were staring at us hard, but that's probably in their job description. "SWB?" I asked.

"Standing While Black."

I laughed a little louder than could be considered good manners, earning me a crooked-finger-beckon from my Pops.

"There are two white cops here and the rest, well, aren't. You can't say that," I said, surfing the bodies toward the seats my father saved for us.

"They're still paid by Whitey. We're on the Branfort side, remember?"

I rolled my eyes. Surge was a victimized black man in his own mind, trapped in a diverse community that never did anything racist toward him. He had to invent things to tell his cousins in California.

"You're late," Pops growled, looking over my head at Surge.

With a playful slap I chastised him for bullying as I snuck in behind his gigantic body. Despite my father's dramatics, he really could be described as a big teddy bear. "Sit, Surge. No way am I staying here alone."

My father shushed me and I sat down without another word.

The board members gathered their tiny brains and melded them together, whispering among themselves until... "We've come to a decision."

"Wait! That's it? You've come to a decision in ten minutes and without hearing what everyone has to say?"

The crowd collectively jostled for a better look at the guy who spoke, mumbling their concerns about his outburst.

"Young man," a rotund woman barked from the council chairs, trying to be heard over the growing din. "The parents here have spoken eloquently enough for your case. We feel—"

The young man in question stood on his chair and pointed his finger at each board member. "We, the students, are the most affected. We deserve to have a voice."

Huh, I thought. The guy kind of sounded like my Pops.

I gave him a quick once-over, wondering, probably like everyone else, whether or not he was legitimate or starting trouble on a dare from his friends. He wore his pants baggy but not thug-y and a hoodie with the hood portion pushed back instead of drawn up over his dark hair. But his face, from what I could see from my side view, was the most startling attribute. I couldn't see if he was hot or anything, but his skin was bright red with anger, like he was really pissed at not being allowed some mic time.

"Could someone please escort this young man out?"

"He has a right to speak," someone shouted.

"This has dragged on long enough," someone else countered. And the fighting began.

By then, the local police had their hands on the guy who started the disturbance and jerked him off his chair. I gasped and stood, feeling like I should do something to help him, but what?

"This is bullshit," the guy yelled.

His gaze searched the crowd for support and landed on… me of all people. I tried to encourage him with a "right-on" smile, but our moment of camaraderie was broken by a mass of bodies as people stood to argue with each other or get a better look at the drama.

A really old, fragile-looking man banged his gavel on the oval table at the back of the room and rose to make an announcement. "Settle down, people. Settle down."

A cop was whispering into the young guy's ear while giving him a quick pat down. The other officers were motioning with their hands for everyone to sit and regain control of themselves. There was still grumbling, but the old guy who seemed to be in charge spoke over the noise.

"This outburst does not change the board's verdict! Due to the city's current financial crisis, we have no choice but to close both Kennedy and Branfort. The students will move to a central location in Three Rivers, and attend what used to be known as Three Rivers Academy."

My Pops hates it when I swear, but for once he didn't say a word as I jumped out of my chair, my former confidence in Kennedy's stability shattered. "That's fu—!" Of course, he probably couldn't hear me as total chaos broke out at City Hall.

Three

For weeks all everyone talked about was the school closings and the impending relocation to Three Rivers Academy, which used to be a school for dumb kids.

Well, we were all about to move in, so what did that say about us?

My brother, Warp, said he wasn't going to a school for 'tards but Pops flicked him in the ear and said something about karma. So I kept my mouth shut.

Warp seemed to lack that ability.

He called an emergency meeting of our parkour group once everyone was home from summer vacation, to complain about the move to a new school and to talk tactics. Tactics for what, I wasn't sure, but it couldn't be good.

For twenty minutes he rambled on about which gangs to avoid, based on rumors he heard, and which groups were all talk. I wanted to say "you mean other than this one?" but I knew Warp would see my joke as a challenge and up his presence level in school to prove to me he could be feared.

Pride, in high school, was the seed that destroyed entire groups, Pops said. I was pretty sure he was spot-on, so I decided to keep my snarky comments in check.

The "homework" Warp gave us included scouting the new school and becoming familiar with the surrounding terrain in case we came head-to-head with our rivals from Branfort.

Rivals, he'd said. I rolled my eyes. Branfort used to be just another school in our city. Then two years ago, they somehow became public enemy number one.

Now that we were about to shack-up under the same schoolhouse roof, Warp decided to make war plans, another step toward his goal to turn our extracurricular group into his "gang."

Unfortunately, the transformation was nearing completion. If I questioned Warp's instructions, I found no backing except Surge, and we were often outvoted, so to speak. Not that our group had ever been a democracy. There hadn't been a need when my eldest brother formed it. Everyone was united by the love of freerunning and our focus relied solely on the training. We confronted our fears and developed a peaceful show of harmony between the environment and the human body.

All of those ideals were now lost to Warp's ambitions. What a waste. My eldest brother Ander's teachings of respect, honor, and balance didn't even get a once-over at meetings anymore.

God I missed him and the simpler times.

I'd sometimes fantasize about Ander coming home and thwapping Warp upside the head to put him back in his place, but that wouldn't happen any time soon. Away at college, he couldn't afford to take the time off work to come home, and Pops couldn't afford to bring him in for a visit either, since the care of Warp and I sucked up most of his trucker wages.

I wrote to Ander all the time through email. His school supplied computers and, lucky for me, so did my next-door neighbor. The woman was ninety and had better gear than we did in our house. The computer in Pops' room had Windows '93, I think. I didn't even know they had computers back then.

While Warp mapped out the night's practice run in the park's sandbox—complete with crossbones where Branfort students were known to hang—I thought about what I would say in my next email to Ander. "Dear Ander, Warp has gone off his nut. Please advise."

"LL, you coming?"

Surge, Warp, and four other pairs of eyes were staring impatiently at me. I figured I must've missed the inspiring huddle formation at the end of the meeting with a war yelp on three.

"Yeah, sorry."

Warp gave me his special glare. "If you fall behind because you weren't listening to the route, we're not waiting on you."

I rolled my eyes. "Whatever."

So, of course, I fell behind. Surge doubled back for me and gave me a quick rundown of the night's path, but I would've been content to fly solo. I disliked order anyway.

"What the hell?"

He squinted toward the group in the distance and my gaze followed. Our crew had paused on the ledge of a wall, looking down. My brother wasn't visible.

Oh God...did he tank? Serious injuries in street improv parkour were expected, but Warp was one big callus. Nothing but a life-threatening injury would slow him down. My heart raced ahead with assumptions and a cold coating of dread poured down my arms. He might be a douche-bag sometimes, but he'd always be my brother.

Oh please, let him be okay. I couldn't stand losing another piece of my family. After mom, we all held each other up like a house of cards. If one more fell…

The moment we climbed up the wall to join the others, I went from being worried about him to wanting to strangle him. My body shook from the swing between moods. Or maybe it was the suppressed urge to smack the dumb out of him.

Warp stood a few yards away from a *writer*, a graffiti artist, holding a can of spray paint in each hand. My group had obviously interrupted whatever it was the guy was making, and since my brother took issue with all writers, he couldn't resist stopping to harass him.

"What are you doing over this way, Branfort? This is Kennedy Country. You're gooping up our walls with your chicken-scratch."

"Technically, this is TRA Country, Kennedy. I'm checking out the turf, same as you, I'm guessing."

I jumped off the brick wall, landing close to my brother and his adversary so I could run a little interference. Looking at the design, I thought it looked cool as hell.

Instead of simply tagging his crew's name or his own call sign, he was making a masterpiece against a subtle swirling vortex background. Off to one side, beaming sunrays parted billowing clouds, glistening off the central face of a pretty girl with long dark hair and greenish-brown eyes. Below he'd written a name in bubbled letters:

"Heather."

I hadn't realized I'd said the name out loud until everyone looked at me, including the writer from Branfort. When our eyes met they held each other like some sappy girly movie at an intro moment.

Wow.

I recognized him right away, too, but pretended I didn't so I could take a second to check him out at close range. He had hazel eyes and dark-brown hair with a little patch of pure white on the side. Yes, we'd definitely run into each other before, but now that I saw him real good, I knew the school board meeting hadn't been the first time I'd seen him.

A little over two years ago, he and his family were on the TV begging for a witness to come forward in his sister's murder. Her name was Heather.

He didn't have the white patch in his hair back then and he'd grown into his nose, but I knew him to be the awkward little brother on TV.

The guy I saw now was nothing if not Depp-fine. What was his name again? Bran, Bren…? I looked at the small sig in the bottom corner of the piece on the wall. *Haze*. Huh. I was way off.

Or, like the rest of us, he had a street name. But if someone didn't pull him and my brother apart, Haze was about to get a new nickname, Native American style: Smear.

"Are you kidding me right now? You stopped the flow to gawk at his artwork?"

"This piece of shit doodling ain't artwork, and this asshole needs to learn we're not gonna tolerate amateur vandalism on our blocks."

"You're being a jerk, Warp. Can we keep going, please?"

I watched Haze spin the cans in his hands, as calm as if he wasn't surrounded by a bunch of guys who wanted to kick the crap outta him. "You should listen to your girl," he said.

Warp wrinkled his nose. "That's my sister."

"Really?" Haze's eyes twinkled a little and a corner of his mouth curved. "Good. I saw you at the meeting, right?"

Good? What did he mean good? My stomach squeezed. "Um, yeah."

His grin seemed to cover his whole face. "It's real nice to see you again."

I couldn't decide if Haze was brave, or utterly special-ed. We were in the midst of a serious turf issue and he was instigating a pickup.

"Don't look at my sister like that!" Warp growled.

Surge laughed so loud and hard he was doubled over, apparently enjoying Haze's ballsy-ness. Warp and I glared at him but he only laughed harder. The other members of our group held back their cackling...barely.

"Like what? You got a problem with people thinking your sister's beautiful? I'd think you'd be used to it." Haze took a step back probably so he could face me *and* keep my brother in sight. Or maybe just completely drive Warp nuts by giving me the once-over. "I could create a masterpiece with her face alone. Look at those shiny brown eyes and high cheekbones flushed from running. Or maybe something else?" Again, he smiled the smile that I swear all boys learn in sixth grade: Cute and full of promise. "She's an artist's muse."

Warp took a step and so did I. "Stop," I said in a voice hopefully low enough to sound authoritative, but neither of them seemed swayed by it.

"And the blue stripe down the side? Rebellious but doesn't take away from the dark brown perfection that is your hair."

Artists. Unafraid of words and lethal when using them. If I were the type to swoon, I'd have face-planted right there—even knowing that he'd said what he did to rile my brother.

Surge, at this point, was gonna need a de-fib if he couldn't catch his breath.

"You think that shit's funny? You mocking my sister, you fucking fag?" Warp cussed, trying to get Haze's attention, but the writer's eyes were set firmly on me, his smile as genuine as though he'd meant every flowery word.

"I like it," he finished, tracing the side of his own face to indicate my blue strand.

Warp's right eye twitched and I felt his muscles coil under my hold.

I liked Haze's approval because he was the first person who said anything positive about my lock of blue hair. Still, for goading my brother, his sanity was in question.

"Thanks," I said lamely.

My gratitude came out more clipped than I intended, but I was glad it didn't come out like a sigh.

Past his limit, Warp pushed me out of the way and stepped up to bat, grabbing the front of Haze's shirt in his fists. "I said stop eyeballing my sister!"

"Get your hands off me before you get hurt," Haze warned.

Dropping his paint cans, he grabbed my brother's wrists and looked as if he were going to do something of a karate nature. My brother's position sucked, to say the least.

"Warp! This is getting absurd. No one's going to think you're the big bad, picking on someone who's clearly outnumbered."

The air around Haze and Warp trembled with suppressed testosterone. Neither looked ready to back down. I knew sooner or later someone was going to pop. "Surge, do something."

Standing up straight, Surge rubbed his thumb over his nostrils and sniffed, collecting himself. "My cousins always say, never interfere in a cockfight."

I glared at him.

"A'ight, a'ight. Come on, Big W. You're making your sister freak."

"Then take her outta here!"

I folded my arms over my chest, hoping I looked pissed with a dash of violent intent. "I'm not going anywhere!"

A door in the alley slammed open, banging against the wall, and a dark silhouette appeared in the archway. "Ya'll better get off my damn property!"

I squinted at the intruder but couldn't make out more than a lump for the head. The gun, though—crystal clear.

Four

Funny thing about teens who are constantly accused of being trespassers—we all know the sound of impending death when we hear it. Like cockroaches exposed to light, the second we heard the familiar pumping action of the shotgun, we scattered.

"Surge," my brother yelled.

"Got it," Surge answered, claiming responsibility for me while Warp and the rest of the boys ran up the side of the apartment building to take the attention off my escape.

I scaled the brick wall and teetered on the top, irrationally concerned for Haze, who was left behind to collect his paint cans. With a speed that said this wasn't his first criminal excursion, I saw him drop the cans into his antique doctor's bag, snap it closed, and sling the homemade shoulder strap over his back. He then ran at the wall and leapt, his quick feet and forward momentum carrying him up the face and close enough to the top to vault over the ledge to safety—all without taking buckshot to the ass. Nice.

Not that he couldn't stand to learn a few tricks—

"LL! Let's go."

I brought my attention back to Surge as he took my hand, and we jumped.

Livia Menesa stood in my kitchen a week or so later, munching on the last bite of her Pop-Tart while waiting for me to walk with her to school. As I entered the room, I caught the tail-end of my father's explanation/rant as to why I didn't attend the first week of classes and winced. Poor Liv and her bleeding ears. Pops could go on for hours on any topic, let alone one he felt strongly about.

I poured two cups of coffee and handed one to her.

"And I was right, too!" Pops was saying. "Two shootings last week before they put metal detectors at the doors and security in the parking lot. What if one of my kids had been killed? I'd go Rambo on that damned school board! You can trust me on that."

"Pops." I groaned, as I grabbed the coffee cup from his hand and set it down. I'd cleaned up enough sloshed coffee after the arm-waving tirade he performed for me an hour earlier—a performance I didn't wish to repeat. "Rambo? Really? You need to watch your blood pressure."

I had no idea if he had a blood pressure problem, but if he didn't, he would soon if he kept working himself up so much.

"Hey Liv," I added.

She acknowledged my greeting with a smile and winked before turning her attention to her cup of coffee. I could tell by her pinched face after each sip that Pops brewed it. *Puts hair in your nose*, he'd say. Why anyone would want that was beyond me.

"My blood pressure is fine. It's my anxiety that'll put me into an early grave."

"The gangs are targeting each other, not random people. And the school is better prepared now for any violence. It'll be fine." I sipped from my cup and gulped. Yup, he made the coffee. I longed for Warp's mud.

"And you can't get caught in the crossfire?"

"I could get caught in the crossfire anywhere. But I'm quick and I'm smart and I have two older brothers who are well respected." Though I wasn't so sure about Warp anymore. The more he changed the more worried I became that one day he'd make enemies with one of the gangs on the other side of town. The gun-toting kind.

Pops sighed, his shoulders slumping over his coffee mug. "What kind of father can't take his kids away from danger?"

Livia shifted uncomfortably, and I smiled to reassure her that things weren't going to get too sappy. "A good, hardworking father. Three Rivers isn't so bad. And besides, I'm sixteen. By the time the streets are overrun with criminals and the cops become trigger-happy and jaded, I'll be in college like Ander."

He snorted, but patted my hand to let me know he appreciated my "go Pops" cheerleading.

I wrapped my arms around his shoulders and squeezed. "I've got my cell, Pops. Call if you get worried."

"Your dad's really freaking, huh?"

Liv and I walked to school together every day at the end of last year, and though I missed out on the first week this year, our routine picked up as usual. Which was good. Without Liv, I'd have to hang out with my brother and his friends.

"Yeah. Pops has been hard on himself since Mom died, but with this school merger, it looks like his guilt is getting worse. He's got a job that has him gone for awhile, so that's not helping. God. You shoulda seen him last week when I came downstairs dressed for school."

"Of course there had to be a few punk wannabes shooting each other in the parking lot. I bet that *really* helped put him at ease." Liv switched her book bag to her opposite shoulder, almost taking out a kid speeding by on his bike. "Whoa!"

"I woulda laughed if you clothes-lined him with your pack."

"Wouldn't be the first person this bag has defeated. I practically keep my locker in here."

I grinned. "And an entire beauty salon."

"School violence is no excuse to slouch on appearance." She threw a lock of gold over her shoulder and posed. "What d'ya think?"

"Pfft. Like you need me to add a puff of breath to your inflated ego."

"Ouch, bitch." She elbowed me and I laughed.

Livia was one of the most sought after girls in our old school. With her long wavy blonde hair, Mexican mix-breed tan, and pale blue eyes, she was the perfect example of the hotness that blended ethnicity brought to the humanity table. Which also meant every girl secretly hated her because their boyfriends made fools of themselves in her honor.

Me? I knew having her as a friend probably meant any boyfriend sneaky enough to get around my brothers was in danger of falling prey to his baser instincts where Liv was concerned. But it'd be a good way to sift out the little wormies wiggling around in my flour bin of life.

I looked in the direction the bike-rider went and noticed an antique doctor's bag bouncing on his back.

"Oh, hey! You know who that was? That's Heather's brother! I ran into him last week."

I felt like a moron the instant I brought Heather's name up. Last year, Livia told me the two of them used to hang before Heather was killed and that's why she didn't have too many friends. She'd withdrawn to escape all the morbidly curious questions she got every day.

I couldn't blame her. And here I was digging up the buried bone.

"Gah. I'm an idiot. Sorry, Liv."

She laughed a little and dismissed my apology with a shake of her head. "It's sad that she's gone still but I'm okay to talk about her." A serene memory visited her face but I didn't want to pry my way into it. "You would've liked her. She was a lot like you. Adventurous to a fault."

"No such thing as being adventurous to a fault." I snorted.

"Heather wanted to be a writer, like her brothers, so she went out on her own to some dark alley to practice and wound up dead. I would say that's a huge fault."

Going out on her own had been insanity, not adventure. But it's considered unkind to speak ill of the dead, so I let it go.

I watched Haze turn a corner and ride out of sight. Not for the first time over the last week, I puzzled through the few facts I knew about him, obsessing over each little word he'd said.

"I wonder if he blames himself. If that's why he's got that white patch of hair," I said, thinking aloud.

"How hard was this run-in you had with him?"

I shrugged. "My brother harassed him, and he taunted Warp by saying how beautiful he thinks I am all poetic-like."

"Wow." Liv seemed to mull that over for a minute. "And Warp didn't hit him?"

I laughed and hooked my arm through hers as we walked up the sidewalk toward the entrance to the school. "I know right? Too much to hope that Warp's growing as a person?"

Liv made a noise filled with doubt and changed the subject, but I wasn't listening.

"Hey, Vertigo!"

My brother caught up to Liv and me in the hallway and draped an arm over each of us.

"It's Liv." She corrected and brushed Warp's hand off with a dramatic sigh.

Ever since Liv and I started hanging out, my brother had been trying to hook up with her, and to my amusement she dodged his every attempt. The male version of Liv, Warp could've had anyone he wanted back at Kennedy High, too... *except* for Liv. I think that's why he tried daily to get her, switching between blunt proposals and kindergarten antics. He obviously picked the latter for the day.

We found out Liv was afraid of heights the first time we took her out with us. She turned a little green on the roof of our apartment building when we showed her how to jump one story down to the housing complex beside ours.

Ever since, Warp called her by her new "street name". I guess he thought it was cute.

"I'll see you in art class, Ellie." She waved.

"What? No love?" Warp asked. Liv rolled her eyes before jogging down the hall toward her locker.

"I love how you choose to ignore the fact she's not interested and keep going for it. It's a little brave and a lot pathetic, Warp."

"Whatever, *Ellie*," he teased, and I winced. My brother knew how much I disliked being called that.

My full name, Emanuella, sounded very Sexy-Latina-Hotness; except I don't have an ounce of Latin American in my blood. My mother was half black, half English and my father was all purebred Southern-cracker-white. I took after Pops, except more tan, which prompted my mother to often say how much my name fit me. "My best friend was a Latina super model," she'd say. "The name will make you great, too."

When I won my first trophy in gymnastics Mom gave me the biggest hug and said, "See! I told you, Emanuella, a great name for a great girl."

Without Mom around, it was hard to hear my full name without feeling pain.

"Liv doesn't like the name LL, said it reminds her of the rapper guy, so we compromised with Ellie. For her. You start calling me Ellie, and we're going to have issues."

"Aww," he said, ignoring my threat. "You've got a new BFF."

I would've argued the title, but Liv and I hung out a lot more lately. I didn't see her spend as much time with anyone else as she did with me and vice versa. We never said we were best friends but we never said we weren't either.

"And you scared her away when she was supposed to show me around." I glanced down at the locker number I wrote on my hand, then to the row of lockers on either side of me. "Great." I was locker 112 and the lockers near me read 1175.

Warp grabbed my hand and tilted it toward him to see the number. "Back hall. But I think you should have Liv come over later to make a map of the school for you."

I elbowed his ribcage. "I know where this is going. You're gonna ask me to have a sleepover and try to get her drunk while Pops is outta town. Not gonna happen, *John*."

He glared at me for using his real name, and I matched his look. If he'd been Ander I might have considered folding, but he wasn't.

"I think you should walk to school with the crew from now on," he declared.

I blinked like a fielder hit upside the head with a ball he didn't see coming. "Hello, random. Why? So you can hit on Liv each morning."

"I think it would be safer."

"No. I walk with Liv—alone. If you're going to start trouble this year, then I definitely don't want to walk with you."

"Pige—LL," he started.

"No, Warp. I mean it. I'm not walking to school with you. I feel safer lately when you're not around, because all I see when I look at you is your self-destruct button."

The muscles of his jaw tightened and I turned and walked away. I wasn't sure what happened to Warp to change him so much, but I hated...absolutely hated, what he was becoming.

I'd been so lost to my thoughts, watching each step my feet took, I failed to notice a door beside me opened inward until a hand emerged from the void to wrap around my bicep.

"Whoa!"

Someone tugged my arm and whipped me into a dark closet, slamming the door closed. My assailant and I were in complete darkness.

Who was it? Did he have a weapon? See me talking to my brother and decide to make a statement right away by cutting on me? Shit.

This...was not good.

My heart throbbed in my throat as I thought about the conversation I'd just had with Warp about safety. The irony-bat was in full swing aimed at my head.

Plink!

The light came on overhead and I found myself staring into the amused hazel eyes of Haze. "Scare ya?"

Yes!

"Nope."

Needing a moment to breathe-out the panic attack, I glanced around with what I hoped was casual curiosity, as though being yanked into a small dark space by a hot guy happened once a week. "This is an art supply closet."

"Yeah," he said, without taking his eyes off my face. I tried not to notice.

"Don't you need a key to get in here?"

"Yeah."

I frowned. "You stole the key?"

He laughed and I felt it trickle straight to my gut. "No. I'm the art teaching assistant and Mrs. Peris loves me so I'm allowed in here whenever I want."

So much for the art teacher from Kennedy keeping his job. I wasn't too broken up about his layoff since Mr. Galan and I hadn't seen eye-to-eye.

"Well aren't *you* cool?" I smiled.

"You're easily impressed. I should tell you how often I sneak in through the art room window at night and leave you awestruck."

"Now you're lying your ass off."

"True story." I wanted to ask more about late night B&E but he seemed to have questions of his own he itched to ask. "I haven't seen you in school. I was afraid you went private."

He was afraid I went private? Cue the return of the erratic heart-thumping. "Oh. No. My dad's a bit psychotic, that's all."

"My parents were freaked, too. They drove me to school every day last week after the shootings. Practically ran over the entire student body to get me as close to the door as possible."

I grinned, feeling suddenly giddy. Haze talked to me as if we had a long-standing friendship and chatted over lunch instead of him kidnapping me from the hallway and imprisoning me in a closet.

I would've been a fool to think he did it because he liked me.

I sensed an ulterior motive coming on.

"I'm not going to tell my brother."

His forehead puckered. "What?"

"You're wasting your time if you think I'm going to run to my brother and tell him about this so the two of you can use me as an excuse to beat the hell out of each other."

He stared at me so long I started to feel uncomfortable.

"Is that what you think I'm doing?" he asked.

He made a mistake assuming I was doing much thinking at all. My brain had been on autopilot the second he turned on the light. "Uh…yeah."

"Then you're dumber than I thought."

"Hey!"

Grinning, he folded his arms across his chest and leaned back against the metal supply shelves lining the wall. "I pulled you in here so your brother *wouldn't* find out. So we could get to know each other and figure out if it's worth making trouble for ourselves."

"Oh." The supply closet got smaller.

"There's a lot going against us. You're from Kennedy and I'm from Branfort. I'm a graffiti artist…"

"A writer," I said, letting him know I wasn't ignorant of his extracurricular activity.

"Yeah." He smiled. "And you're into the freerunning? Or do you prefer to call it parkour?"

"It doesn't matter. You can call it either. Kinda like soccer and football, yanno? And anyone who practices it is call a traceur."

"Cool." Haze said. "Good to know. My point is, this school isn't ready to see us mingling together. Every group of kids is tense and ready to take out perceived competition to gain the true power here."

I thought of Warp. "That's for sure."

"So..." he pushed from the shelves and gave them a tap. "Supply closet it is."

I thought about what it was he proposed and couldn't help but question his intentions.

He must have sensed my hesitation. "I just want to get to know you, LL."

"LL?" How did he know that name?

"Isn't that your name? I heard one of your friends call you that when you stood on the wall making sure I got away. Thanks, by the way."

Oh God. Why couldn't the floor swallow me?

"Do you prefer something else?" He kept talking to me, oblivious of my self-esteem melting into a pool at my feet.

I cleared my throat. "No. LL is fine. And do you go by Haze?"

"If you like. Brennen is my legal name."

I really liked that name! But I wasn't going to gush over it in front of him. "Cool."

I could feel the incoming awkward silence and shifted, but he seemed perfectly at ease. His confidence was a little annoying, actually. "I, um, don't wanna be late. I have no idea where any of my classes are, soooo..."

"Do you have a free period this year?" he asked.

"Fourth."

"Fourth...I can do fourth. Same closet? 'Cause it's the only one I have a key to."

"Right." I blushed. One question burned in the back of my brain and it fell out of my mouth before I could add garnish to it. "Why?"

"I'm only just getting to know most of the teachers here, but give me time. Their keys shall be mine!"

I bit my lip, trying not to giggle. Only idiot flighty bitches giggle. "Why do you want to get to know me better?"

He reached forward and tucked the single strand of blue hair behind my ear. The tip of his finger grazed my skin and I stomped on the urge to shiver like a love-struck goon.

"I meant what I said last week. I think you're…beautiful. As shallow as that sounds, attraction is the beginning of most relationships, isn't it?"

Logic. Ugh.

"I suppose."

He seemed unaffected by my wariness. "If you hate me, no harm. No one but us knows we even talked. And, hey, feel free to tell me to get screwed right now if you'd rather."

I thought about it for a minute. Haze. Hot guy, talented, bold…I'd be an idiot to say no. "All right. Fourth period."

Of course, I'd be an idiot to fall for someone, knowing it could start a war.

Five

"What's it like in your world?"

I blinked, and focused on the face hovering over the black lab table talking to me. My biology teacher, Mr. Fewd, squatted down so he could peer up at me. I could only see from his nose up. He, and the rest of the snickering class, awaited my answer.

Still in a daze, I said the first thing that came to my newly awakened brain. "Shiny." Like his bald-ass head.

Mr. Fewd frowned and I felt guilty for a split second. It didn't last long, though.

Students from the dawn of school time to the present all knew the truth. Teachers aren't real people. They're part of the school system that brings us all down. Besides, they wouldn't take the job if they couldn't handle the massive amounts of verbal abuse thrown at them every day. Still, I'd answered reflexively without intending to insult him.

Unfortunately, that argument wasn't enough to keep me out of the principal's office. Of course, Liv's giggling hadn't helped either and I became the recipient of a red paper pass straight to the "doom room."

I held my books to my chest as I walked the post-apocalyptic-like hallways. Last year, you'd often run into kids haunting the corridors, goofing off and taking advantage of little to no authority shepherding wayward students about. After the shootings, though, no one wanted to be in the halls. Not alone.

I wasn't entirely alone. I had company in the form of the blue-haired mafia standing in the alcove near the emergency exit. Their job was to keep skippers from skipping and to check hall passes, which they rarely did. Maybe it was because they knew most students were afraid to get in trouble when it was dealt with so severely now, or maybe they were afraid of the students knowing that at any moment, one of us could lose our respect for life.

Either way, from what I could tell, the hall maids now got paid to hang around a plastic chair all day gossiping about the happenings in the teacher's lounge. They were comfortable knowing if I did manage to get past them, the parking lot officers would just walk me back in none-too-gently and throw me into a chair in the office.

As I passed the group, I held up my piece of paper, not at all shocked they barely nodded before returning to the huddle. No wonder tax dollars went to new school safety measures. Any toddler with a pad of construction paper and a pair of scissors could've bypassed that effective security system.

Shaking my head, I continued my death walk to the doom room.

The usually transparent front of the principal's office had a ton of red cut-out hearts taped to the glass. On each was a scrawled message to one or several of the gang members who died in the parking lot incident last week. For me, this was an abrupt reminder of the violence bubbling up from underneath us all and I found myself drawn up short before entering.

I had guilt again, and this time it didn't fade like it had with Mr. Fewd.

This disposable monument made me feel more deeply than any of the TV news spots or newspaper articles I read about the tragedy. The inadequately expressed mourning trapped on crude artwork was a testament to the total screw-up the city would never admit to. Even I'd blown it off, pushing the deaths to the back of my mind as I floated around the new school preoccupied with finding my classes, meeting up with Haze, and building my friendship with Liv. I hadn't whispered so much as a word of sympathy for those who were destroyed far too early because of the school merger.

I bit my lip and stared at the names of the victims. I didn't know the kids since they'd been bussed in from even farther than Kennedy or Branfort, but it didn't make me any less sad.

I thought about the moms, dads, and siblings of the deceased. I thought about their friends forced to walk over the very sidewalk where the victims died and see the chalk outlines, even though they weren't there anymore.

Every day.

The school as a whole had no time to digest the devastating events or to remember and mourn.

Since the deaths were on the sidewalk off the main parking lot, the school didn't have to close. The board did, however, let the students go home early on Friday for a half day of grieving, patting themselves on the back for their generosity.

The community wasn't pleased.

The local paper accused the district of insensitivity, railing against everyone from the school janitors straight to the mayor. The school board shot back with this wall of hearts and extra counselors on staff for the next month. As if a month would erase the blood stains.

As if strength was in pretending no one could be faulted.

We, the students, knew, and the parents were beginning

to understand that the death of the young men could've been avoided if the board had taken into consideration the potential for gang violence. But they hadn't, out of ignorance. Or maybe they just didn't care.

Well, I cared.

I lifted my hand and traced the crookedly cut edges of a paper heart and swallowed hard. If Warp wasn't careful, I would be scrawling my own goodbye message in Sharpie and adding my lament to this wall of sorrow.

The thought scared me, bringing tears to my eyes.

In the past few years, I'd lost much of what I'd grown up knowing, and now I was losing my brother, too. For the moment, Warp was only emotionally distancing himself, but soon...oh God, soon it might get worse.

I didn't realize I'd been crying until I felt a gentle hand squeeze my shoulder. I jumped and hurriedly wiped at the tears beneath my eyes before facing whoever consoled me. And because my luck sucks large, I found myself looking into the kind eyes of Haze for the second time that day.

I sniffled and had enough self awareness to wonder if I looked like a melted M&M.

"Did you know them?" he asked in a low whisper.

I shook my head. "Not at all, and yet, as cheesy as it sounds, I know them very well."

A lopsided smile complemented his gorgeous face, instantly curing my crying problem. "How very poetic of you," he said, and I wondered if he was mocking his use of flowery words last week. "I get it, though. It's hard not to relate, or see our future in these cheap hearts."

The way he talked, I knew he drew parallels to his own loss a few years ago and I had no idea how to say sorry or if I even should. I settled for a lame answer.

"Yeah." Not my best. "Can we talk about something else?"

"Sure." His hand dropped from my shoulder and I wished I would've just fumbled through the topic to keep physical contact. "We could talk about you skipping out of class." He tsk'd. "Not very responsible of you, LL."

The growing weight of biology knowledge made my arm feel like it would fall off any second. I shifted my books to my other arm and flashed my "doom room" ticket. "I have a right to be here! I have a naughty pass." I waved the red piece of paper in the air between us hoping the draft would dry up my nose.

Haze looked from the pass to my face, lifting a skeptical brow. "You're here because you're in trouble?"

"I blame the light reflection off Mr. Fewd's solar dome. If he hadn't face-blasted me with it and seared my eyeballs, my inner thoughts would've stayed inner."

Haze burst into laughter and I felt my face flush with pride.

I made Warp or one of his friends laugh all the time, but making Haze crack up had to be the best feeling in the world. His opinion mattered to me, and I wanted it to be a very, very good opinion. One worth defying my brother for.

"Nice," he said, sobering. "I'll never see a solar panel again without thinking of Mr. Fewd, but I forgive you for the image."

"You're such a nice guy," I teased. "So, what are you doing out of class? Did you get in trouble?"

"Nah. I'm never in trouble." The way he beamed triumphantly led me to believe it wasn't that he was never in trouble, just never caught in the act.

"Right. Right."

"I came down here to switch my schedule."

"They screw something up?"

"Yeah. They didn't give me fourth period free."

Anything cool I might've said shriveled up and died right there. I realized what he meant. He tweaked his schedule just so he could meet me in the art closet. Holy sh—

"Miss Harvey."

My head snapped up when I realized the door to the principal's office stood open and the principal himself waited for me. Whoops. Damned wireless networks. Since each classroom was outfitted with a laptop linked to the principal's personal PC, taking one's time to get to the main office was no longer an option. "Modern convenience" was a misnomer for computers, in my opinion. Especially when they outted me for lingering in the halls.

"Sorry, Principal Meisen. I saw Miss Harvey grieving and detained her to offer a shoulder, yanno, in case she needs it."

Principal Meisen smiled his patient smile. It made me think that he had paranormal abilities in lie-detecting. I was willing to bet his keen eye is what saved him from getting the axe when the schools merged, too.

"That's very kind of you, Mr. Craig. But I'm sure you wouldn't want to miss any more Trigonometry."

"How do you remember my classes? Truly, you have a gift, Mr. Meisen."

"I have many gifts. Hope you only experience the one," the principal said and then turned toward me, sweeping a hand in the direction of his office. "Miss Harvey, if you wouldn't mind."

Haze grinned and saluted me. "See you later, Miss Harvey." He nodded to the principal. "Mr. Meisen." And then he left me alone to my fate.

By the time third period neared its end, I had a full-on panic attack brewing.

What the hell had I been thinking, agreeing to shack-up with Haze in an art closet? What if this was all a setup to embarrass me? What if I went to the meeting place, tried the handle, and found it locked? Visions of me standing outside the door trying every secret knock from every movie I'd ever seen passed before my eyes. No matter which knock I tried, one thing remained the same: I was pathetic at the end of every version.

"Pssst! Are you going to answer me back or what?"

I blinked Bonnie Hefden into focus, noticing her dramatic lean over her desk's edge and I wondered how long she'd been trying to get my attention.

Great. How many times was I doomed to zone-out on Haze-related crap? I wasn't a dreamer by nature, but apparently being attracted to a guy shut off a few switches in my brain-unit.

"Uhm. Sorry. What?"

Bonnie nodded her head toward my elbow. A small, folded piece of paper jutted out at me. Damn. I hadn't even felt her tuck it in there, which meant I wasn't only heart-deaf but numb, too.

Mrs. Rosnek wrote a sonnet on the board which gave me the chance to open the letter without fear of it being read aloud.

> *Coach Mann emailed Wenda with her permission to practice under the assistant coach from Branfort, so we can all get to know the girls from the other school. That means we're go for launch tonight. Cool, huh?*

The note implied this had been a planned event with back and forth emails, which was strange considering Wenda told me at the coffee shop we were going to practice individually. What a lying little—

"So?" She whispered behind her hand, ducking when Mrs. Rosnek peeked behind her shoulder.

I tried really hard not to be annoyed by Wenda's blatant attempt to exclude me, and I knew Bonnie, in all her cheery airheadedness, hadn't intended to start a problem. She simply didn't know I wasn't wanted.

I wasn't invited. I wrote back and handed the note over.

What do you mean? Didn't Wenda call you?

No.

Bonnie bit her lip and stared down at the letter. Next time she handed it to me, she stared hard waiting for my answer.

Why?

Pfft. Why?

Kennedy High School Gymnastics team had scraped by, winning the last regionals, and though I didn't want to admit it at the risk of sounding conceited, the win wouldn't have happened if it weren't for me.

Besides Bonnie, the other girls, especially Ramona and Wenda, all hated me with a *Titanic* passion because of that meet. I'd pushed them beyond their limits. I dared them, challenged them, and I even talked a little bit of smack until they were all performing at their best—if only to shut me up.

In the end, my scores took us to the top of the podium, but the success came at a price.

Pops reassured me the girls would get over their grudge or eventually see the value in what I did. But that was because he always supported me, no matter what.

I knew different. I'd crossed the "no-I-in-team" line, and had become Kennedy High's own Svetlana. With attitude comes consequences and, though it bugged me that the girls included me in extra events like slumber parties and bake sales only when Coach Mann was around, I knew I'd done what was necessary to get noticed and get my chance at a scholarship.

I folded the note and buried it under my book, out of sight like the hurt I felt knowing the rest of the team went along with Wenda's plan. What was done was done. I focused on the book in front of me and tried to remember that the reason I went to school wasn't to be class president.

The bell rang and I jumped. It was time.

My former nervousness over meeting up with Haze was now intensified by the feeling that I didn't belong…anywhere. People who knew me…didn't like me. They didn't get me. Why would Haze be any different?

Stalling, I waited for everyone in my row behind me to file out of the room before I stood. This class went by so fast. Too fast. Everything Mrs. Rosnek lectured about was now lost somewhere in the void between my temples due to a bizarre time warp. My ears were ringing, and my head was throbbing now, too.

I shoved my book into my bag, grumbling as the note from Bonnie fell to the ground, reminding me again of my lack of popularity. If I wasn't worried someone would find it and read it, I wouldn't have bothered wasting the energy to pick it back up.

"I'm sure Wenda just forgot to tell you. It's a bummer, though. I really hoped you'd come 'cause I think we get more done when you're around. And it wouldn't be cool if someone from the Branfort team took a leadership role." Bonnie chattered on behind me, following me out of the room.

I should've been grateful for her enthusiasm since, unlike the others, she obviously appreciated my mat-side manner. But my self-pity was like the treasure-protecting dragon in the book my mother used to read me, greedy and not easily slain. I wanted all the girls to like me. Not one.

I looked over my shoulder at Bonnie and did my best impression of an indifferent smile. "Well, I think the other girls might not feel the same way. Maybe they want to try a quieter practice." More than likely they wanted to get to the new girls on the team first—add some more members to the LL hate club.

A perplexed look overtook Bonnie's face and I knew any second she would ask me another question. Ugh! I didn't want to talk about it anymore.

Luckily, once we entered the main hall, I noticed Liv standing there, bouncing on the balls of her feet with barely suppressed excitement.

I might not have many friends but I did have one really good, very timely, one. Some of the sadness creeping in crept right back out.

"Talk to you later, Bonnie." I excused myself before practically running to Liv's side.

"Tell me everything! What did Mr. Meisen say? Wait, what's this?" she asked, plucking the note from between my fingers.

"Oh, that's just a note from Bonnie."

I watched her eyes scan the letter before handing it back. "Here, I thought you actually wrote me. What the hell was I thinking?"

Liv loved to overdramatize. She knew better than to take my lack of correspondence as an insult. I simply didn't write people. If I had something to say, I'd say it in person, not in a damned note that anyone could snag. The last thing I needed was my business to end up on some moron's Facebook.

"Yeah, what the hell *were* you thinking?"

She grinned at me, but it faded with her next words. "I didn't know you had practice tonight. That sucks, I totally wanted to go see that new "everyone dies including the planet" movie at the 'plex."

"I don't have practice tonight. Wenda and some of the other girls do."

Even though I felt Liv staring at me, I pretended to be preoccupied with my class schedule. I doubted she was fooled. "You know," she started, "I could have some of my freshmen fans blow up the gymnasium."

"Gah!" Despite the disturbing mental image, I couldn't help but laugh. "Be careful how loud you say that! Mr. Meisen is on the prowl for anyone acting overly aggressive. I'm pretty sure terrorist bombing falls under that category."

"Speaking of Mr. Meisen, let's hit the library. You've got fourth period free, right? We'll plan our night tonight and you can spill about your field trip to the office. Tell me you didn't get detention for pointing out Mr. Fewd's glossy bowling ball of a head. Seriously, when you said that...*high*-larious." Liv went on and on.

And that was the first time I stood up Brennen "Haze" Craig.

Six

"So who has you thinking thong instead of panties?" Liv asked me forty minutes into our library voyage.

If I'd been chewing gum, I would've swallowed it. "What? No one!"

"Oh come on," she teased, inching closer across the table. She tapped the eraser of her pencil against the page of my open Biology book. "You've been staring at the same page for twenty minutes. Only men can distract so easily. Take my ex-boyfriend, Damien, for example." Her head turned subtly in his direction, so I took a look.

I recognized his shaggy hair but not his face. In all her old pictures of the two of them, Liv didn't leave too many of his facial features unscathed. I found it interesting to see what he looked like without a Bic mustache and horns, and with his eyeballs intact. "I thought you said he graduated."

"He was supposed to. Real winner, huh?" She snorted and shook her head. "He's arguing with his newest victim, I see. Probably because there's a big party Saturday and he wants to be single for it. And here I sit, on his ex list for over two years and still angry enough to imagine him tripping and impaling himself on his pencil."

I nodded.

"His *unsharpened* pencil," she added.

I grinned a little, nodding again.

"Through his eyeball." She paused. "Into his brain."

I waited for a break in her bitterness before steering her back on track. "You had a point in there somewhere."

"Oh, yeah." Liv laughed at herself and touched her pen to her own opened book. "I haven't turned the page, either. That's how I know you're thinking about a guy."

Wow. Outted by my Biology book.

I thought about telling her right then about Haze, but after standing him up in the closet, I had no idea if he'd ever speak to me again. I had zero interest in confessing my crush only to have him ignore me for the rest of my time at Three Rivers Academy.

Also, I had to admit that talking to Liv about boys was a little intimidating. A male didn't exist she couldn't have, but for me, dating was a little more traumatic. My eldest brother did a fantastic job of scaring the boys away from sixth to eighth grade and Warp picked up the mantle once Ander left. Now, no one would come near me. I'd have to get a tranq-gun and blackmail photos to get a guy to visit my house.

The way Liv looked at me made me feel a little unnerved. Maybe it was guilt, but I swore she could see straight through my lies. My Pops had the same "I-know-you-did-something-wrong-but-I'm-waiting-for-*you*-to-admit-it" look.

I had to say something. So I sighed dramatically and leaned my head back, looking at the ceiling and hoping I looked frustrated instead of panicked. "Like Warp would allow me to date? Psh. But it's not a boy that's on my mind, Liv. I'm worried about my brother." When forced to lie, use as much of the truth as possible. I saw that in a movie or a television show or something. Worrying about my brother wasn't on my mind as much as the Haze situation, but only because I was getting used to Warp's antics.

"He's acting out. Looking for fights. One day he's going to mess with someone who's bigger and better and they're not gonna fight fist to fist. I miss my level-headed dorky bro that I didn't have to worry about, yanno?"

Liv reached for my hand and wrapped her fingers around my fist, giving it a squeeze. "I can talk to him if you like. See if I can get him to calm down some."

Given my brother's infatuation with Liv, I didn't think it was a bad idea. "You can try, but he seems determined to make himself infamous."

"I think it's a g—" She gasped as Damien nudged her chair with his hip, sending her ribs into the side of the table. Liv's face twisted in pain.

I was outta my chair so fast it flipped over. "You piece of shit! Picking on girls make your dick bigger or something? Is everyone here impressed?" I gave anyone who snickered a glare in Liv's defense but I needn't have bothered. Liv—delicate-as-a-flower Liv—recovered quickly, and with the aid of my Biology book, she came up behind her ex while I had his attention and christened the back of his skull.

Damien fell to the floor, his hand instinctively rising to ward off a second blow, but Liv calmly turned away from him, her face rosy with victory. Her humiliation of her ex-boyfriend complete, she relinquished her weapon to the table once again and bowed.

I wasn't the type of girl who found humor in violence, but watching Liv take down a jerk nearly twice her size had me laughing.

"Thanks for letting me borrow your book, Ellie," she said, right before the librarian descended and Liv received her own bright red doom room ticket.

At least I wouldn't be the only one in detention after school.

I was still grinning about Liv and Damien when I walked into Art class.

The room seemed smaller than it should be. Too many tables were all mashed together, forming a circle with only a foot or two of sidling room in between them. The only way to get to the teacher's desk or the small supply closet to the right was to suck-n-hold the gut in.

If I wasn't claustrophobic before, I was feeling it now.

Lining the wall to my immediate left was a series of filling cabinets bogarting all the space out of the room. Actually, these suckers were like burly cousins of the typical filing cabinets. Six feet tall and five feet wide with tons of one-inch-deep drawers, each cabinet had a number on it (the hours Mrs. Peris had students) and each drawer the name of a student.

I squinted and moved closer, feeling a strange sort of validation when I saw my name.

Every year of school, I'd always had this irrational fear of being in a class I wasn't supposed to be in. The anxiety lasted all through roll call until the teacher would call my name and I could breathe again. Thank God my last name didn't start with a Z or I'd pass out before they got to me.

But with this class I didn't need to worry. There was my name, right under the cabinet labeled Fifth Hour.

Relieved, I repositioned my book bag over my shoulder and moved toward the back of the room, heading for an empty seat. I bumped a few people with my bulbous backpack and murmured my apologies. It wasn't *my* fault I had to bring it. I hadn't seen my locker since before first hour. I swear it was like that castle that disappeared all the time to keep anyone from finding it.

I glanced toward Mrs. Peris' desk in hopes of getting in a brown-nosing smile, but my view was blocked. A boy leaned over her desk chatting, or if we were all lucky, possibly plotting a new table arrangement.

Well, there went my chance to get in a little teacher ass-kissery.

Speaking of asses, I caught myself staring at the guy's backside and blinked. When the hell did I turn into a butt-girl? Usually I'd look a guy over and move on, but with this one, I was gawking like I'd never seen a fine shape before.

And it was fine!

Swimmer's shoulders, lean waist, defined—but not scary—arms. Nice!

"Miss...Emanuella Harvey, is it?"

I pulled myself into reality when the teacher spoke to me.

A second later I wished I lived in my own little world, because on my planet, the student I'd been checking out wouldn't be the guy I'd stood up in the closet.

Haze performed the suspicious brow-lift thing, and I wasn't sure what it meant. Of course, I would spend the next few days obsessing over it. Was he making fun of my name? Was he chastising me for the no-show? Did I draw on my face with my pen on accident?

Did he suspect I was checking out his butt? *Oh God...please let me have pen on my face.*

"Y-yes."

"You look a little lost, dear. Take any seat you like, I don't assign them and I encourage my students to move around. Different perspectives are imperative to a lifetime of open-mindedness."

Though I wanted to say "Okay, Confucius," I settled for less.

"Uhm. Okay." I tried to smile and ignore Haze without looking like I was trying to ignore him. Not easy to do, but when in doubt, go with the duh-face.

I moved to the back and plopped my bag down on the table, busying myself with straightening the books inside of it.

I didn't look, but I knew he stood behind me. My aura twitched with full on hot-guy-alert. "What's up?"

"Mrs. Peris has instructed me to bring you up to speed on what we're reading and the techniques we're applying to the still-life scene over there." He moved next to me and pointed to the draped cloth full of fruit, ready to be painted, sketched, or whatever the hell.

"Okay." Could he hear my heart echoing up my throat every time I opened my mouth? It was best to keep my answers short, just in case.

"I promise it won't be too painful. I do have to go get you a sketchbook from the supply closet though. You remember where that is, don't you? West hall? Big sign that says Art Supplies."

There was no hope for it, I had to face him and what I'd done, or rather, didn't do. I turned, expecting a snarling beast, but met his toothy grin instead. It was contagious. I had to bite the inside of my lip to keep from full-on grinning like an idiot.

At least he didn't seem mad. That couldn't be a bad sign. In fact, he seemed to be teasing, and like all the other times we'd met, all my awkward uncomfortableness faded. Oh I was still flip-flopping on the insides, but I was calm enough to engage in a banter-fest.

"Yanno…I didn't get a very good look at the door the first time. I kinda got sucked into it blindly."

"Closets do that sometimes."

"Do they?"

Nodding, he gave me the once-over, his gaze shimmering with mischief, and I daydreamed what it would feel like having his arms around me when he looked at me like that. Pure heaven. "If I were you, I'd expect to get sucked into one on a regular basis. I've heard once they're drawn to you, you're never safe."

Aaaand I couldn't think anymore—about anything—except how drawn I was to *him*.

"Lemme get that book for you."

Yeah—yeah, good idea. Him going away before I made a complete idiot of myself was good stuff.

I watched him walk to the door and then move aside to let someone through.

"Hey, Bren," Liv said, as she came into the room. "Nice to see you again." Her voice quivered awkwardly, like she didn't mean a word, and I couldn't blame her. Talking to the brother of her deceased best friend had to be a little nerve-wracking.

"Hi, Liv. Nice to see you, too," he answered.

"I didn't know you had this class."

"I'm the teacher's aide for this hour."

"Oh. I didn't see you in here last week."

"Last week I was in the lounge doing some mailing for the upcoming art contest. This week I should be in class, though."

"Cool," Liv said, and I could almost feel her willing me to bail her out.

I didn't fail her. "Hey, Liv. Back here."

"See you later, Bren," she said dismissively but not unkindly. Then her face brightened with relief and she waved at me. "Ellie! We'll be sharing a table at the doom room. Woot!" She laughed.

I grinned and glanced briefly at Haze catching his sexy smile before he left on the hunt for my sketchbook.

"Like this?" I asked, moving my hand so Haze could see the picture I sketched.

He hadn't been very talkative since his return; he was all business, keeping himself at a distance. At first I thought he was angrier than I'd thought, and he had every right to be, but then he winked at me. My "WTF" must have shown on my face because he wrote *Liv's watching* on my sketch pad in pencil.

Ah, I wrote back and from that moment on I kept up a great show of being engrossed in sketching. Occasionally I'd look up and grin at Liv, feeling bad she was forced to sit at the opposite end of the room.

Mrs. Peris wanted me to get caught up, and Liv, being Liv, talked excessively the first fifteen minutes of class until the teacher finally punished her by reassigning her seat for the day.

"It looks good." He answered. There was a hitch to his tone, so I knew he was trying to be nice.

I made a face at him and he cleared his throat to mask a laugh.

"You're not very nice." I did feel a little disappointed. I wanted to show him I could be good at anything. All I showed him is that I could be good at anything except drawing.

"But I'm very honest. That counts for something, right?" When I glared at him, he smiled. "Not everyone is an artist, but if you're serious about it, you can be. Most people take this class to goof around with their friends." He looked pointedly at Liv.

I shrugged. "She likes art, and she's my friend. If I didn't take it, we'd only have one class together."

"Understood."

"I do appreciate talent, though. I may not know how to make pretty sunrays shine on a pretty face, but I can look at it and know it's beautiful."

Haze seemed a little uncomfortable with my praise, but he only showed it for a moment. "So, you're Emanuella, LL, and Ellie?" Haze asked in a whisper, interrupting my thoughts.

"Uh huh. So?"

"You have enough aliases to warrant an FBI investigation. I bet they have an open file on you at headquarters."

I tried very hard to hold my grin in, but he didn't make it easy. "LL is my street name, Emanuella is my full name, and Liv insists on calling me Ellie to be different. All caught up now?"

"Should I make up my own name for you, too? Ema? Nuel? Ella?"

"Manu?"

"Oo! That's a sexy one. Manu."

I kicked him under the table. If he was going for inconspicuous he needed to stop trying to make me laugh. "Stick with LL. Your shins will thank you for it."

Typically, he just grinned.

I met up with Liv at the end of class so she could walk me to my locker. "Did Brennen say anything to you?"

A panicked flutter in my chest made my voice a little higher than usual. "About what?"

"I don't know," she said. "Anything about me, I guess. After Heather's death, we hadn't spoken. I don't want him to think I was being bitchy or anything."

"He didn't mention it. I wouldn't worry too much about it, though. Her death was hard on both of you. Talking would only be a reminder, so maybe silence was what you both needed then. I say start slow, and talk to him once in a while. Especially if you're interested in him."

I threw that last in out of curiosity and prayed my voice sounded more casual this time. I didn't want to battle Liv for Haze since I was pretty sure, once she set her sights on him, my chances slimmed dramatically.

"What? Ugh! No! I wasn't asking because I like him. I just feel bad I didn't keep in touch. I'll say hi to him when I see him instead of avoiding him from now on. If he wants to talk to me, he will, right?"

I may have risked looking like a nimrod for suggesting she might be into him, but I was glad I did.

"LL!"

My brother bellowed from the opposite end of the hall, his loud voice echoing embarrassingly down the full length of the corridor. Everyone stopped to look at me.

I sighed and waited for Warp to get closer before talking to him. "Why are you yelling?"

He crossed his arms over his chest. "Did you think I wouldn't hear about you and that asshole? That you could sneak it by me? What the hell were you thinking?"

I gagged on a heart-attack. Oh my God! He knew!

Seven

All Warp was missing, as he stood there with invisible steam coming from his ears, was a tapping foot.

"If you're going to air your brotherly bullshit to the entire school, at least tell me what the hell you're talking about." I had no idea whether or not I sounded convincingly blasé, but one could hope.

"It's all over school that you got detention for hitting Damien Cox with your Biology book." What? Oh, thank God, oh thank God. Warp didn't know a damn thing. I was giddy with relief.

I glanced over at Liv. "His last name is Cox?"

Grinning at me, she nodded. "Fitting, isn't it?"

I laughed. "You're a hot mess, yanno that?"

"LL, I'm serious," Warp barked. "Since Pops is on a job, I'm responsible for you and you go around picking fights with a notorious punk from 3-Town Vengeance."

Liv failed to mention that tidbit in the library. Not that I was worried about the gangsters coming after me or anything. I hadn't been the one to biff Damien in the back of the brain-holder, but from that point on, I'd think of standing next to Liv as an extreme sport.

"Ellie had nothing to do with it, you bullying ass." Liv poked a finger into Warp's chest, successfully distracting him from me. "I hit Damien with her Biology book and received a detention. Ellie got a detention for insulting Mr. Fewd's gem-like head. Get your stories straight. And Damien doesn't run with Vengeance anymore, considering most of them are in *jail* for the shootings last week." Liv crossed her arms over her chest, smug at giving Warp a dressing down. "Now I think you should apologize to your sister."

I almost giggled. Liv had no clue. Warp would rather gnaw off his arm than apologize. When he turned toward me I didn't move, stunned he seemed about to do what Liv told him to.

"What the fuck you looking at Branfort?"

...Or not.

I spun around to see Haze standing close by, on the edge of the growing crowd.

Oh, hell. My heart instantly revisited my throat and I thought I would vomit right there on Warp's school shoes.

"The back of your sister's head, waiting for her psycho brother to shut up so I can hand her the book she forgot in class," Haze answered.

Warp lurched forward. Oh, double hell.

"Come near my sister and I'll kill you."

"Hey!" I yelled at Warp and forced him back with a shoulder to his chest.

"I'm not trying to molest your sister, Kennedy. I'm trying to give her a damned book. You really wanna do this shit here?" Haze looked around pointedly before bringing his gaze back to my brother.

Even as I surveyed the area, students were stopping and asking questions.

I groaned. "Jesus, Warp. What the hell is your problem? If this is your plan to keep me out of trouble with Pops gone—epic fail."

"Haze? You need something taken care of?" A baritone cut into the scene. The owner of the voice loomed behind Haze, glaring at my brother with his gigantic muscled arms overlapping like logs on a fire.

"There's nothing to take care of, Decay," Haze reassured his friend while keeping his eyes on Warp.

"You sure?" Decay asked.

"Sure he's sure!"

I practically sagged with relief when I heard Surge's voice break through the tension. "Just a misunderstanding up in here. Tha's all. Wouldn't want it to escalate."

Surge came into my periphery from the right, and though he spoke rationally, there was no mistaking the promise in his eyes that he would spring at both Haze and his crewmate, Decay, if they pushed.

The potential for violence hung in the air like smog. I could taste it every time I breathed in. "Okay, okay. I forgot my book in art and *Branfort* brought it to me because he's the teacher's aide and has to. Can we complete the transaction without the drama so I can do my homework later?"

I gave my brother a little shove back and walked around Surge to grab my sketchbook from Haze.

I didn't dare look at his face lest everyone standing around would become witness to my growing crush.

"Thanks," I mumbled.

"You're welcome, Manu," Haze said in a hushed whisper.

The corner of my lip twitched, wanting to smile but I managed to keep it at bay long enough to unleash it on Surge instead. The school would be safer if everyone thought I was grinning at him. I made my way back to "Kennedy Country" and stood next to Liv.

"Umm, disperse with a quickness," Surge warned a nanosecond before Mr. Fewd pushed through the crowd.

"Is this a fight? Are you all fighting?"

My throat went dry. The words "no-tolerance" shot through my head and I saw us all getting expelled. They'd call my father on the road and announce that his children had been sent home from school and he'd have to come to sign papers or go to a court-martial-type hearing, or whatever the hell they did to unworthy students.

I didn't breathe or blink, like failure to move would make me fade into the background and come out of the incident unscathed. *Nobody here but us chickens.*

"Are you saying that because I'm black?" Surge accused loudly, throwing everyone off for a second. "Oh, I get it. A black guy stands around to deliver an important party message and you assume I'm starting something? I'm crying racism, my man, ray-ciz-zem!"

Mr. Fewd looked put out, but only for a minute. To his credit, he collected himself and got back to teacher mode. "We don't allow party announcements in school, either, Mr. Lawrence. Let's go visit the principal's office."

Looked like Liv and I would have some company after school.

"I'm saying! LL! Being around you brings me trouble," Surge grinned at me, his beautiful smile stretching his lips from ear to ear as he walked into the doom room after regular school.

He passed the attending teacher, Mr. Stratt, slapping a high-five before sitting on the top of the desk I was sitting at. He threw a wink toward Liv before hunkering down to look me eye-to-eye.

"What?" I asked defensively. "You can't possibly blame me for my brother's psychotic outbursts."

"Sooo, you didn't beat the shit outta Damien Cox with the *Introduction To Algebra*?"

"Language," Mr. Stratt warned without looking up from his copy of *Sports Illustrated.*

"Sorry." Surge shrugged. "Well? What do you have to say for yourself, young Lady of the Ledge?"

I grinned and simply pointed at Liv who raised her hand.

"Guilty," she said.

Laughing, Surge reached over and gave Liv a pound of pride. "Right on, baby girl. The shit I hear about that dude makes me itch to beat his roof in."

"Most of it's probably true," Liv grumbled under her breath.

Surge didn't seem to want to pry for once. The rumors he heard must've been really bad.

"So? What did you do to get in here, LL?"

"It's so minor I'm embarrassed to admit it," I said.

Liv cracked up. She had no qualms about recounting the story. "She was zoning out in Biology and Mr. Fewd tried to sneak up on her. He peeked over the table and she said his head was shiny. It was classic!"

Mr. Stratt chuckled and I looked to the front of the room to grin sheepishly at him.

"So what was your infraction, Mr. Lawrence?" Mr. Stratt asked.

Out of the corner of my eye, I caught sight of someone through the wedge-like window on the classroom door walking down the hall. I waited a moment and saw the blur again before it reversed and aligned with my viewing angle.

Surge regaled Liv and Mr. Stratt with tales of his hallway exploits, and they laughed at the appropriate moments. I did, too, reflexively, but I couldn't break the stare Haze locked me in until he smiled and gave me an up-nod before walking away.

Oh, boy. My lips hurt from smiling and my stomach tingled like I'd swallowed a bunch of Pop Rocks...over an up-nod! Yeah, this was bad. And I had the rest of the imprisonment period to think about how wonderfully bad my crush was.

Surge and I dropped Liv off at home. He continued on with me to my place, insisting that 3-Town Vengeance might be down but not out, and he needed to watch my back. As far as I knew, we didn't have any problems with any gangs yet, but if Surge wanted to embellish the situation as an excuse to walk me home, I was cool with it. Other than Liv, he was my only friend, so I didn't mind hanging out. There didn't need to be a reason.

"So. You got something going on with Brennen Craig, huh?"

Did he see him outside the detention room door? No, he couldn't have. His back had been turned. I figured he was taking a stab in the dark and reminded myself to react accordingly. "Really, Surge?"

Hands out to his sides, he was the picture of innocence. "What?"

I laughed and shook my head. "Come on. I just met him the other day when Warp was trying to beat the crap out of him for no reason. And now he's the teacher's aide for my fifth hour." I stared at him like he had a couple of drugs in him as we walked. "Based on that information, I don't know *how* it took you so long to notice my obvious love affair."

"Sarcasm works on your dopey brother, LL, bless him, but it don't work on me, ya'll. I saw him that day at the wall, checking you out like you were a fine bottle of wine he wanted to decork."

"Ugh! Surge." I slapped his arm.

"And then today in the hall, he wouldn't look at you, and you wouldn't look at him but I heard him call you Manu."

"So?"

"Soooo. A man only names a pet he's planning on keeping."

"You know, I always wanted to be compared to a dog. Thanks."

"You get what I mean, quit playing and answer the question."

I was running out of hedge room. "What question am I supposed to be answering? I can't dig through all this crazy."

I crossed the street and Surge skipped backwards so he could continue his stare of accusation while keeping up with my pace. The stupid grin across his face was as wide as the Nile. Or how wide I thought the Nile might be.

"The Lady of the Ledge doth protest too much, methinks."

I suddenly wanted to burn all things Shakespeare. "Okay fine! I think he's cute."

"Pfft! It's more than that, ain't it?"

Shaking my head, I stopped and leaned against the privacy fence lining the sidewalk. I tilted my head, waiting for him to look directly at me. "Are we doing serious, for real? Is this what you want? Me to confide some dark secret for you to run to my brother with?"

Surge pursed his lips and scratched at his neck. "Look, I'm concerned. You're my girl, yanno? Well, not my *girl* girl, but you know."

"Are you my friend? Or are you my brother's friend?"

Sighing, Surge mimicked my lean. He closed his eyes for a second and then stared up into the sky. I watched his inner battle through the interpretive dance of his Adam's apple. "I'm your friend, LL," he said, and met my gaze.

"Then why don't I know shit about you? All we talk about is parkour and what I'm up to, and when I ask about you, you always crack a joke and hide behind the laughter. Now, you catch something some guy says to me, and you're grilling me like we're girlfriends about to dish. I'm supposed to believe you're asking because you care and want to put some more blocks on the building of our friendship?"

"Look, I'll be honest, I would've been outta our group last year if I hadn't promised Ander I would look after you."

Great! Not Warp, but Ander. I'd wondered why Surge always looked out for me, stepping up to my brother when he became overbearing. Also...I wondered how Ander would dare go off to school with only Warp to look after me. My eldest bro had practically clubbed anyone who looked at me sideways. Part of the reason my friend-pond needed a pity feed, but I didn't need it filled with my brothers' friends.

"Well, you can tell Ander that I can take care of my own self and he doesn't need to indenture someone to spy on me."

Hands up in surrender, Surge stepped in my path as I moved to go around him. "Wait, wait, LL. Ander might have asked me to look out for you, and I might have originally done it because I felt I owed him one, but I don't tell him your business."

"Why did you feel you owed him one?"

"Because Ander made my life better, LL. The worst portion of my life to date, and Ander gave me something no one else could."

I bit my lip, wanting to know every tiny detail of this story that I was sure would be interesting, but I held back the questions. "What?" Okay...maybe just one question.

"Understanding of who I am."

I studied Surge's face for a long time. The way he spoke about my brother, and the soft smile that tilted the corner of his mouth...holy crap. "Surge, are you like...gay?"

"Way to throw a label out there, LL."

"Whoa, whoa. I'm not throwing labels. I'm asking a question. Being gay isn't a label if it is who you are."

"But I don't know who I am, girl. That's the point. I like girls, and sometimes, I like guys."

He stared at me, waiting for me to have a comment, but I couldn't come up with one. I didn't care if Surge was gay or straight, I dug him either way, but I was afraid if I said something wrong, was either over- or under-supportive, whatever good Ander did for him, would be erased.

"Okay."

The grin he gave me, let me know I didn't screw anything up yet.

"I thought I had to make some sort of life decision. When I first had a crush on Ander, I obsessed over how to tell my parents I was gay. I stopped talking to girls I was attracted to because I thought they were making me more confused and messed in the head. When I got overwhelmed...I ran away from home and hung out on the roofs, skipping school... feeling sorry for myself."

"Ander found you?"

"Yeah. He sat down and didn't say anything to me except: 'There's nothing you can say that will make me think less of you. I'm going to stick with you until you tell me why you're out here.' I called his bluff for a couple of hours. He didn't leave. He just sat there. So I tried a different approach. I told him that I liked him."

I was glad Surge was sharing so much with me, but it was a lot to process. "What did Ander say to that?"

"He said thanks, but no thanks, peddle your gay juice elsewhere."

I'm sure my mouth dropped open by a foot. "What?!"

Surge pointed and laughed. "You shoulda seen your face!"

I wanted to kick him in the ass. "So, you're not gay?"

Still grinning at me, Surge shrugged. "I wasn't lying about the story, just that last bit. I wouldn't put any labels on my jacket yet, LL. I just don't care to. And that's what Ander did for me. After we talked for a long time about my confusion, liking girls and all too, Ander told me to take a deep breath, and enjoy being who I am. I don't love anyone. I don't need to define myself one way or the other. I'm just open to whichever direction love comes at me. I don't need to cloud my high school experiences with inner turmoil by making statements I'm not sure about. I just gotta let life roll at me. That is what Ander taught me. And that, is what I am trusting you with."

For the first time since I'd known him, I felt close to Surge. I finally felt like he let me know him...even though "him" wasn't defined.

I closed the distance between us and gave Surge a big hug, complete with squeeze. "Thank you for trusting me with that."

"I've always trusted you. Just didn't really know you were interested in knowing that much about me."

"I am interested. I feel like we get each other, yanno?"

"Yeah, I know. And I hope you know now that you can trust me with anything you might wanna talk about, cuz I ain't about to jeopardize my situation with the coolest girl in town for nobody. Not even Ander. I've got your back, a'ight? Don't play, cuz you know I do."

"So, you still want to know about Haze?"

"Not so's I can run to Ander with it. And definitely not to say some shit to Warp. Don't tell me anything until you feel you can. But if you and Haze hook up, there could be a world of violence. So until you talk real to me, I'd take it as a courtesy if you'd at least let me know if I need to start ducking. You know the black man dies first every time."

I groaned and rolled my eyes, but was glad to see his confession didn't create an awkwardness between us. "Three Rivers is sixty percent black, Surge. I'm black. You saying I'm gonna die?"

"Psh! Girl, look at your daddy. You're white with some Oreo dust."

I had to laugh. He wasn't wrong. Coming from anyone else, I woulda thrown a punch to defend my parents' breeding decision, but Surge could insult anyone and it would sound good. "Yeah, yeah."

"So, you and Haze..." he prompted.

"I've known him for a total of an hour."

"Boy works fast." When I glared he backed off. "A'ight, okay. Like I said—just tell me—"

"...if you need to duck. Yeah, I got it."

Eight

"I can't believe you're out on a school night past nine." Liv beamed at me as we stood in line for overpriced popcorn and partially melted chocolate-covered raisins. "I love when your dad isn't home!"

I smiled but I couldn't really get behind her excitement. I loved having my freedom but I didn't really feel like I lived under my father's thumb like most kids. As far as dads went, mine was pretty cool, so anarchy wasn't on my to-do list. Guess I needed to work on my teenage angst or something.

Liv interpreted my silence as annoyance and hurriedly backpedaled. "Oh, I know he just cares more about you than most parents around here. I'm not trying to dig on Pops or anything. I mean, I barely even see my life-donors. I'm not sure they'd even bother to come home if I landed in the hospital."

I stepped up to the counter and placed my order but kept my ear tilted toward Liv as she lamented over her parental apparitions. "Although, they did come home last year when the neighbors called the cops about a break-in at my house."

"I didn't know someone broke into your house."

"No one did." She smiled but I could see the sadness beneath the painted surface. "It was all me."

I couldn't hide my wince. "Yikes."

"They were terrified of getting arrested for child neglect, so they both took turns staying home for a month."

"Well that was good at least, right?" I wasn't sure trying to make her feel better about her parents' behavior was a good tactic, but I didn't feel comfortable not saying anything in support.

"Are you kidding? I wanted to make them panic, not stay home and glare at me. I couldn't wait for them to leave again. Rosahlia is all the guardian I can handle. She comes, she cooks and cleans, and doesn't try to get in my way when I want to do something. She does kinda nag, though. Hey, isn't that—?"

Liv pointed off toward the ticket booth and I followed her finger. Yup. My luck from the rest of the day stayed consistent. "Yeah. Haze."

"I'm used to calling him Bren, but I'll try to remember Haze. You know me, I could give a rat's ass about that street bullshit." And then as if she remembered who she was talking to she added. "Except you, Ellie."

Feeling suddenly happy, I laughed openly, a part of me wondering if Haze would recognize the timbre of my voice and home in.

There was no home-age.

"I know you dig what I do. Don't sweat it. Maybe one day you'll get over your fear of heights."

"No way. I'll leave all the cool acrobatics to you. Hey, they're looking over here. Think they'll come over?"

Sexay Home-age after all! I kept my happy feet from dancing. "I have no idea. Maybe you should wave, Liv. You said you wanted to start slow with talking to him again. If he sees you looking and you don't wave..."

"What? Like I have no loyalty? He's with a bunch of his writer buddies. And after today's near-brawl in the hallway...?"

"Look at you with your graffiti jargon. I'm impressed."

"Ellie." She snorted. "I had no idea you thought of me as a complete idiot."

I laughed. "Sorry, sorry."

"I was best friends with his sister and she was a graffiti artist, or trying to be before..." Pursing her lips, she busied herself yanking a few napkins from the holder.

Damn, I hated the whole situation. I never really knew what to say or how to say it when it came to Heather.

"I'm sorry. Not trying to bring that stuff up."

She slapped my arm. "Don't be sorry, newb. Oh, they're looking over here. Ugh, he's with Decay and Racker. Not my favorite people. Say the word and I snub them now and ruin their night."

Liv could be full of self-importance sometimes but I dug that about her. Glad to be out from under the dark topic cloud, I laughed and shook my head. "You know my brother, itching to start a fight. This whole feud is bullshit so wave all you like."

She did and the three guys answered. I remained Switzerland and gave the cashier my full attention.

"Feel better?" I asked.

"At least we know they're amicable and not about to attack me because I'm with a tracy."

"Traceur," I corrected, and received Liv's infamous *whatever* look. She knew I couldn't stand the word "whatever," or the attitude that usually accompanied it, but she didn't seem to mind doling out the smirk. I gave her an E for effort and the finger.

"Your phone's ringing," she said, and reached for the refreshments the cashier handed to us.

Who would be calling me? Warp was busy with the boys; Pops had already called to check in. I didn't know anyone else really.

As I fished my phone out of my pocket I irrationally thought it might be Haze. It took me a second to calm down and rationalize that Haze couldn't be calling for two very good reasons. One, he stood across from me without a phone to his ear and two, he didn't have my cell number.

Oh! The picture of my older brother beamed up at me from the phone and I smiled.

"It's Ander. I gotta take this." I couldn't keep the excitement out of my voice. I hadn't talked to my older brother in over a month. Maybe longer since the last few months went by in a blur.

Liv laughed. "Okay, go, go. I'll save you a seat, but your bro owes me for the damage walking around solo will do to my reputation."

Beaming a smile at her, I held the phone up to my ear. "Helloooo?" I pressed a ten into Liv's hand to reimburse her for the goodies and walked toward the bathrooms where I could hear better. I caught a quick glimpse of Haze as I walked past, and noticed he was staring at me scowling.

Why was he angry?

"I said 'hello, little sister!' Are you spacing out on me? I'm the one whose brain is supposed to be academically fried."

"Oh! Ander, sorry, I was navigating away from the refreshment stand. You know how brutal that can be."

Ander laughed and that was all it took to make everything right in my world.

My eldest brother was the kind of person everyone wanted to be near. A natural leader, he took any erratic or chaotic situation and smoothed it out. He did this with people, too, as both Surge and I could attest. When asked who I would take with me on a deserted island, I always got funny looks when I would say my brother, Ander. "Um, okay, sick," they'd say until I learned to lie, but in truth, Ander would have my stranded ass off that island eating a prime rib dinner within a day using only a shoelace.

He simply excelled at puzzle-solving and squeezing order out of chaos.

In four years, Ander had carried us all through mom's death while stopping the growth of gang activity on our blocks by introducing everyone to parkour and giving them something else to exert their energy on. Something new, cool, and time-consuming.

Parents loved him, kids respected him...and Warp was screwing it all up.

I listened to Ander tell me about his college experiences. He managed to find a few other traceurs in Florida and start a parkour group there but he missed us. He missed me and Pops and Surge and even Warp.

"Speaking of Warp, how's his inner struggle going?"

That's what I loved about Ander. He didn't bother with bullshit.

Laughing, I switched my phone from one ear to the other, looking around the near empty concession area. Poor Liv, she had to go into the theater all by herself. I'd have to make it up to her later.

"Warp is...well Warp. Pops kept us home to see what the school merger would bring about. Then the shootings last week ended with 3-Town V losing a big chunk of their invaders to jail or death. The other gangs aren't making much trouble, so Warp has decided to step up our crew's appearance. I'm worried, Ander. He's taken a personal dislike to the graffitis from Branfort."

Ander sighed into the phone. "I'm not surprised. I'll talk to him, Emanuella, okay?"

I hated talking to him about Warp and the situation at home because I knew he'd feel responsible, and if he thought about it too much, his school work would suffer. I kinda worried he wouldn't want to call anymore if I made things sound too dire or melancholy every time he dialed my cell.

"No. You don't have to. You know how I get. I worry about whether the sun will rise tomorrow, as Pops says. I just miss you and although I love Warp to death, he's no substitute."

"I'll call Surge."

"Really, you don't have to."

"He's my guy in town." I smiled because I knew now why Surge would do anything my brother asked. "Besides," Ander continued, "he has a knack for getting people out of trouble."

I thought about the hallway incident. "You're not wrong."

"Well, I should probably get to my lab class. Oh! I hear Surge gave you another street name. You never did like Pigeon."

"Ugh, don't remind me."

"Lady of the Ledge...I dig it."

I grinned at the phone. "Yeah, I do, too. Everyone calls me LL."

"It fits you. Okay, LL," I could hear the smile in his voice. "I'll call you again, sooner this time. And try not to worry too much about Wharf."

I laughed. Ander loved to tease Warp by calling him Wharf instead. It used to amuse us to see how many shades of angry maroon Ander could get Warp to turn.

"Okay, Ander. I'll talk to you soon. Miss you, love you."

"Miss you, love you, too, little sister."

And then he was gone. It was hard not to feel a little sad but I was super glad he called.

"Who was that?"

The masculine voice threw me for a second, and as I looked up at Haze's face, the first word that came to mind was, *figures*.

"What?"

"On the phone. Who were you talking to?"

He asked casually but I could tell he was interested in a way that most boyfriends would be interested in who rang their girls. The sadistic side of me wanted to prolong his agony. But karma and all that crap. "My older brother, Ander."

He smiled, and I might not have been a boy genius, but I was pretty sure I saw some relief on his face.

The smile faded into a frown, and I noticed I'd lost his attention to something over my right shoulder. Before I could turn and see what bothered him, he pressed himself into me and smushed me against the wall with his body.

"Hey," I complained. Kinda.

"Shh," he urged, and buried his nose against the side of my neck. Goosebumps tweaked my arms the second his hot breath fogged the sensitive flesh beneath my ear. I heard him sniff in the scent of my hair and I was glad I used the cheapo tropical shampoo at the dollar store. I had to wash my hair twice, but it smelled really yummy.

What the hell was he doing? Why was he doing it? Not that I really cared, but curious, I peeked over his jacket collar before ducking right back behind its safety. Damn.

A few feet from us, a few guys I'd seen around school walked down the corridor. They were writers, too, but they weren't part of Haze's crew. I guess he didn't want them seeing us together, which probably meant Warp's plan to carve a rift between them and us was working.

If that were the case, Haze would be seen as a traitor talking to me, and I, his whore. This could get ugly.

They outnumbered us four to two and might have weapons. Unless Haze was the type to carry an automatic in his pants, we'd lose if a fight broke out. I shivered in fear. "Shit." Nerves made my voice shake.

"So. What did you talk about? Me?" Haze pressed harder into me, like he was trying to keep my attention off the situation and onto him. It worked. Clouding the thoughts of panic was the invasion of his smell and the heat of his body radiating into my bones.

Focus, LL, I chided.

"Yes," I croaked, and cleared my throat, reaching for the sarcasm I knew was in my brain somewhere. "That's the first thing I brought up to him. How some graffiti writer yanked me into a closet against my will."

Once the guys turned the corner, Haze stepped back. The grin on his face didn't waiver, despite the near-death experience. As usual, he seemed unfazed. "And what did he say to that?"

I slapped him in the arm. "You're deranged, you know that? Why are you even talking to me? The longer you stand here the more likely we'll get caught. And the movie already started." I realized I was babbling by the look of amusement on his face. I sighed. "I just mean that there are a million reasons why you shouldn't be next to me right now."

"And there is only one that keeps me here."

Holy hell. He worked hard on that swoon factor. "Uhm," I said profoundly.

"I'm not leaving until you promise to meet me in the closet tomorrow. And you'd better mean it."

"I meant it last time," I defended. "But I couldn't get away without being noticed. You can understand that, can't you?"

"I do understand. That's why I'm continuing to risk our safety and look like a disloyal asshole by coming over here. So promise me."

"Okay, okay, I promise."

"'Ey! Haze. Come on, man." Decay leaned out of the door to the movie theater and eyed me oddly. The WTF look he gave Haze made me cringe.

"Not good," I said, wondering if I'd have to decapitate a rooster to change my luck around.

Haze grinned. "Nah, he's giving me that look because he's missing the previews. They're his favorite part."

"Oh." I felt relieved...sorta, but Decay gave me the heebs. I couldn't be sure that Haze was right about his friend's glare. I saw something much harder than annoyance at missing the Coming Soons.

"I'm coming!" Haze yelled to his buddy before winking over his shoulder at me. "See you tomorrow."

Tomorrow. Things could only improve, right?

Nine

I woke long before my alarm went off. Stress will do that, they say. From five until seven in the morning I slept in ten-minute increments, which couldn't be healthy. I tried to counter it with a banana for breakfast but I could only choke down half.

Today I'd be spending quality time with the enemy in a closet. The herd of mutant butterflies in my gut flew upwards, heading off any attempts to swallow and leaving that panicky tang taste in my mouth.

If I remembered right, the closet wasn't very big.

"How was the movie last night, Pigeon?" When I shot eye-daggers at my brother's head he held up his hands. "Sorry. I meant to say LL. My fault."

"Uh huh." He'd call me Pigeon like Ander always called him Wharf. On some ancient paper somewhere, a rule was written saying siblings were supposed to be pains in each other's asses, I was sure of it.

"So you didn't answer me. How was the movie?"

"It was fine." I grabbed my book bag and tossed my half-eaten nanner in the trash as I passed him.

"Just fine? LL, wait."

"Can't! Gotta meet Liv halfway." Of course Liv didn't know that I had to meet her, but lying was better than admitting I'd been too preoccupied to note much about the movie, other than the action scenes were many and very loud. Loud enough to annoy me when I was trying to think.

Liv looked surprised to see me walking toward her house from mine.

"You aware you're going the wrong way? Your internal compass broken this morning, sweetie?"

"My brother."

"Ah. Harping on you about going out last night?"

I shrugged. "Something like that. With Pops gone on a run and Warp in charge, he likes to play the father."

I ranted the rest of the way to school and Liv was kind enough to listen, grabbing my hand and squeezing when I became misty-eyed over missing Ander. I even tried to apologize for leaving her lonely for awhile to chat with him at the movies, and like the billion other times I tried, she slapped my arm and called me silly.

We arrived at school in record time. Only to see a squad car speed away from the curb with a student or two stuffed into the back.

"I wonder what happened."

"Who the shit knows these days?" Liv snarled. "I sure wish people would stop screwing around before they push the school board into doing something even more dumb."

"What could be more ignorant than putting two rival schools together?" I asked her.

She shrugged. "Separating them again."

I thought about arguing with her screwy logic, but then I remembered the red paper hearts and found it impossible not to wholeheartedly agree. To go back to the old schools now would be like a slap in the face to those lost in the violence of the merger. Like...Oh, whoops, sorry, guess we'll find more money somewhere like we shoulda done in the first place.

Nah. We were in it now.

"Hey, I gotta go beg for an extension on this test for Government. I'll see you in Bio?"

I nodded but couldn't respond vocally.

When Liv walked down the hall in her barely there skirt and off-the-shoulder shirt ensemble, everyone's head turned... except *his*.

Haze stared my way, returning Liv's hello automatically but without breaking eye contact with me.

So, of course, I turned away.

Honestly, I felt he knew enough about my feelings without me having to confirm them with a nice shiny blush across my cheeks.

I busied myself at my locker, hoping to give him enough time to pass behind me before I lifted my head again.

Something brushed across my butt, and I looked around for the culprit, glaring straight into the eyes of...Decay. Haze's right-hand freak looked over his shoulder at me with a canary grin while Haze spoke to the guy on his opposite side, oblivious to the feel his boy copped.

Decay hung his tongue suggestively out of his mouth, lapping at nothing while rubbing the front of his pants. A stubby finger lifted and he pointed at me, then tipped the finger toward his junk.

Ew.

I turned back to my locker, feeling dirty and dizzy with fear, hoping the assmunch didn't see my shiver.

So far, I was of the mind that Tuesdays suck. Not only did Mr. Fewd give a pop quiz, and I suspected that was for my benefit, but Liv wanted to hang fourth period. She managed to talk her Government teacher into giving her an extra day of studying by blaming her parents somehow. That meant I would have to blow off Haze. Again.

I could've told Liv I had plans, but I wasn't ready to share my flirtation with Haze. Not yet. If nothing came of it, I didn't want anyone to know I'd even thought about it. I chose to think of it as caution instead of cowardice.

Clutching my book bag, I neared the closet and tried the handle. It was locked. Briefly, I wondered if Haze was tucked in a corner somewhere, watching and laughing with his buddies, their phones capturing the YouTube experience. I quickly turned, deciding to get the hell out of there.

The door opened and a hand tugged me inside.

Before I completed my spin around to face him, I had to admit to myself that I still doubted his intentions. Haze seemed to be on the level and, without proof, I inwardly accused him of being a sneaky jerk.

Maybe that made me the sneaky jerk.

I looked into his eyes and smiled, feeling comfort and excitement until he pulled me against him and brushed the corner of my mouth with his lips.

What the—? I drew in a deep breath and stiffened. His kiss so unexpected I did the idiot thing and froze.

In my head, I played through his possible motives for wanting to kiss me, and the fact he might actually want me came in dead last on the list.

After a moment, my lack of response brought him up from the chaste kiss.

He looked down at me. "Too soon?" I blushed and wanted to scream, *No!* but my voice was held hostage by my tight throat. "Okay then." He grinned and his hands fell to his sides.

Disappointed, and more than a little annoyed, I silently berated myself. I *wanted* Haze to kiss me and I just made the biggest ass out of myself by acting like a scared virgin. Didn't matter that I *was* one! Timid girls didn't get the hot boys, no matter what the movies said.

"After last night I got a little excited, I guess. Let's just start out with a non-threatening talk."

"Okay," I managed to say after chiseling myself out from the wall of self-hatred.

"Glad you could make it." He sounded sincere.

Oh. OH! That reminded me I couldn't actually "make it." Ugh. Guilt times ten. "Yeah…about that…"

"No way! Are you ditching the art closet hour? How come? If it's the attempted kissing thing, you can smack me in defense of your honor if you'd like. I'm cool with it." He smiled at me crookedly, in that sexy way and I felt my plan to meet up with Liv wad up like a paper ball and sail toward the virtual trash can.

"No. No, it's not that. It's Liv. She wanted to hang out," I said weakly.

"Psh. Liv will understand…" When I rolled my eyes he added, "…if you lie to her. Unless you want to use Liv as a reason to run from me. But hey, I can totally understand loyalty. You'll miss out on some cave-drawing fun, though. I planned to open up a few jars of paint, sniff the fumes and get down on these walls Neanderthal-style. It won't be as fun alone and of course, I might get so paint-stoned I fall and crack my skull open only for some janitor to discover me later, half-conscious covered in rotten egg-smelling blue, red, and yellow goo."

"Who sniffs paint anymore?"

"Not anyone I wanna know." He smiled. "But people do dumb things when they're lonely and bored."

I bit my lip to keep from laughing, aware that the hallways had quieted and my laughter would carry. Man, he was fighting dirty, insinuating his future injuries would be my fault for leaving him. But I liked it. "You know what?" I felt nervous, knowing I was about to choose a boy over my best friend. "Liv will understand." Eventually.

My worry over Liv's reaction diminished behind Haze's wicked grin. Guys knew how to work their cuteness to get them whatever they wanted. Or so my Pops told me a year or so ago in one very awkward conversation. Now that I stood in front of Exhibit A, I totally understood what he meant. The thought made my smile widen.

"What are you grinning at?"

"You're grinning, too," I pointed out.

"Yeah, but yours looks devious."

I laughed as quietly as I could, remembering where we were. "Not devious. I was thinking of something my Pops told me."

"You're in a closet with me and thinking about your dad?"

"Jealous?"

"You caught me." He held up his hands in a guilty gesture before reaching for a jar of paint to fidget with.

"I was thinking about all the warnings my father has given me about boys and their intentions when they get me alone."

Haze thought about that for a second and then shrugged. "He's not wrong. But I'm not the type to throw myself at a girl, willing or not. Er…usually. You seem to be the exception."

"Uh huh." I could practically hear Surge. *The man doth protest too much.*

"Say what's on your mind, LL. Ask me."

He lifted himself up with one hand onto a piece of plywood thrown over a laundry sink in the back and sat down, leaving the upturned bucket for me.

"Okay." I took a deep breath. The conversation had the ability to turn into an insult-fest, and I wasn't looking forward to it. Diplomacy was needed and I wasn't sure I was qualified to use it. "Put yourself in my shoes. I meet you while my brother and his friends have you surrounded and ready for a pummel."

"I can handle your brother," he said, flipping the jar of paint between his hands. The tone of his voice didn't come off as cocky but confident, confirming my suspicions that day.

"Yeah. You've had some training?"

"My parents have always been a little protective. They realized they couldn't keep me locked up in my room, so they decided to send me out in the world with a little leg up."

"What are you trained in?"

"I have a black belt in karate, and a green belt in jujitsu."

"Cool."

"It's helped. But street fighting and arena fighting are two different things."

"Right," I said and nodded.

"What about you? I saw you flip off that wall to get in between your brother and me, and I have to say...dayum."

He might be more mature than most of the guys I knew, but he was still boy enough to be a flirt! "I'm a gymnast," I told him.

"Hot! You any good?"

"I won all-around at regionals. I should get a scholarship out of it next year as long as I avoid injury."

"When's your next practice? Can I come watch?" His question matched his leering grin.

I smiled a little. "Maybe some day. Right now there's a whole lotta weird with the two teams merging and all. There's gonna be a struggle for power soon."

"Oh? And how do you know that?"

"Because I plan to initiate it." I grinned when he laughed. "I have to. Most of the girls on my team can't stand me, thanks to Wenda, and I think she's going to start working on the Branfort team and get them aboard the LL hate train."

"Sport politics. I guess you know how good you are by how many people hate you."

"I guess."

The topic was starting to depress me and he seemed to sense it.

"So. We're both go-getters. No wonder we're digging each other."

What a cocky bastard! "You don't know that I'm digging you."

"You're in a closet with me."

"It's a big closet."

He laughed. "And you're risking your brother's wrath."

"I could just be curious."

The look on his face said he clearly didn't believe me. He threw my words from earlier right back at me. "Uh huh."

He had me, and he knew it. I was in the closet because I liked him and I suspected we'd make a good match. We both had activities that society viewed as good, and activities some considered beautiful but were viewed as bad by the majority. For me, parkour and gymnastics were close cousins but karate and graffiti showed the range of talent Haze had. For that reason alone, he was squee-worthy.

We talked about silly things for the majority of the hour. Favorite foods, colors, music, movies...all of the things that usually come out over months. We rushed through the mundane questions, wanting to know our compatibility now.

Our "courtship" didn't have the luxury of time. If we were discovered, even later today, we'd have to make a snap decision as to whether or not we wanted to go forward with a relationship or cut it off to satisfy our respective crews. A light dating process was pretty much impossible.

We both knew that, and Haze inviting me into this art closet was a loud admission on his part. He liked me enough to take a risk. I knew that meant I would have to start trusting him.

Toward the end of the hour we came back to discussing our activities, specifically freerunning.

"You should teach me."

I didn't think I heard him right. "You wanna learn parkour?"

"Yeah. I figure, like my karate stuff, parkour will help me in the grid."

"It can't hurt. Especially while running from the Po-po."

He did that skeptical eyebrow thing. "Do a lot of running from authority, do you?"

As embarrassing as it was to admit, I had to nod. "Parkour is too new to the cops to be understood, I guess. They call us trespassers but I think it's because they don't know what else to say about us. We jump on buildings and run along the roof, then hop from fire-escape to windowsill and down before they can blink. They aren't sure if what we're doing is wrong, they just know we're doing something they don't approve of. So the tickets usually read trespassing."

"Escaping is probably easy."

"It can be. But Warp had a cop pull a gun on him before. A rookie fresh outta the academy. I thought Pops was going to explode."

Haze grinned. "Your dad…or Pops, sounds like a formidable dude. I'm surprised he didn't take someone out."

"His brother's a cop in Metro Detroit. In high crime cities, cops are a little jumpy. Everyone trying to kill them every day and all. I can understand their asshole-ery, I suppose, yanno? And Pops taught us to respect police authority while pushing our limits. It's a weird balance that sometimes gets screwed. Warp, these days…" I silenced myself and shook my head. I felt a sense of loyalty to my brother, knowing he wouldn't want me talking about him behind his back, especially to a guy he'd taken an instant dislike to.

"You're worried about him."

It wasn't a question, since he'd obviously read concern on my face, but I didn't want to talk about it.

Probably sensing my reluctance, he changed the subject. "So when are you gonna teach me?"

"Uhh…"

"Unless you're too busy?"

I wasn't busy so much as under the heel of a very protective and prone-to-violence brother, but teaching Haze meant spending more time with him. I'd have to find a way.

"You're damned crazy, girl!"

Surge and his plainspeak always made me grin.

"Oh, come on! You'll love it, Surge."

"Going behind your brother's back to train a guy he wants to beat the crap out of? I'm not loving it at all."

"Haze probably wouldn't lose in a fight against Warp."

Surge stared me straight in the eye with his unamused chocolate browns. "Focus, LL."

I laughed and sat down on the curb at the corner. We were a few feet down from my house, but I wasn't ready to go home yet. I needed to convince Surge to help me with teaching Haze parkour.

"There isn't much to do. It's all about teaching him the technique, how to fall, how to land, and all that. Everything else comes from him, so I'm pretty much asking you to call an ambulance when he cracks his head or sprains something."

The corners of Surge's mouth crinkled in that disapproving way of his, which usually indicated his eventual cave.

"Look," I pressed on. "I'd do it myself but if I went off on my own, Warp would want to know why. He'd get all up in my business and then freak if he found out. A huge war between writers and traceurs would—"

"Okay, okay," Surge conceded in a huff as he sat down next to me. He hooked an arm around my shoulders and squeezed harder than was necessary. "You're a pain in my ass, LL, but I love ya. Not much I wouldn't do for you."

I turned toward him, grinning. "It's a mutual thing, Surge."

For a second, I thought I saw some of that sexual confusion Surge had confided to me cross his face and wondered if he was contemplating sneaking a kiss to see how it felt. Or maybe I had it all wrong and he just had something really important to tell me.

A horn honked several times and we both turned our attention to the car.

"What the…?"

A half-block away, a true beater of the eighties revved its engine. Tires squealing, the car took off from the stop sign and roared past Surge and me at the corner.

I caught a glimpse of Haze in the passenger seat, staring at me with a look of confusion and possibly hurt. I frowned, and felt the impulse to yell, "It's not what you think...he's kinda gay," but there wasn't time, and I wouldn't destroy Surge's trust, no matter how helpful it would be for me. With Decay at the wheel, the vehicle sped down the road, fishtailing in an attempt to show Surge and me how cool the idiot driving thought he was.

"Wasn't that your boy? He didn't look thrilled."

"He's not my boy," I said. When I noticed Surge's eyes on me, I caved. "Yet. And if he isn't thrilled, then he has his own assumptions to blame."

Despite my outward attitude, inside I hoped Haze would let me explain before giving up on me for good.

Ten

All morning I had the feeling people were looking at me weird.

By mid-afternoon, I knew for sure I wasn't paranoid, because everyone *was* looking at me weird. I sat in English Lit scratching the back of my neck, feeling like bugs were crawling up my spine.

What the hell was everyone's issue?

In second period, I'd told Liv about my heebies and she checked me from head to toe. No embarrassing bleeding, toilet paper, or wardrobe malfunctions. And my hair...well, I had a blue streak in my hair, but that wasn't exactly a new development.

"I don't know, Ellie," Liv had said. "There isn't anything different about you for them to stare at. Want me to start eye-gouging?"

Even now in English Lit I grinned remembering the conversation. Liv's violent solutions to every problem rivaled my brother's, and if the two of them could be in the same room with each other without bickering, they might make a good couple. Of course, I'd bite my tongue out before saying such to Liv.

Bonnie cleared her throat, practically hanging off her chair as the last minute of class ticked by.

I thought about ignoring her but rudeness isn't my thing. Even though she probably had more fun news about Wenda's newest hate campaign, I broke down and glanced her way. She pointed at the clock and held up her index finger, wanting me to wait. Apparently, Mrs. Rosnek had spoken to her about her constant note-passing and jawing during class so she was counting the seconds.

Once the bell chimed, she was on me.

"Oh my God! The pic is making the cell rounds. It's really cool! Who did it?"

Okay, I was officially lost in Bonnie's babble.

"Huh?"

"Looks like a cool anime cartoon of you painted on the side of the pizza shop on Evans Street."

Come again? "What...pic?" My mind raced, wondering if I'd taken any cell phone pics of my ass or something. Considering I barely used my phone, because everyone I knew, except Ander, was usually within shouting distance, my logic won out over instinctual panic.

"You mean you don't know?" Bonnie bit her lip and squee-d. "I'm totally going to the bathroom to send it to you. Put your cell on vibe! Oh, and text me back!"

And then Bonnie ran down the hall, eager to be the first to show me this pic. My mind ran up and down the humiliation checklist, wondering which one of many pranks was pulled on me. Perhaps someone doctored a pic of me. Probably photoshopped my head on some animal body and sent it around as a cruel joke. It'd have to be someone from the gymnastics team. No one else hated me that much.

Decay.

Crap. I'd forgotten about that jerk.

My phone vibrated in triplicate, letting me know I had a message. I berated myself for shaking as I pulled my cell out of my pocket. Taking a deep breath, I clicked to accept the image and blinked.

The side of a pizzeria came into view with a graffiti piece of me painted on it. Beneath rays of the sun peeking between unfinished clouds, my large-as-life face grew out of a swirling background on the side of the building. All of my features were slightly exaggerated, and the blue streak in my hair cascaded from the center of my forehead, down my nose before dramatically sweeping to the side near my ear. Bonnie was right, I looked really cool and—beautiful.

But it also looked like Haze couldn't keep a secret to save his life. OMG, dumbass much?

If my brother saw this…

Oh, hell.

At least I knew why everyone took turns staring at me all day. They wanted to know who the artist was, and they figured I knew, but no one braved coming right out with it.

I hurried to my locker in hopes of getting in and out before true trouble could descend, but I'd barely opened the gilled door when it was slammed shut by my brother's shoulder. Standing behind him was Liv, her brow creased in worry, and I figured she'd found out about the graffiti this past hour too, and, like my brother, raced to my locker to see what was up. I wanted to tell her everything right then, but she was with my brother. I couldn't help but wonder if she was *with* my brother. On his side.

"What the hell was that for?" I hoped I sounded befuddled. That was a good word…befuddled.

"Care to tell me why that Haze guy is creating a replica of your face on the wall of a pizza delivery place?"

"Whoa, what?"

Liv gripped Warp's shoulder and guided him back long enough to slip in. "There's a picture floating around of your face up on the wall."

"I just saw it myself and I have no idea who would throw me up on any wall."

"It's that asshole, Haze, challenging me. I know it." Warp's face twitched with every angry word, but there was something else. Something in his eyes made him look almost excited. I was right to be worried. Warp was going to use this graffiti to start a war between crews. Shit! I needed to call Surge and tell him it was time to duck.

"What are you talking about? No one is challenging you! I don't think you're—"

"It's not up to you to think," Warp countered.

I whipped my book bag at his shoulder, taking satisfaction in his stumble back. I could only hope I knocked some sense into him. "Haze doesn't even know me! It's not him."

Warp blinked at me, his color changing from red to purple like my father did when he thought someone was lying to him. "He knows you're my sister!"

"Like everyone else out of Kennedy!"

"If not Haze, then who?" he asked between clenched teeth.

Liv, too, looked at me with a curious tilt of her head.

"I have no idea."

"You're lying!"

"Hey!" Liv jumped in, and I was relieved to lose Warp's rage-filled focus as he turned his glare on her.

"You have no idea if it's Haze. You're stabbing out there with a wild guess. It could be other members of his crew, or someone unrelated to them, with a crush on Ellie," she defended, but her keen eyes frisked me for the truth. "I'm your best friend, and as far as I know, you're not with anyone, are you?"

I felt glad that I wasn't going to have to lie. For all intents and purposes, as my father would say, I wasn't technically "with" Haze. "I'm not with anyone! For all I know this is someone trying to start trouble. That guy Haze doesn't strike me as the type to start a war or to waste his time painting me on the side of a pizzeria. Not even to get you mad, Warp."

"I'm going to find out who painted it," he promised.

"Knock yourself out." I'd hoped he wouldn't go too far in investigating.

After Warp stormed away, Liv grabbed my arm and squeezed, staring hard into my gaze. "You'd tell me, right?"

I could see the hurt, and I gave her a big hug. "You're my best friend. Of course I'd tell you."

I was totally going to hell.

Haze barely had time to jerk me into the closet before we were both running over each other.

"What the hell is the matter with you? You paint me on the side of some pizza joint?"

"Who was that with his arm around you on the corner of your street yesterday?"

"What?" we both asked simultaneously.

"Okay, you first." Haze took a seat on the laundry sink again and I followed suit on my bucket. "What are you talking about?"

I took out my phone and pulled up the photo, handing the cell to him. His eyes rounded and then narrowed.

"That isn't mine. I'll take care of it, though." He tossed my phone back to me.

I caught it and took another look for myself. "I thought… it was you. Even though it's not completely finished, it looks similar to the Heather one I saw you do. Warp thinks so, too."

He cussed softly.

"Exactly." I nodded. "Now he's demanding to know about us, making assumptions it's you trying to use me to start something with him."

"If he comes to me with it, I'll tell him the truth. It wasn't me."

"If he comes at you with this, you should run because I'm doubting reason is on his to-do list when talking to you."

His bottom lip bowed as he blew an annoyed sigh into the front of his hair. "I wouldn't do something like this, LL. I wouldn't jeopardize getting to know you better. Now, things are getting out of control."

I had a feeling he was about to back out and the thought made my heart race. I didn't want to give this up. "I guess our closet-time-fun is over, hm?"

The smile spreading across his face made me relax a little. He obviously thought I was a nub for saying such a thing. "I don't care how hard it is on us. I'm in it. I dig you. More than I thought I would and I'm not going to let someone bully me out of what I want."

He hopped down from his perch and grabbed my hands, pulling me up to face him. I suddenly felt—silly. Like a little girl playing at being an adult when I didn't know the first thing about the grown-up world. I'd thought, once I knew where Part A docked with Part B, I was in the know on relationships and the steps would come naturally. It suddenly dawned on me, in that moment, there was more than one Part A.

"But," he continued as I tried my hardest to hear over my erratic breathing, "…I don't want you to think my decision should be yours, or that I'll think badly of you if you wanna skip out on this. I know your brother makes your life difficult, and I'm making things worse. I don't want that for you."

Men. Did they all know how to be romantic *and* take control in the same breath? I thought of Ander and the girls he used to bring around, back before he had scruples. Yup, all men. Even my saintly older brother.

That damned Sneaky Gene was trying to manipulate the situation again and I wasn't above beating it with a stick.

"I'll decide what works for me." I informed him, but my agitation with his high-handedness didn't bother me enough to pull my hands out of his. "You're right that things will be a little harder, but I have to have faith that everything will work out. I don't like hiding things but I guess I have to right now."

"We both do," he reminded gently.

"I wanted to tell Liv, but I'm not sure if she has much of a poker face. Besides, if we don't really know for sure if we're going to—um, be together—"

When did the conversation turn into a bad episode of a nighttime soap opera?

"Can we just do the wait-and-see thing?" I asked timidly.

The award-winning smile was back, and with his nod I released the breath I held onto.

Which turned out to be a happy accident.

The moment I relaxed, he moved in, mouth first, capturing my lips in a kiss that literally made me dizzy enough to fall into him.

He wrapped his arm around my waist to hold me steady and tilted his head to get a better angle on my mouth. I whimpered. I actually whimpered, which gave his kiss Redbull wings, and in he delved, tongue first.

Whoa! I hadn't meant to give him a blatant invitation, but after the initial shock wore off, I realized I was glad he took it as one.

I folded my arms around his neck and pulled myself up to deepen the sweep of my tongue against his. Wow. Mouthwash, heat...and the purest energy I ever tasted. I lapped at it all, thirsty for this kiss to continue but after a minute or two, Haze eased away.

Our puffy saturated mouths hovered near, sneaking in tiny kisses between excited breaths. How much time had passed? A minute? An hour?

"Did the bell ring?"

Haze gave a quick, preoccupied laugh and dropped his hands to my waist, pushing back until there was a little distance between us.

"So, who was that guy you were with?"

Haze looked at me as if I proposed he have dinner with a family of preachy Creationists.

"I want *you* to teach me," he said. "Not some guy who probably fantasizes about kicking my ass."

"Surge isn't the type. He's a nice guy. And I can't go missing every night from the crew without my brother thinking much about it. A couple of nights I can say I'm practicing at the gym with the girls, but the other nights he expects me to be near him. Surge and I are known to go off on our own sometimes, and on those nights, we can hang with you."

His mouth tightened. "I hate that we can't just...be."

I smiled. "I hate it, too, but until we can get a good handle on the situation, we're doomed to play it safe for a little while."

"Do you see the situation, LL? Because where I'm standing, we're wasting time on hoping anyone will understand us."

"When did you get pessimistic?" He shuffled his feet, obviously embarrassed by being called out on his sudden, negative nancy-ness. "If things work out between us—"

"I think I proved that they have." He leered, seeming more like himself.

I playfully slapped his arm. "If things work out between us," I repeated, attempting to sound more stern, "then I'll bring in the big guns and clear a way for us. We only need to wait for it."

"What do you mean 'wait for it'?"

"Because the big gun, in this case, is my big brother and he's not due home for a while."

"And he's going to do what?"

Slipping out of Haze's hold, I sat down on the bucket and peeked up at him. "Honestly? I'm hoping he'll kick Warp's ass back into reality. Or at least be able to bully him into admitting to whatever chip he has on his shoulder. And I'll have him put pressure on Warp to accept us."

Haze looked doubtful. "I don't know about that. I don't feel comfortable having your big brother try and mesh out our shit."

"The other alternative is what? Violence? Will either of us be able to live with ourselves if one of our friends winds up on that hearted wall out there? I can't take that chance, Bren."

He smiled, catching the fact I used his real name. In my opinion, certain situations demanded the use of it.

"I know, Manu. Okay. First things first, though. I'll find out who put your character up on the wall and I'll buff it tonight."

"Why? I kinda wanna see it."

My enthusiasm seemed to bother him for some reason. "No, you don't."

"I'm sure it will look cooler in person instead of on a cell."

"LL," he said in all seriousness, "there are only two reasons why someone would throw up a piece of you—to either make a tribute or bring you down."

"Psh. Why would anyone wanna bring me down? Unless they're on the gymnastics team."

"They may not be after you. They might be after your brother, and you by extension. He's made a few writer enemies out there."

I tried not to get freaked out by what he was telling me, but the possibility couldn't be denied.

Still, if he was right, and this was an attempt to declare war, I wasn't sure I could continue on. It was better to find other reasons.

"I think you're too worried about this," I said. "Maybe it's real simple, like someone trying to set you up, or out our relationship. The fact is, you don't know."

"No one knows about us! The only one who saw us together is Decay, and his focus is nature. He's not as 'all city' as he would need to be to make a piece like that. I dunno, I guess it's possible he did some talking to the crew." He sighed and reached down, cupping the side of my face. "You're right. I don't know what's going on, but I'll figure it out and make it gone. If your brother takes issue with you over this, let me know and I'll meet with him."

How cute! He didn't actually say "no one messes with my woman," but I heard it anyway. And the cutest thing of all? He actually thought it was possible to talk to Warp and walk away unscathed.

Eleven

I shouldn't have been surprised that by the time I got home, Warp was waiting for me in the living room, happily livid.

I wished I would've taken Liv up on her offer to come play mediator between us again, but I was tired. Tired of tiptoeing around Warp and his bipolar behavior. If he was determined to lecture me, then I'd be equally determined to let him know where he stood.

"Emanuella! Who the hell are you involved with?"

"I'm sick of this conversation, Warp." I tried to walk past him, but he grabbed my arm and turned me to face him. His lips were curled in a snarl, nothing like the brother I had known years ago…when we were all happy and learning to live again without my mom.

Warp was heading back to that ugly place.

"I'm sick of you not telling me shit!"

"I tell you nothing because you can handle nothing!" I squared off with him, having to look up a little to meet his enraged eyes, but I managed it. I wouldn't be bullied. "Every time Pops leaves, you get worse than usual. Like you're afraid I might suddenly turn newb and get myself hurt."

"This spray-portrait of you is why you need to be dealt with. You're into something and you won't tell me what. You're not letting me protect you just like Mom never said anything to Pops about how fucked in the mind she was. You can't bottle up like that, Emanuella!"

"Give me a break." I rolled my eyes. I loved my mother. I missed her very much. But Warp had a habit of using her death to berate my behavior, and I was pretty sure she'd want me to give him a verbal smackdown for it. "You always try to use Mom against me, like that will make me tell you my innermost secrets. Mom was ill. She couldn't handle her thoughts. She died because something was wrong with her head. Not because she didn't share her feelings often enough. I'm not going to sit here and let you try to guilt me into giving you a story I don't have."

"There is a story. I ain't dumb. I told you I'd figure shit out, and you know what? I already found out the paint used on your portrait is only sold at one store. Did you know that?"

"No I didn't, Detective."

"And guess whose crew is closest to the locale? That Haze asshole and his buddies."

"So what?"

"I'm just saying, stay away from him."

My instinct told me to tell Warp to mind his own business and stay out of mine but that would only ensure he stayed glued to my ass. "Does that make you feel better? Saying that? Coming at me with all of this flimsy evidence? Do you hear yourself? You found out the paint used is sold at a store that Haze's crew uses. Like no one else could Google map their way to the store, genius?"

Warp's lips pursed. "Don't push me, Emanuella."

Don't push him? I could barely see, I was so angry. Stumbling for something potent to say, I pulled out Haze's words from earlier and used them as a weapon. "I will push you, Warp! Because someone has to. And I'd rather it be me than someone you piss off."

"What are you talking about?"

"I'm talking about you looking for trouble." He was about to blow me off, but I was too mad to let that happen. "You ever stop to think if I get hurt, chances are, it will be your damned fault?"

He flinched and dropped his grip on my arm.

"No, I doubt you've thought about that at all." Shaking my head, I shouldered past him. As far as I was concerned, the conversation was over.

"I'd offer to skip Government but you'd probably only stand me up again," Liv said, walking to fourth hour the next day. She tried not to sound too bitter about my disappearance the day before.

Fail.

I knew it bugged her because she'd been one-word-Wanda on the walk home and to school in the morning. I hadn't realized she could be so touchy, but I guess I couldn't blame her. She'd told me her parents didn't want to be around her, and maybe she thought me ditching her for one hour meant I was no better than her parents.

My heart added an extra beat to its rhythm thinking about the reason I stood her up, but I was able to maintain normalcy and continue the conversation. "I'm sorry about that. But hey, what good is a gymnastics scholarship if scraping by is all I'm ever going to do? Study hall is important."

Liv smirked, but dropped it. "Speaking of gymnastics, I heard that girl, Wenda, got shot in a drive-by last night."

My face became anemic. I know because I felt every drop of blood ooze down my body and settle in my toes. "Oh my God. Are you kidding me?"

Liv looked at me as though shocked I'd ask something so stupid. "Not something I would joke about, Ellie. What does it matter? She's not dead, she's in the hospital, she's luckier than the freaks on the heart wall. A kneecapping is better than dead."

I knew some of the dead gangbangers by reputation only, but this bit of violence concerned someone in my squad. "Shot in the knee? God, her career is over. She must be crushed. I should go check on her and send her flowers or something."

"Screw that, Ellie. She bad-mouthed you behind your back, led the other girls into keeping secrets from you—like the meet-up with the new girls on the team, I say you sign a 'from all of us' card and get over it. Besides, she was jealous of you before. How do you think she's gonna feel knowing that she can't compete for a long time if ever again?"

How do you tell someone you wish them well when they'd gone out of their way to make your life hell? Liv was right. Any gesture I might make would be perceived badly. "Wow. It feels kinda weird."

"Yeah." Liv shrugged. "I just hope your dad doesn't find out when he gets home. He'll put you on lockdown and we'll never go out again."

I knocked on the door and felt the familiar warmth of his hand snake around my wrist and tug me into the closet.

After spending an entire evening fantasizing about his mouth on mine, and an entire night dreaming about it, the reality was rather mind-jumbling.

I barely had the time to draw in a breath before he kissed the sense from me, steering his mouth to the left and then to the right, searching for my response, which I was only too happy to give.

We came up for air at some point, but not until well after our lips were swollen and our hands probably numb with our death-grips on each others' clothes. I couldn't be sure, but I suspected my Imagine Dragons tee had wrinkles at the small of my back to match the ones I had ironed into his shoulders with my fists.

Whoops.

"Thanks, I needed that," I admitted, and snuck another kiss to his chin.

He ran a finger down the bridge of my nose to the tip. "Glad I could service you." He grinned. "Having a bad day?"

"I'm having a weird one. One of the girls on my team, Wenda, was shot in a drive-by."

"Jesus. I'm sorry, Manu." He leaned his head against mine.

"I'm sorry she was shot but it feels weird because we don't like each other much."

As if he knew what I needed, he shrugged. "You didn't shoot her, and you're not wishing she were dead. It's okay to not care that she got shot."

"I don't know if I can say I don't care. I don't know how to feel about it. I know…it sounds psychotic, but a part of me feels…responsible. I wanted to strangle her myself, I wanted bad things to happen. I…"

"Hey," he comforted, smoothing his hand up and down my back. "You're not friends. She made you angry, wasn't very nice to you, and you wanted her to get what she deserved. That's normal! You can't blame yourself because this massive shit-hill of a city made it so. The truth is, the people in power don't wanna look down at the kids getting shot, beat up, and dying at their feet, because of this school merger. They don't wanna admit they're to blame, which they are. It's not us, Manu. It's them, and until they turn the tide of violence, shit like this is gonna keep happening. You're not to blame because you didn't like her," he repeated. "It sucks she was hurt. Leave it at that."

I nodded and enjoyed his comfort in silence, trying not to think of anything but what he'd said and allow it to wash my guilt away.

Of course, after twenty or so minutes, I could only handle so much of his nearness before my thoughts turned to picturing him naked.

Whoa. I blushed and decided to hide it while fidgeting with the shoulder strap of his doctor's bag. "So, planning on going out tonight? I was going to invite you to meet up with Surge and me at Tucker Park."

"I wasn't able to go out and erase your character last night. I'm going to do it today while everyone is here at school."

I laughed. "And how do you plan to sneak past the hall Nazis?"

"I don't have to. My parents are cool. I told them what I wanted to do and they called me out."

Well, that was weird. My father would turn purple if I asked to skip school, and then he'd dip into his lecture on why rules and structures were important in the real world. I loved my father, but sometimes he really did try too hard. I guessed it was because he wanted more for us than what he had.

All parents say that, but only some obsess about it. Pops was a definite obsess-er. "So, you'll meet up with us tonight? Six-thirty-ish, okay?"

"Yeah, sounds good, Manu."

Apparently he didn't plan to wait the whole hour, anxious to get the deed done. His lips brushed over mine again and I was lost. Sometimes, I suspected his mouth was covered in some addictive substance. I could never get enough and right after a kiss ended, I wanted another, and another, and another.

Sadly, the make-out session was short-lived.

"Tonight then," I said, once the thrill of his kiss died down and I could breathe. With a nod he ducked out of the closet.

Five minutes later, I was outside of Liv's Government class dancing the cha-cha until she noticed me and came out to play.

Twelve

"Maybe he ain't coming. He heard it was gonna be me, and instead of admit he was scared, he decided he would give you some lame-ass excuse tomorrow." Surge walked across the monkey bars. When he came to the end he did a little turn, while dropping down through the small square. His hands gripped the bar at the last second, jerking his descent to a halt. He proceeded to swing from one bar to the next, the way the apparatus was intended to be used.

"I told him you'd be here, dork. He'll be here," I said without certainty. I didn't think like Surge. I knew Haze wasn't afraid of him. But that didn't mean Haze didn't run into the law while trying to clean up some graffiti. The irony almost made it impossible *not* to have happened.

While I rested on the parallel bars, draped across them like a sheet on a couple of clotheslines, I watched as Surge effortlessly moved from one side of the monkey bars to the next before making the leap to the nearby catwalk.

The best place to learn parkour was a small arena, and playgrounds were the best, as long as you didn't make a bunch of noise that provoked the neighbors into calling the cops.

I knew that the difference between parkour and freerunning

was spelling to most people, but to me, freerunning seemed a little more specific to what we actually do. If you were going from one point to another out in the world off the beaten path, *that* was freerunning. The rest of the terminology debate was lost on me. The flow and the freedom I felt while practicing was all that mattered.

"Looks like he's decided to brave the Surge," Surge said looking off into the shadows.

I lifted my head in time to see Haze wandering up, his doctor's bag hanging between his shoulder blades.

Surge gave a little show by jumping off the catwalk onto the poles of the swing set, his legs spread and feet docked to hold himself up without effort. Showing off for the new guy. Was he trying to intimidate Haze or impress him?

"Hiya, stranger," I smiled and let the top of my body free-fall, depending on my knees to hold me up. Using the momentum of my swing, I straightened my legs and landed on my feet, heading toward him.

I hoped I looked as impressive as Surge, but didn't have to worry much as I saw Haze's eyes take on a mix of respect and something a little more primal. He probably felt a lot like I did when I saw what he was capable of doing with a few cans of spray paint.

"Sorry I'm late," Haze mumbled, eyeing Surge as he pulled me in for a quick hug. I'd told him Surge knew about us, but I couldn't blame him for being too cautious.

Stepping away from me, Haze held his hand out to Surge, who clasped it without hesitation.

Bonus! Good sign. I was surprised at how easily they seemed to take to each other, before I realized neither had let go of the other's hand. They kept squeezing, waiting for the other to cry uncle.

"Ugh! Really?" I stepped into their embrace, forcing them to let go. "Unbelievable."

"Calm yourself, LL," Surge said with a grin. "We're letting each other know where we stand."

Haze grinned and I found myself wanting to smack the both of them.

"Must be one of those jokes where I'd need a penis to get it," I said.

"Let's get started," Haze said and clapped his hands together with enthusiasm. I briefly wondered if he'd be that excited after his first hospital visit.

Right before I turned away, I noticed a crack in Haze's smile and made a note to ask him about it. He arrived late and not in the best of moods. Something was up.

Once Haze started bleeding, we called it a night. For the last few hours Surge and I showed him the basic concepts of parkour, from ideals to moves, then we stood back and watched him jump around on all the activities of the playground without a routine. After all, improvisation and quick-thinking breed the strength of mind needed to freerun. Or so Ander often told those he taught.

But all the quick-thinking in the world can't save the inevitable face-plant or, in Haze's case, the introduction of nose to metal pole.

Cussing, he landed flat on his back, his nose trickling blood. I winced and ambled over, ignoring the snickering from Surge.

"Welcome to the fun stuff, bro. I'll let LL play nurse while I run to the store for ice and some mango smoothie goodness. Either of you two want?" Surge pointed two fingers at us while walking backwards. Haze shook his head and I nodded. "Cool." Surge waved and scaled the playground fence.

I turned my eyes back to Haze. "You all right? Feeling woozy or anything?"

"I'll live, LL. I just haven't had a bloody nose in a while. A tournament when I was in sixth grade, I think. I forgot how much it sucks."

"Is it broken?"

"My pride? Yup."

I thwapped his arm. "Your nose, freak."

He wiped his nose across his sleeve and stared up at me with a grin. Blood smear and all, he couldn't help but remain hot.

"Nah. I doubt it will even bruise noticeably. Which is good. Hard to get girls with a battered face. Might hurt when I put on my respirator, though."

"Get girls, huh? I think you're wrong about that broken nose."

Laughing, he sat up and pulled me by the hem of my hoodie onto his lap. "I only care about getting one girl."

"Getting something you already got seems like overkill."

He buried his hand in my hair and brought my mouth down to his, kissing me while laughing. I'd never been kissed that way before but there was no question I loved it. I loved everything where he was concerned. And his lips made me forget all about asking after his earlier frown. Which could mean only one thing:

I was the queen of all fools.

Haze waited for Surge to come back with ice and my smoothie before he gave me a quick kiss and claimed he had to go. I chewed on the inside of my lip, coming to terms with my feelings for Brennen Craig while watching him leave.

Once he was out of sight, Surge came up behind me and squeezed my arms into my chest until I involuntarily squeaked.

I laughed and sent a warning elbow into his ribs.

"Harsh, girl!"

I knew he wasn't as hurt as he pretended. Especially since he stumbled back and clutched his middle like I threw a UFC punch.

"Yeah, yeah. So what do ya think?"

Surge stood up straight, his Oscar performance interrupted by my question. He ran his tongue around the inside of his mouth and then shrugged. "I don't know, LL. I just met the guy. Unlike you, holing up in some school closet for hours every day, I haven't had the time to form an opinion."

I shook my head at him and cracked open my smoothie.

"I'm serious, baby girl! I'm not as convinced as you that he ain't the one that painted your face for all to see. Some of my cousins are the best writers in Cali, so I know a thing or two a'ight? I know that they all can tell who did what by the style. Everyone is different, like Monet is different from Van Gogh. The lines, the style…it looked a little like the clouds we saw Haze painting on the wall that day."

"Come on." I groaned, folding my arms across my chest. "You saw his work for like, a second. There are similar styles between some artists that would need closer inspection to see the differences. Besides, do you really think he'd ruin a chance for us to be together by making an homage to me on a noticeable wall? I mean, I don't know exactly what he feels, but I'm pretty sure he likes me enough not to cause problems for me."

I walked over and sat down on one of the swings, drawing my hood up over my hair. The single strand of blue waved across my nose, unruly as ever, reminding me of the piece causing me so much grief. I always said the lock had a mind of its own. I kinda wanted to give it a personality all its own, too, which is why I dyed it a vivid color.

I shivered when Surge sat down on the swing next to me, but my reaction had nothing to do with him. When the sun goes down, the late September nights became downright cold.

Of course, coming out of the winter, I always thought the same temperature was tee-shirt weather.

"I didn't mean to make it sound like he don't like you, girl. I just think maybe he likes you too much."

Surge probably took my silence as anger, but I felt fine. His suspicions about Haze meant he cared about me, so I wouldn't hold a grudge against him.

"Sounds like you think he might want to start trouble with my brother or something."

"That ain't off my map completely," he admitted, "but I see the way he looks at you, and that's what makes me a little concerned is all."

"Paranoid, you mean."

"Well, Ander will kill me if I let something happen to you. That's enough to make me a little 'noid, I'm saying."

"Yeah, I get ya. It's all right. Keep your eye on him if it makes you feel better, Surge. I want you to be comfortable with this." I leaned on the chain links of the swing and rested my chin on my grip so I could stare over at him. The genuine concern I saw in his face humbled me. "I'm glad you're my friend."

"I'll remind you of that if I have to tackle your boy like a 'roided quarterback."

Thirteen

"Your brother is still really mad at you, huh?" Liv turned her head to stare at Warp's retreating back. For the second time in two hours he'd walked past me without saying a simple hello. Rudeness was nothing new for Warp, but I knew him well enough to know he was still stewing from our talk night before last.

Pops had returned from his job a full day early, so we hadn't had another argument like I'd been expecting that last day or so. I wondered if Warp's anger would ever subside enough to where we could have an actual conversation or if I was doomed to be subjected to his 'tude for all eternity.

Liv and I arrived at my locker and I unloaded all but my third-hour books.

"I think he's just mad because I made him feel guilty pointing out the truth and all."

"You're not gonna do your Bio homework in Study Hall?"

"Nah. I'm going to work on my art project for once. I need something that isn't going to make me pull out my hair today." I planned to work on it with Haze in the supply closet but left that part to myself.

"Ah," Liv said, seemingly mollified. "So why do you think your brother feels guilty?"

"He was accusing me of getting myself in deep with someone and not telling him. He's so sure that I've done something wrong and got mixed up with the wrong crowd."

"Like you have time in between his stalking, hanging with me, parkour and, oh yeah, school!" Liv rolled her eyes.

"Exactly. I told him, with his territorial attitude, he could very well be responsible for the reason my face was on some wall."

Liv sucked in a breath and wrinkled her brow in uncertain disapproval. "I don't know, Ellie, I think you might have gone too far with that one."

Slinging my book bag over my shoulder, I turned and walked to my third hour knowing she'd follow me. "No. I hope me saying it will make him more careful about who he upsets."

"You want him to not piss people off? I don't think he can help himself."

"Liv, if he makes a bunch of enemies, they could use me to get to him. I don't want to be involved in some pointless war. I had to say something, cuz I don't think he thought about his bullshit causing me trouble before I said something."

"I guess. If you think mentioning it might keep him from doing something irrational." She didn't sound convinced.

"There isn't much I wouldn't lower myself to do if it meant keeping my brother in check."

"I don't blame you," Liv said.

A typical noncommittal response that made it possible for her to skip to the next subject. Not that I minded. I didn't like talking about my arguments with my brother.

"Are you spending the night tonight?" she asked.

"Can't. Pops is home, and he always likes us to be 'in house' when he's around."

"Oh. Well that's cool, I guess."

"Yeah. Warp isn't on me when Pops is around, but I have less freedom, too. It's a vicious circle, as Mr. Fewd would say." We both laughed.

Liv stepped in front of me and gave me a big, reassuring hug. "Things will get better. Maybe your brother will cut the crap now that your portrait is erased." She released me and frowned at my frown. "What's wrong?" she asked.

I couldn't think of anything to say. Over her shoulder, I spied Haze and one of my gymnastics team members intimately entangled.

Cathy. The dirty slut.

Five seconds ago I was antiviolence. Now, the urge to run down the hall and face-stomp her into the linoleum crawled into my skin and played over and over in my mind.

"Ellie, what's going on? You look—unhinged." Liv turned and saw the same scene. "Check out the whore-jacket. Yikes! You'd think Bren would have better taste."

I hated that I felt my eyes sting and knew if I so much as blinked, I'd have a telling wet trail down my face. Next came the shakes as I fought the impulse to brutalize the bitch throwing herself on my secret boyfriend.

Was he my boyfriend? It wasn't as if we had verbally said so. Although Haze did tell me he only wanted one woman. Maybe he was being purposefully vague so later down the line he could cruelly say "I didn't mean you, silly girl."

I swallowed and looked down as I felt Liv grab my hand and squeeze hard. "Snap out of it," she chastised.

But I couldn't. "I..."

Down the hall, Haze stepped into my line of sight, his face impassive as he started talking to Cathy, who stood on her tiptoes and planted a kiss on Haze's lips.

I was going to be sick. My stomach roiled and I took a step back, feeling the sharp slap of betrayal.

I think my hateful gaze penetrated the distance and called to him, because in the instant after he moved back from her, he turned his stare to me. A strange expression claimed his handsome, treacherous face and he subtly shook his head.

Whatever his message, I couldn't absorb it through the sudden hardening of my heart.

"Jerk," I whispered, and damn if I didn't blink.

A single tear rode the wave of my cheek down to my chin.

"That's it. You have some explaining to do," Liv said, tugging me off toward the bathroom with a grip so tight it hurt. She could've done anything she wanted to me and I wouldn't have cared—I wouldn't have felt it. My entire body was numb with heartbreak.

I don't remember much about my climb through the girls' bathroom window or the jog a few blocks down to the local fast-food joint, but once I sat down and sucked on the straw of my pop, I finally realized Liv was munching a burrito while glaring at me.

"What?" I asked defensively.

"You promised me you'd tell me if there was someone. But now I know you lied to me. You've been hooking up with Brennen behind my back! I thought we were friends. Best friends!"

"You're jumping to conclusions, Liv."

She threw her unfinished burrito down on the wax paper wrapper. "You were in tears when you saw that Cathy whore hanging on him and kiss him. I'd like to think that I'm not a complete dumbass and can add simple Scooby-Doo clues together."

"I had a crush on him. I didn't say anything because it isn't anything. And seeing him and Cathy together..."

Liv stared at me before taking an angry sip of her pop. She sprayed a little as she jerked the straw from her mouth before she finished sucking.

"You're not the type to crush without a reason. He looked at you and shook his head, Ellie. Why would he do that if you two weren't a thing?"

My heart pounded hard with hope. "You think he didn't want Cathy on him?"

"Oh, Christ. Look at you. You're completely oblivious."

"It doesn't matter. It was silly to think we could be together, anyway. I'll get over it."

I could feel Liv's leg shake from my chair. "You're missing the point, Ellie. No matter if you guys were ever going to be an item—why didn't you tell me? Why did you hide it?"

"It seemed like Haze liked me, too, but I couldn't be sure, and I didn't want to look desperate if he was using me as a tool to start a fight with my brother. You gotta understand that."

"Yeah, I do."

"So why are you so mad?" I asked.

Liv leaned over the table a little to look me straight in the eye. "Because you didn't trust me to keep a secret."

Ugh! She was right. On dictionary.com under "horrible friend" my mug shot would be in the right column.

I was never the type to shy away from admitting I screwed up. I should've trusted Liv with the news about Haze and me. I should've come out with the truth and revealed the whole story. The supply closet, my first non-awkward kiss, the night I spent teaching him the basics of parkour with Surge.

But I didn't.

"I know. I suck. But you're the most beautiful girl in school, guys throw themselves at you. I didn't want to seem inferior if I couldn't even keep this one guy."

She shook her head at me, but I saw her shoulders lose some of their tension. Apparently compliments were ways to defuse the Liv-bomb. "Now you're being a dork. Like I'd ever judge you based on your slut-level. Come on. Give me some credit."

"I will."

She looked away from me, so I reached across the table and grabbed her hands to pull her back to the conversation. "I mean it. From this point on, I'll give you more credit. I'm just not used to having a best friend so you have to give *me* a little bit of time to get used to spilling my thoughts out to a living diary, all right?" I added a squeeze of my hands on hers and attempted at a smile.

"Sheesh. You look constipated. Maintain the frown for a little longer until you can grin and mean it."

I snorted. "It could be a while. I'm feeling kinda foolish right now."

"It'll pass. And I should know. I've fallen for the wrong type too many times not to know how quickly the disappointment fades when you have a friend at your back."

I nodded.

"So, what are you going to do?" she asked.

"I don't know. I'm guessing he isn't interested anymore."

"Hm. When did you two find time to talk anyway?"

Being a bad person was a disorder I couldn't help. Why else would I keep lying to my best friend? I tried to console myself with the excuse I was trying to keep her from being hurt. If she learned I skipped out on her to have a conversation with Haze, I wasn't sure she'd remain my friend.

"That's the thing, we spoke in art class once." Half-truths paved the road to purgatory. "And then between my classes."

"Oh, so this was a preliminary crush?" When I nodded, she sighed. "Cool. I thought after the way you reacted in the hallway he was sneaking into your room at night or something."

I wish. "Nah. It's just—I've never really liked anyone before him."

"Ahh, my poor innocent BFF."

I rolled my eyes. "Yeah, yeah. Hey, shouldn't we get back? Fourth period will start soon."

"Screw it. My Government teacher loves me. Let's skip over to get some ice cream. I think it's clinically proven to keep hormones and heartbreak under control."

That was the second time I stood up Brennen "Haze" Craig.

Tink.

I breathed in through my nose and stretched. The alarm clock seared red numbers into my eyeballs. 13:27. Huh? I blinked. 12:37...okay that made more sense.

Tink.

What the hell was that?

I rubbed at my eyes and threw my legs over the side of my bed. Holy hell, it was cold in my room. Whenever Pops was home, he turned the thermostat to I've-got-penguins-for-children.

Tink.

I flicked on my nightstand light and listened. Nothing. I looked over at the small windows of my bedroom and shook my head. No way.

Tink.

Yes way, the noise said. And with my heart pounding, I walked to a window and pulled aside my threadbare curtains.

Haze stood halfway into my yard so he could see over the porch eave into my bedroom but remain in the streetlight so I could see him perfectly. Instead of smiling at me once our eyes met, he threw the remaining pebbles into the bushes and disappeared. Was this some new twisted version of ding-dong ditch?

A second later, he crawled across my tattered roof and glared at me through the windowpane.

A single finger pointed at the slide lock in a silent command to let him in.

Tempted to do exactly that, I held my ground and shook my head. He'd expected this, raising his knuckles as if he were going to knock. Ugh! Calling my bluff was so unfair. He knew I wouldn't risk Warp or my father hearing him.

I opened the window and stepped back, resisting the urge to throw myself at him the instant his messy dark hair and angry eyes came into the light. Standing at his full height, he shut the window against the cold and faced me. Frown or no, he was hot as always. Bastard.

"You can't be here," I said in a low voice.

For so many reasons, his presence in my room was wrong, the most important being I wasn't sure I could control myself with him so close to my bed should he try and take me to it. God, I was a Cathy wannabe.

"Here is the only arena I have for our big fight since you obviously plan to call things off by avoiding me," he vehemently whispered.

"I'm not the type of fool to let you kiss me in the closet so no one knows, then flirt publicly with one of my teammates so your friends don't think you're gay."

I might have laughed at the look on his face if I wasn't worried that it might be the last time I saw it. "Do I come off as the kind of guy who worries about what other people think? My crew is full of a bunch of man sluts who get drunk at parties and make fools of themselves. That isn't me, LL. I like to hang out with the guys, have a few beers, but I like being in control of myself and my actions. I have confidence in who I am as a person. I don't need to impress anyone with how many drinks I can slam without passing out or how many girls I can bang in any given weekend."

"That makes your flirtation with Cathy worse, Bren."

"Flirtation? I helped her with a problem in Trig. I stayed after class to talk to the teacher, and when I came out, she pounced on me from behind. At first, I guess I was delusional, thinking that it was you trying to surprise me."

"Like I'd do that. Looking desperate isn't something I practice."

"Yeah, I realized that after a minute and, of course, the blonde hair flying into my face was an obvious second clue."

I folded my arms over my chest. "So why didn't you hurl her across the hallway into the lockers when she kissed you?"

"Seriously, LL?"

"She woulda deserved it." I pouted.

"Yeah, she would've, but I don't beat up on girls, even one whose attention is unwanted."

"Exceptions should be made."

He grinned at me, closing the distance between us and wrapping me in his arms. According to the movies, I should push at his chest and pout some more, but all I wanted to do was feel the bliss of loving him without complications or jealousies.

"If she had tried to put her hands on my junk, I would have made with the kung fu, but tops, she was just annoying. Everyone in that hall knew I wasn't interested in Madam Birdlips, except you."

Remembering what Liv had said about Haze shaking his head at me, I tried to look at what happened with better eyes. He mistook my silence for disbelief.

"It's true. I bet if you ask Liv she'd back me."

Sighing as if I were letting out all the steam from my earlier anger, I conceded. "You're right. Seeing Cathy on you made me feel weird and I overreacted. I don't need Liv to tell me that. Besides, she's busy being upset with me for not telling her about us."

"Oh."

"I told myself I kept quiet because I was afraid to trust her or she might say something to someone on accident. But I don't really know why I didn't tell her."

He shrugged. "Because you thought I was a man-whore, after you for a game of fetch?"

"That was part of it, I guess. But I've never really had a best friend before. One that didn't have a penis, anyway."

I tried not to smile when Haze frowned. "I like it better when you have friends without penises."

I ignored his jealousy, but put it away for smile material later. "I always feel as though Liv is trying to teach me things. Like she takes it as her responsibility to keep me from messing my life up. Like Warp. I guess I'm used to shutting people like that out."

"Decay's like that, too. He's been a writer longer than me and he's taught me stuff along the way. Like wearing a respirator and making consistent lines and stuff. I think sometimes, that makes him feel like he needs to keep schooling me, even though I'm good now, I don't need all his advice. So sometimes, I don't tell him everything 'cause I don't wanna hear it. Liv is who she is and you need to decide if you can deal with it or not. But, if she tries to change you, ditch her."

"Oo. You're so wise and opinionated." I teased.

"I know, right? Listen, Liv can be overbearing. Heather used to get into fights with her sometimes over it, and honestly, I wasn't sure why the two hung out as much as they did, until Heather told me some of the shit Liv's parents would do to her."

"Yeah, she told me about this time when she reported a fake robbery just to get them to come home because she was lonely."

Haze shook his head. "It's messed up how they punished her."

"She didn't tell me that part, just that she was glad they were gone."

"Heather told me they tied Liv to a tree and left her outside all night so she would know what being lonely really meant."

"Jesus!"

"Yeah. Heather felt bad for her. Said she'd never do anything to make Liv feel alone, so the two of them, despite their fights, were pretty inseparable. But my sister was pretty easy to get along with. If you think Liv is going to try to push you around…well you push back. No girlfriend of mine is gonna be bullied."

I felt my throat tighten and I looked up into his beautiful eyes, the deepness of our conversation lost behind one word. "Girlfriend?"

"Yeah, Manu," he whispered the silly pet name, and I realized I didn't mind it. "You're my girl, and no dollar special, park bench whore like Cathy is going to get in the way of me proving it to you."

Stretching on my tiptoes, I met his mouth and slid my arms up his muscular biceps, encircling his neck. I pulled myself closer at the same time he cinched his arms around me.

Bliss. I was vacationing in his kiss, inhaling the scent of his cheek. He smelled so good. Like adventure and mystery. The unknown lay with him and I wanted to explore all of it.

The floorboard outside my door creaked and I barely had the sense to break off the kiss before my doorknob turned and in walked my brother.

Fourteen

My hands slid down to Haze's shoulders where I held on for dear life. We all stood there in silence, allowing for the shock to settle. Warp's eyes drifted from me to Haze with murder screaming from his dark gaze.

He began to shake, lifting his finger to point an accusatory finger at Haze. "You—you dirty bastard!"

"Shh," I scolded, moving away from Haze to intercept my brother's approach. I grabbed his finger and jerked his hand down. "You wake up Pops and I'll kill you."

"The way you killed me now, Emanuella!? Shacking up with this piece of shit writer...the enemy? How could you do this? No, no, I don't wanna hear any bullshit you might spew to save your boyfriend's ass."

"I don't need her to save my ass. I got this, easy." Haze's voice was low, but I could tell by the tone, he was ready to hard-play.

I looked over my shoulder to see him step up to the line. Oh, God!

"Hey, hey." I moved to the side so I could press a hand to both heaving testosterone-y chests. "Can we be rational about this for one second? Warp, I know how this looks but you have to trust me."

"I knew you were dating this guy. I knew he was the one who put your portrait up, but you lied to me. You tried to make me think I was the one responsible."

"I didn't paint that shit!"

Warp's eyes turned from me to Haze. "I saw the lines, man. It's your signature as clear as if you tagged your name on it."

I frowned. "How do you know his signature?"

Warp shook his head slowly from one side to the next. A typical stall tactic I'd seen him use with Pops countless times. "Are you ignorant or something? You were with us when we saw him painting his sister's face on the wall. You didn't recognize it?"

"Someone took a bite from me—copied my style." Haze growled. "I didn't have anything to do with painting LL's piece."

"And the bloated one I found tonight? I suppose you had nothing to do with that either, huh?"

I frowned and glanced back at Haze, who looked as dumbfounded as I felt.

"What the hell are you talking about?" Haze asked.

"Your act might fool my sister, but not me. I know you're using her to start the war, but you know what, asshole? I didn't need the push. From here on, I'm on you and yours."

I felt sick to my stomach. Five minutes ago I had been happy, knowing that Haze didn't want Cathy, he wanted me. Now, his visit had opened the door for Warp's war, where my brother hoped to gain city infamy. Red paper hearts dotted my blurring vision as tears filled my eyes. This couldn't be happening...but it was, and no amount of denial on my part was going to fix it.

I remembered Haze's distance when he'd come to parkour training, like something was weighing on him. Maybe he had seen his signature on the piece he'd gone to erase and was worried about who was framing him.

"No, Warp, stop it. Just give me time to figure this all out, all right? Haze says it isn't him and I believe him. Maybe it is someone in his crew trying to create problems or someone else trying to take out other crew competition. Please. There could be many reasons for this. Even you," I reminded him in a last ditch effort to get him to see reason.

He laughed at me, his bitterness like the shriek of a screech owl to my ears. "Nice try, Emanuella." Warp looked past me, sneering at Haze. "Letting my sister beg for you, coward?"

I held my breath, afraid that Haze would take the bait. "Brennen," I pleaded softly.

Haze's gaze shifted to me, but only briefly. His only focus now was Warp. "You want a huge brawl where the violence will escalate and your sister might become a target? I guess I care about her more than you."

"At least you're admitting in front of her you'd make her a target."

Haze sighed, his fists balling at his sides. I couldn't blame him. My brother wasn't making much sense. When Warp felt angry, logic melted away to reveal dick-a-saurus.

"I would never," Haze argued. "But I can't be held responsible for what other members of my crew or outside crews might do."

"Outside crews? What are you talking about?" my brother asked.

"You think it's only me and my crew that'll jump into the fight? You start a war with one group of writers, they all jump in. I can't possibly protect her from every idiot out there who happens to take a disliking to all things freerunner because they view your attack on my crew as a declaration of war. Why do you think I haven't responded to your bullshit from the other night? Why do you think I held Decay back in school the other day?"

Haze inched closer to my brother, and I was willing to bet a part of him wanted to prove he wasn't afraid of Warp or any of his threats. "I don't do any of this for *your* dumb ass. I do this because I dig your sister and I don't want to see her get hurt because her brother's a hotheaded ass!"

"You don't know nothing about me," Warp yelled and pushed me out of the way.

"And you don't know nothing about me except that I'm into your sister. It's unhealthy, man. You can't try and start a war to keep her under your foot. It's sick."

"I'd rather her be under my foot then hanging with a twisted fool who killed his own sister!"

I'm not exactly sure what happened. The details would be forever fuzzy. I stood there with my mouth wide open, stunned by Warp's blatant accusation and the deep shade of purple Haze's face turned.

Faster than I thought humanly possible, Haze threw a jab into Warp's right eye and followed through with a hard kick to the chest.

Warp flew backwards, falling across my bed. I might've been embarrassed by the amount of stuffed bears that went flying in every direction if I wasn't so sure chaos was about to descend.

Using the momentum of his landing to somersault backwards off my mattress, Warp landed on his feet. He gripped the corner post of my bed and swung himself around until his foot slammed into Haze's gut.

Haze tried to keep his footing, but lost the battle.

In an effort to find something to grab onto, he reached but found nothing between himself and the closet. He tumbled inside, grabbing at my clothes, bringing the suction-cupped bar down on his head.

Yoga padding kept him from meeting hard wood floor with his ass, but from the look on his face, that was the least of his problems. The closet rod, and all its contents, landed in his lap.

"You two leave that parkour crap outside! Not in my house at one a.m.!" Pops bellowed from down the hall. We all froze in place.

Haze's eyes widened as if he suddenly realized where he was…in his girlfriend's house, on the floor of her closet, with all of her clothes piled on top of him and his leg awkwardly propped up by an exercise ball.

I would've laughed if the situation hadn't been so precarious.

Glancing over at Warp, I held out my hand for him to stop his advance on Haze, though I raised my voice to respond to my father. "Sorry, Pops! I'll go to bed."

"See that you do, Emanuella!"

"Warp," I said, stepping in front of him with my palms flat against his chest. "Get the hell out of my room."

"No. How about I call Pops down here and he and I can beat the shit outta your boyfriend?"

Haze made an angry sound behind me but I didn't hear him move.

"Go ahead and call Pops in here. I'm sure he'd love to know exactly what you're up to. I'm sure he'd love hearing your gang war aspirations. How likely is it that he'll send you off to military school in lieu of death or juvie?"

Warp's eyes narrowed at me before he pointed in Haze's direction. "I catch the two of you together again, I won't care about consequences. You got it? It ends now, in this room, Emanuella."

"Fine. Leave," I said, jerking my head toward the door. Let him think whatever he wanted, I wasn't about to make any promises.

Warp didn't move. "I'm not leaving this room, until he's gone. And if I have to, I'll sleep outside your door all night."

"Jesus, John. Stop being so dramatic. You act like you caught us eloping or something and not sneaking kisses." I walked to the closet all casual-like. As if sneaking guys in my room to make out was something I did often enough to not be concerned about it. Looking down at Haze, decorated with my wardrobe, I wondered what my next deceitful move would be. What lie could I possibly hand my brother that he would buy and that would still give me the freedom I wanted? What could I say that would sound believable without turning Haze against me?

"Can we all just slow down the death threats and the beatings until the sun comes up?" I said. "I'm tired. Haze came by to try to get me back after *I* broke things off, Warp. We had one last kiss, that you interrupted—thanks a bunch—and that would've been the end of it. A small fling that you're making so much shit over. You should be embarrassed."

"You should be, LL. Letting this guy use you like some skeezy whore off the block. I thought you were better than that."

Haze made a move to get up and defend my honor, but I turned my head and gave him a look that I hoped begged him to trust me. He sighed and a plaid skirt tumbled down the tilted curtain rod and covered his face.

I smiled despite the dire situation, trying to maintain an air of confidence I didn't at all feel. "Well, I guess you've been thinking of me all wrong." I turned to face Haze fully, putting my hands on my hips like I had no patience left. "You planning on getting out of there anytime soon?"

"I'm very afraid to move right now," he said and lifted the pleated skirt off his head.

"Here." I stooped to pick up the curtain rod full of clothes. "I should make you and Warp iron everything."

"Hey...I'll make your bed if you want, because I put your brother over it, but the closet bit is his fault." He helped me get the pole back into place.

"Not my fault you crumple like paper, bitch," Warp whispered angrily from across the room.

Haze's jaw clenched, but he didn't rise to the bait, choosing, instead, to hand me the clothes that fell off the rod.

"Ignore him. You gave him a good punch to the face first, so your man card is safe in your back pocket." I finished hanging all the clothes on the secured rod and turned to face my boyfriend. I willed him to read the lie into what I said next. "But you have to go, and Brennen, this time you have to stay gone. Warp knows what we both know, too. This just isn't going to work."

I moved with Haze to the window, avoiding his look of confusion mixed with hurt.

"Wait..."

I shook my head and wrapped my arms around him, squeezing as if bidding a final farewell. I couldn't be sure Warp was buying any of it, but I was in it—so it was time to own it. "Meet me in an hour at the park," I whispered, before nodding to the window.

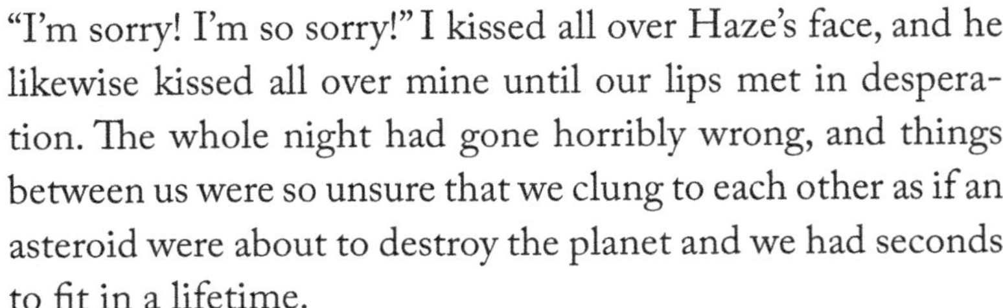

"I'm sorry! I'm so sorry!" I kissed all over Haze's face, and he likewise kissed all over mine until our lips met in desperation. The whole night had gone horribly wrong, and things between us were so unsure that we clung to each other as if an asteroid were about to destroy the planet and we had seconds to fit in a lifetime.

"Brennen…what are we going to do?" I panted against his neck, tasting my own tears of panic on his skin.

"Shh, Manu." He held me for several long minutes, as if he were waiting for the severity of the situation to settle around us long enough to examine it. "This is all my fault. I was so impatient. I couldn't sleep not knowing if you were still mine. I wanted so bad to fix things and now I've made it all worse."

"Don't apologize for coming to me. I was drowning in nightmares of you and Cathy and I'm glad you cared enough to come. And here you are again. I thought…I didn't know if you'd be here. My brother…"

"Doesn't scare me," he interrupted, pulling back just enough to wipe the last of my tears away. "I'm not going to let him threaten me away from you. I was more worried you would let him push you away."

"No. I don't want things to be over, Bren. But we have to be more careful than ever now. I don't know if Warp believed what he just saw or if he was serious about stirring up trouble with your crew."

He sighed. "I hope he just spoke in anger."

The long silence between us as we stood in the park was filled with the tension of the unknown. Too much of the future rested on Warp's reaction to seeing Haze and me together. And my brother was about as stable as the gangs after the merger.

"So, you were able to get away okay? Or should I be preparing for an ambush any second?"

"Warp stayed outside my door for a half hour, then went down to his room. I could hear him snoring when I checked the hall before coming here. We're good."

He dropped his arms from me and took a step back, clearly stressed. "I wouldn't call us good. Dammit!" The woodchips went flying as Brennen kicked them hard in frustration. "I should've respected that he's your brother and let him kick the crap out of me for being in your room. It's what I deserved. Instead I let him get to me, and I start a fight in your house."

"Please." I reached out and squeezed his hand. "There's no excuse for what he said to you. Accusing you of murdering your sister? I'd have hit him, too."

Brennen walked to a bench and sat down, motioning for me to follow him over and sit beside him. I didn't need to be asked twice. I sat and pulled one leg up to my chest to hug while the other dangled, digging into the wood and dirt beneath the bench. I could tell he wanted to tell me something, so I just waited for him to talk.

"When Heather died..." he started slowly, and looked at me, as if checking to see if I was aware of how important the conversation was. I nodded for him to continue. "...I was a suspect. Did you know that? Because I'm a writer and because the cops said I fit the profile of someone who could snap. A hotheaded, overprotective brother. Sound familiar?"

I didn't need to answer but I nodded anyway.

"Because I was with a buddy the night Heather died, I was cleared, but I had a lot of guilt back then because whoever killed her was a writer. And that's my territory, yanno?"

"How do you know it was a writer?"

"She'd been partnering a piece with someone, I'm sure of it—a present for me, I think, since it was a scene I'd tried to paint on my own but my work kept getting erased before I could finish. The only way Heather could've succeeded where I failed..."

"Is if she had someone with her." I nodded as I spoke. "Makes sense."

"Since Heather had no enemies—"

"Do you think it was someone who was after you?"

He nodded and then sighed. "Some overprotective brother I turned out to be. I squeezed so hard trying to keep her from making mistakes, I probably brought on her death."

"Come on. That seems a bit harsh." I reached over and squeezed his hand. "Seriously, Brennen, you can't think like that."

"I can't? She was supposed to be home that night!" He must've realized he was raising his voice, because he took a deep breath and started again, a little more calm. "She loved sketching animals and was good at anything musical—piano, violin, you name it she could play it. She gave all that up. Years of work! I had no idea what she was into anymore, and it scared me. She died because I told on her for lying about being out with Liv the night before and she got grounded. I thought it was good because her behavior had been changing so much in that last month. I don't know...maybe she was just growing but, I hated it."

"You didn't like who she she'd become?" I asked. A part of me could relate hard to the confusion I felt coming off Haze. I disliked who Warp was becoming, and there wasn't much I wouldn't do to try to change him back.

Haze continued, "Back then, I told myself that I didn't like who she was forcing herself to be. That's how I saw it. Someone, or something was bringing about these changes in her. She was sneaking out almost every night. She did her hair differently. She listened to different music. Looking back, I have to admit she seemed happier, but I didn't think of it as her maturing. I thought she was smoking dope or something. I truly felt like I knew nothing about her anymore. Hell, I didn't even know she was attempting graffiti until after she died. She was always the same, always. But then, toward the end, she was adventurous, daring. Wild-hair and all."

"She sounds a little like, me."

"The difference is that I hated rebellion on her. On you, I find it cute because your crazy adventurous nature is who you are. My sister was being something she wasn't." He shook his head, wrinkling his nose in disgust. "At least, something I thought she wasn't."

"I think I remember reading somewhere that she'd snuck out the night she died and your parents said it was unlike her."

"It was unlike her before she hit puberty. Honestly, my parents don't know just how often she used to sneak out, and I'll never tell them. They'd only blame themselves."

I felt so sad for him. He had so much guilt on his shoulders. "Like you blame yourself. Bren, I think you should talk to them."

He shook his head in answer to my suggestion. "It was me who noticed she was gone the night she died. I came home late because I was out with one of my buddies. I could hear music coming from her room. Not classical like she used to play when she was upset and needed to think. But alternative rock. I figured she was mad at me for getting her grounded, so I went to apologize and see if I could get her to talk to me. When she didn't answer my knock, I went in. She wasn't there, so I rode my bike to Liv's, and she was as mystified and worried as I was.

"I called my crew and we all spent all night looking for Heather and didn't find her. When the sun started to come up, I went home, hoping she would be there and we had just missed each other. But instead, there was a cop car in my driveway. It could've caught her out at night and brought her home—but I just knew that wasn't why they were there."

I watched his neck tighten with emotion and reached out to clasp his hand with both of mine this time. "She would've snuck out grounded or not. You said yourself she'd done it many times."

"Yes, but she snuck out, to create a piece...for my birthday. When they found her, they found the piece and it was exactly what I'd envisioned. It was...she should've been mad at me for getting her grounded...she should've..."

When he turned his head up to the sky I could see the liquid pain streaming down his face. He didn't sob, or sniffle, just faced the pain and let it flow. I cried, too, for him. For Heather. For several minutes, neither one of us said anything.

Drawing a deep breath, he leaned over and kissed my forehead. "You and Warp remind me of my relationship with my sister. Maybe in his eyes, you're changing, and he's freaking out thinking I'm painting pictures of you everywhere. He thinks I'm trying to threaten you and he's bringing the might of his entire crew into the fight with the threat of war. I don't blame him, Manu. When I called my crew to help find my sister, I intended to set fire to the city if that's what it took. And I'll do it in a second...for you."

I wasn't sure if I should consider citywide arson a romantic gesture, but I did. "Look, I guess I can understand why Warp wants to keep me safe. And why you jumped up and erased my portrait immediately from the walls. But both you and Warp have to realize that I'm not Heather. I am careful, I'm knowledgeable. I didn't just start cruising the streets a month ago. I've been here for years. You both need to trust me."

He grinned sadly at me, and I saw the gaping hole his sister's death had left in him.

"Can I ask you a question?"

"You just did."

"Yeah, yeah." I nudged him, appreciating his need to lighten the mood with humor.

"Ask away," he said more seriously.

Hesitant, I toyed with my fingers, picking at my nails. "Are you...worried about...I mean...do you think...?"

He pursed his lips together like he knew what I was going to ask and didn't want to hear it. "...Manu, don't."

"Well, there are certain similarities I can't help but notice, Bren! Do you think someone is going to...hurt me?" I couldn't even utter the word murder. It seemed too crazy, but so did the whole situation. If another piece of me was up on a wall, and if Haze claimed it wasn't him—I had a hater or a stalker, and either could be dangerous, especially considering all the territory disputes lately.

"No. I'm not ever going to let that happen."

"But if she was killed by a writer...and someone is painting me all over the place..."

"The piece of you is probably unrelated." I noticed he didn't look me in the eye when he said that, but I didn't say anything. I just listened to him reassure me. "It might be someone trying to rile your brother, start a territory war...who knows? It's only been one. This other piece your brother talked about, we don't even know if it exists or if he was trying to frighten you away from me."

I wanted to believe him. I'd rather someone try to use me to tick off my brother than target me. "I guess that's true, but..."

"Heather was killed by someone she knew. Probably not for a long time, but for about a month or so. She was partnering with someone, and that partner never came forward, so they must've been responsible for her death. It was someone who has something personal to say. The cops called it a crime of passion."

"So you know it's a guy who practices graffiti. That's a place to start."

"The cops thought so, too. It was a weird year for me. I didn't trust anyone except Decay. And I only trusted him because he was away with his family for the summer and couldn't have been dating my sister. One by one, as my crew was interviewed by the cops and cleared, we came together again. But the other writer crews out there, anyone I come across that looks at me funny, I wonder, 'Is this the guy who killed my sister?' It's why I've stayed in the game instead of bowing out. If I lose all my connections, I lose my chance of stumbling on a clue. Maybe one day I'll get lucky and find the person who killed her. Maybe one day they'll slip up and say something over a beer at a party or something."

"It must be hard carrying that wish with you every day. The pressure you put on yourself to make it come true. Is that the reason for this?" I asked, and pressed a finger to the patch of white hair on the side of his head.

"If by reason you mean I started acting out, doing crazy stuff, and managed to get some stitches in my head being an ass, yeah. Not the sexiest battle scar."

"I dunno. I like it," I said. I tugged on my own colored lock of hair. "And I'll keep your wish with me, too. You won't be the only one waiting and listening for someone to slip up."

He stared at me for a second and then pulled me into his lap to kiss the breath from me. A simple press of lips, and I was putty, molding against his mouth and kissing him back with all the emotions of the last twenty minutes.

Opening to the gentle insistence of his tongue, I gave him the taste of me, and he eagerly drank me in. God, I knew I shouldn't think such things, but I wondered if he would mind if I straddled his lap right there in the middle of the park.

"Mmm." He groaned, as if he could read my mind, and gently set me aside. "You better go now before I do something far crazier than just kissing you on this bench."

I tried not to notice as he stood and adjusted the front of his pants. Okay, maybe I didn't try real hard, because I caught every stuttered move he made as he walked me the block back to my house. Just outside my gate he stopped and gave me one last quick kiss.

"So, tomorrow? Tucker Park?" I asked anxiously, unsure if, after all the drama from tonight, he'd still want to meet up with me.

He gave me a genuine grin, back to his old self. "Actually, I think tomorrow we should take things between us to the next level."

I stood there, outside my bedroom window, my mind racing with all sorts of ideas about what "next level" meant. And I couldn't help but smile as I noticed him effortlessly vault over my neighbor's gate like a true traceur.

Fifteen

"This is what you consider next level?" I asked the next night, peeking over my shoulder to see if anyone was about to lynch us. Two kids dressed in black, ten o'clock at night creeping around the school, my arrest record was about to get another page, I could feel it.

Haze felt around the school's windowpane, slipping a finger in the gap I wouldn't have noticed if I wasn't watching. "What were you expecting?"

"I don't know, maybe coffee or something?" When he turned to look at me oddly, I shrugged. "Yeah, I said it! We hang out in a closet every weekday, and a park sometimes at night. I thought you might be ready to get a coffee—like a date or something. Tell me that wouldn't be a step up." Okay, maybe I was hoping that by "next level" he had meant some heavy petting behind the school dumpster, but I'd been willing to settle for a real date—in another city, far, far away from anyone we knew.

"This is next level. You're teaching me yours, now I'm going to teach you mine. It's also a lesson in trust."

"Oh? It looks a lot like a lesson in crime."

He opened the window and motioned for me to crawl in. "That, too."

"I dunno, Bren."

"Trust me not to get us caught, and I'll trust you not to turn me in."

I stood there for a second, weighing the options. If Haze and I climbed into the window and got caught, we'd get busted in more ways than one. I could try to say I met Haze at the school to kick his ass, but I doubted that would fly. Our relationship would definitely be outed—again, and this time, Warp wouldn't buy any of my bullshit acting skills.

Screw it. I didn't feel like worrying about it. Not tonight.

Smiling, I nodded and crawled through the window, damn near falling on my face as I slid across the ancient radiator and landed on the floor of the art room with a plop.

I flinched as Haze's flashlight glared into my eyes a few seconds later.

I couldn't see his face but I heard his soft chuckle clear enough.

"You coulda warned me," I admonished in a whisper.

"You're in this class every day and you didn't remember there's a heating register there? You must get really distracted."

"Yeah. That guy Bernard is pretty hot."

Haze swatted my backside, giving me a nudge toward the gated art closet. The gate was always wide open, so I couldn't help but wonder why Mrs. Peris didn't just take it off the hinges.

"So, you're allowed to sneak in here?"

"Mrs. Peris is actually pretty cool. She thinks some rules are fun when broken. All she tells me is that she doesn't know a thing about it. Which probably means if I get caught, I'm on my own and she'll pretend she had no idea."

"That's kinda cool." Knowing Mrs. Peris approved of Haze coming here all the time, made me feel a little better about being in her classroom at night. At least I didn't feel I was violating her sanctuary.

He swung his doctor's bag from his shoulder and opened the zipper. "Hold this while I fill it?"

I nodded and did what I was told, moving with him into the closet. He took a bunch of spray paints down from one of the topmost shelves and tossed them into the bag. I also saw him grab a couple of pieces of plastic that looked like straws.

"What are those for?"

"They fit on the end of the sprayer and add precision."

"I don't think I'll be very precise tonight."

He laughed lightly and zipped up the bag, sliding the strap over his shoulder again. "Don't worry. A kindergartener could do what I'm going to ask you to do tonight."

"Great, now there's pressure."

He shut me up with a quick kiss to my mouth, and then, as if deciding he liked it, he kissed me again, and again, until he tugged me into him and gave me the good kind of kiss. The kind worth getting arrested for.

I moaned and hugged his waist.

The whole situation gave me such a rush. I was in the school after hours, having climbed in through a window, and I was making out with my enemy boyfriend.

As we snuck back out the window a few moments later, I couldn't help but think adrenaline junkies had nothing on me.

We spent a couple of hours skulking around Three Rivers Academy territory without finding the newest bloated image of me Warp said he'd seen the night before.

"You know, it's possible my brother was just full of shit. Or it was put up on a building that had the money to get it removed right away."

The slump of his shoulders corrected slightly when he shrugged. "I guess. It bugs me, though. If it's not a flattering piece of you, I don't want it hanging around town."

"Yeah me either. I'll ask Surge tomorrow and see if he'll tell me where it is. I don't want to spend any more time looking, though. You were supposed to be showing me some tagging hotness."

"Well I was planning on showing you the 'hotness' once I got rid of whatever your brother said he saw. I didn't plan on it taking so long and dragging you with me."

"Lies!" I grinned. "You just didn't want to be alone. It's okay if you're scared and wanted me to walk with you."

He nudged me and I laughed.

"Yeah, ask Surge. If it's out there, we'll find it soon enough."

I wanted to change the subject. Our night had been fun, running around a good chunk of our side of the city, but the truth of what we were looking for weighed us down. I wanted to get back to the fun side of our relationship.

"So what would you like to do with me tonight?" I purposefully loaded the question to get a smile and a topic-change. It worked.

"I had a cool idea the other day, and I thought maybe you could help me with it."

"Sure," I said. "What do you need?"

Tugging me into the nearby alley, he looked up and down the walls like a portrait artist might a blank canvas. Though the street lights gave off enough light to see well enough, he took his flashlight from his cargo pants pocket and searched the shadows.

"We need to find the perfect spot. If we put it too close to the street, someone will clear it within a day. I want it to last longer than that."

"You want what to last longer, Mr. Cryptic?"

Grinning all proud of himself, he jerked his bag off his shoulder and set it on the ground, squatting over it. The flashlight illuminated a piece of trash as he set it aside so he could unzip his bag.

"See? Now we're getting to the good stuff." I clapped my hands together and rubbed them against each other all sinister-villain-like. After putting the little straw thingy on the end of the nozzle, he gave it a couple of shakes and handed the spray paint to me.

I noticed the green-colored dot on the can's label. "Your favorite color," I said, remembering our closet conversation.

"Mmhm. And this—" he took out another can and repeated the process before holding it into the flashlight's stream, "—is yours."

I felt the muscles in my cheeks bunch with a blush. "Yup. I'm a huge fan of yellow. I remember this one time, I painted a wall in my room yellow with finger paint."

He picked up the flashlight and his bag and walked with me toward the back of the alley. "I bet that was fun to clean up."

"Who said I cleaned it up?"

The way his mouth moved around a smile was pure magic. I hoped I never stopped amusing him.

"Stand up against the wall right there," he commanded, and when I pointedly stood still he added, "please."

My hoodie stuck to the bricks behind me, so I knew I was pretty close to the wall. He handed me a face mask and motioned for me to put it on. I could feel my breath create moisture against my mouth, and couldn't help but wonder if the sides of my mouth would have red marks and make me look funny after I took it off.

"Press up against the wall and hold still."

"Um, why?"

He laughed. "Trust me. Close your eyes and hold your breath when you feel me around your head, all right? You have a mask on, but no reason to breathe when I'm that close to your noggin anyway."

Trust is a hard thing for me, but I took a deep breath and held myself still as the hiss of the paint can came near one ear and then another. He positioned my arms down to my side with my right angled slightly outward and then continued to trace my body.

"Okay," he said, releasing me.

I stepped away from the wall and grinned at the child-like outline of me in yellow on the wall. "That looks awesome."

"Now take your can and do me."

"Do you, huh?" I bit my lip and played on the sexual innuendo.

"Well if you want that," he paused, letting my mind wonder about what he'd say next, "you're going to have to wait. I'm just not that kind of guy."

"Uh huh." I laughed.

Once he was in position, I gave him the mask and traced his body like he had mine, with a few minor mishaps until I came to his left hand. "Your hand is going to overlap with mine."

One of his eyes popped open and glanced at me. "That's the idea, Manu."

"Oh." Well wasn't I just a dumbass?

I finished spraying around his hand and down his leg. "Okay, you're done. I think I got too close a few times and got some on your clothes."

He stepped away from the wall and turned to look at our hand-holding outlines, pulling the mask off his head. "That's why I told you to wear something you didn't mind losing. Just be careful getting back to your room. Don't let your brother see you or he won't believe the gymnastics excuse."

I nodded absently.

"So what do you think?" he asked.

Words didn't come right away. I could only stare at the sugary sweetness that was our painted bodies immortalized on the wall. Or…temporarily immortalized. Chances were good someone would eventually paint over or remove our little drawings, but the fact they were once there would be enough for me.

"This is—really cool, Bren."

Grinning at me, he switched paint cans and took off the extensions. "Since you like yellow so much, why don't you paint a sun?"

"Um. Tracing is one thing, but—"

"Oh, come on. Just hold the paint can a little away from the wall and draw like you're five again. We're not trying to impress anyone. Just have fun."

"Okay," I jerked the mask out of his hand as he held it out to me. "But if you laugh, I can't be held responsible when I kick your ass."

The sound of his laugh echoed in the alley, Haze-in-stereo style. Kinda neat. "I'll keep that in mind."

With a nod, I aimed my paint can and tried to draw a circle. I choked at the bottom of it and it dripped a little. "Yikes."

"Sun has rays. That's an easy cover."

The thrill of doing something different than usual felt nice. Doing it while being next to Haze felt even nicer. I painted a few lines out from my circle and filled in the center, stepping back to see what I'd done once I finished. So I wouldn't be an artist, but it wasn't too bad. With a little bit of practice I could probably tag with some of the weaker crews.

I glanced over to see what Haze was doing and laughed. "Wow, that's interesting."

The trunk of the tree was obvious, what with a little hole in the center for squirrels; its big branches were shaky but they worked. Once he started spraying in smaller branches and twigs…he had a hot mess.

The can of paint dangled from his fingers in defeat. "Yeah. People, buildings, flowers, I can do all that. Ask me to draw an oak and I choke."

"Oo. Rhyme time."

We both laughed. Haze took the can of paint and the mask from me and dropped both into his bag. Looping his arm through mine, he pulled me closer to him.

"I guess I'll leave the hippie crap to Decay."

I looked at his mouth. "Guess so."

"I just want you to know, if I'm going to do a tribute to you, to us, I'd make it personal, and for you and me alone. I'd never risk what we've got until I could be sure it was safe for everyone to know."

"Oh, I know that."

"Are you sure?" When I nodded, he smiled and kissed the tip of my nose. "Good. When everyone knows, I'll make a huge mural, to show the world that you're mine. And I'll paint the true beauty of you, Manu."

Sixteen

"You're not nearly that fat," Surge said, looking sideways at the infamous bloated piece of me Warp had told Haze and me about.

"Gee, thanks, Surge." I elbowed him in the ribs and touched the art to see if it was tacky.

"How did your brother find this? I don't think we've been down here on a run yet."

"He probably heard it through the thug-line or stumbled on it." I stepped back again to survey my sprayed image. The edges of the piece seemed a little sharper, the swirl of paint in the background a little sloppy. My face...stretched and some unfinished cracks, or twigs or something, looked like they were going to poke me in the eye. The writer must've been in a rush or methed out. "You know, this isn't very flattering. I look kinda...piggish."

"Maybe it was dark. Or they sniffed a little too much paint, yanno? If they did this at night I'd still say it's impressive, but as a depiction of the fine Lady of the Ledge, it's way foul." He threw off his backpack and rummaged around for a flavored water.

All morning we had combed TRA territory looking for the giant "LL re-creation" Warp claimed to have found night before last. The one Haze and I had searched for all night last night and couldn't find. If we'd gone one more street over, we'd have found it.

The sun burned high noon before Surge and I stumbled on my graffiti-stalker love-note. Now that we saw it, I wished we hadn't.

"So, now what?"

He swirled some water around in his mouth and spit it out. "This is your show, girl. I think we have to recognize the skills and admit someone was trying to make you look unfine, so it's up to you. You wanna get some supplies and erase it?"

"Why? Whoever it is will only make another one. At least I know where this one is. And it's on the side of a building long dead. I'm guessing if we erase it, the next one will look even worse."

"Throw in some yellow zits and crossed-eyes type deal?"

"I wouldn't doubt it." I sighed and put my back against the brick. "I'm trying not to let everything get to me but…"

"I know, baby girl." He ambled over and slid his arm between my neck and the wall, giving my shoulders a squeeze. "We'll figure out what's what."

We were quiet for a bit. And I couldn't be sure what he was thinking but I suspected it ran along the same lines as what I contemplated. How do you get an unknown graffiti artist off your back?

"You just gotta react the opposite way of what they want."

I nodded.

Surge straightened, dragging his arm out from around me. "I've got an idea."

A can of black paint, a black eye-liner pencil, and an hour later, we were back at the graffiti crime scene.

"I feel dumb," I admitted.

Surge tapped the side of my face, the black eye-liner poised near my nose. "Quit moving or I'm going to color in a few teeth on accident."

"Sorry," I mumbled. "I just don't know if I can do this."

"Look, you gotta pretend this shit is funny to you, LL. They want you to take it serious, so if you don't, they'll move onto another target they can bully."

"Or I'll come off to the entire school looking like an idiot."

"Pfft. You're friends with me. Everyone in the school already knows you're an idiot for that alone, girl." He scraped a few more pencil lines across my face and then stepped back.

"How does it look?" I asked.

"Like you're mocking the improvements I made to your character!"

I looked over at the mustache he'd painted on the wall image of me and grinned. Other than holding the can too close, making some of the black paint ooze down the front of my artsy face, he did a decent job.

"Now go stand next to it!"

"Yanno, I think we violated an ethical code about adding to someone else's masterpiece."

Surge grinned and held up his camera phone. "If they were trying to be accurate, then I'd hardly call that shit work a 'piece.' Okay now, blow out. Try to make yourself look fat. Yeah…yeah. Awesome!"

Surge took the picture and sent it to my phone—as well as everyone else's. The whole of Three Rivers would have my funky photo in an hour.

"Oh God, I feel sick."

"You'll be fine. Everyone will laugh and have a good time with it thinking you're goofing around. Except the artist."

"Writer," I corrected automatically.

"Whatever. The *writer*," he said with dramatic emphasis, "will cry at his failed attempt to bully you and find another, more vulnerable target."

"Surge, what if the reason this one's fat is because it was made by someone else? I know it has similar lines and style but...what if ripping Haze's style and making fun of me become trendy things to do?"

He stared at the graffiti for a long time before answering. "It don't matter how many pictures start poppin' up, we'll take them all down, LL. Trust me."

Other than Saturday night's graffiti date with Haze and Surge's brilliant Sunday afternoon prank, the rest of the weekend had been spent watching the distance between Warp and me grow in silence. By Sunday night his eye had developed quite the shiner, thanks to his tussle with Haze on Friday, and he'd told the crew to go on a run without him for the first time ever, hoping to hide the various shades of purple for a day.

Warp's hiatus made it easier for Surge and me to go off on our own to meet Haze. The night passed with only a couple of burgeoning finger blisters and a nasty bruise on Haze's shin.

Despite his injuries, he had a natural aptitude for freerunning and I was proud of him. I decided against saying so, though, lest I sound like his mom or something.

Pops left after midnight for another cross-country trek that would "bring in Christmas money," which meant he'd be gone for a while again. I could always tell when Pops felt guilty about being away because he'd put a name to the extra money he'd bring in. "Warp's birthday trip." "Easter Dinner trip."

I wanted to tell him the same thing I always did. "Don't worry, Pops. You're leaving me with a stand-in dad. I'll miss you but I'll be fine."

Not this time. I couldn't reassure him. Not when I was feeling so inexplicably uneasy.

The picture Surge and I sent out seemed to get rave reviews, but I hadn't had to face anyone yet. Not to mention Warp was so damned mad at me I wondered if he wouldn't snap under the pressure of Pops being gone. More than his usual snap-age, anyway.

All I could bring myself to say was, "Whatever, Pops."

I'd meant it to be flippant, but I knew I didn't hit the mark when I saw the stress age my father's face before my eyes.

"I'll be fine, Pops," I whispered now on the way to school.

Late. Late for Pops and late for school after waiting all morning for Liv to show. She never did. Obviously, she was still a little sore at me for not telling her about my crush on Haze.

"Hey, Emanuella! Nice picture." Someone yelled as they sped by me on the sidewalk. The guy didn't look familiar.

Sending out pictures to the entire student body might not have been a good idea, after all. At least it wasn't as bad as Susie Tamer's boob-episode of last year, but, hello—nerve-wracking.

I'd vowed never to take a picture for a boyfriend of mine over the phone, no matter how much they seemed to "love" me. Susie's case was the perfect reason to stay away from *that*.

By fourth hour I'd seen so many renditions of my face on disproportionate bodies I wanted to hurl. My cheeks hurt from forcing a smile all day, and all I wanted to do was fall into Haze's arms by the time I made it to the closet.

I knocked and he jerked me inside rougher than usual. "Um, ow. Ya bully." He dropped his hand and I rubbed my arm.

"What the hell were you thinking?"

Haze's face wasn't made for anger, and it was kinda scary seeing it there. I wondered if my assumption of his inability to commit murder was accurate.

"Don't yell at me! I've had a rough day and you're *not* going to make it worse by jumping down my throat."

My theory about turning his offense to defense didn't work out so well.

"LL, I'll yell at you all I want when you do something as suicidal as challenging someone you don't even know."

"We're going to get caught if you don't shut up." I tried to calmly point out.

It helped bring his voice down but his anger didn't budge.

"You can't cross out someone's work and not piss them off!"

"I didn't cross anything off. Surge painted a mustache on it. We thought if we showed I found it amusing instead of being victimized by fat jokes—"

Haze dragged his hand over his face and stared up at the ceiling like I was trying his patience. "I get it." He snapped. "But it's a serious infraction. You're pretty much telling whoever did the work that you're at war."

"Oh, come on, this isn't a gang-sign marking territory. It's my face."

"It doesn't matter that it isn't a sign if the person who painted it feels it's a territory issue. As bad as the portrait was, they might have really put their heart in it, and for you to make fun and to touch it…dammit. This is why I handled the last one. There's a way to do it. And your way—not it, Emanuella! We can only hope it's some newb idiot expressing a crush. Please, in the future…"

"Don't touch anything." I started to feel a little worried. What if Haze was right? What if I did something really bad and made myself a target?

"Yeah, because this…" he said holding up his phone with the picture on it, and sounding like he wanted to yell again. "Not. Very. Smart."

"You know what, Haze? Maybe not by your standards, but I'm not going to sit here and be victimized. If whoever it is thinks I started a war then…then…. Good! Maybe they'll actually show their face, the coward. I don't know what I've done to be the butt of their jokes, but I'm not going to put up with it! I'm sick of all this crap! I'm sick of my brother, I'm sick of school, and I'm sick of pretending that you don't exist outside of this closet! Maybe if I could show you were my boyfriend, the person painting my pictures would cut it out!"

The lines around his mouth softened and he pulled me in slowly for a hug. "I'm sorry. This is all so messed up. I feel helpless because I can't come out and openly challenge whoever is screwing around until all the territory crap is settled, and when I saw the picture—"

"Have you seen the doctored text-pic with my painted head on a dog's body? That's my favorite." I smirked.

"Who cares about those? My photo was on TV, so you can imagine the hurtful crap some heartless kids put out there."

"Yeah." I remembered hearing some of those really nasty things the kids were saying about him. It bothered me more, now that I was his girlfriend, than it had back then. It also made me feel pretty silly getting all stressed out over the pictures of myself I'd seen. "I'm not bothered by that stuff as much." I was, but I'd get over it.

"Then what stuff?"

I shrugged. "I just want to be normal. I wanna be able to go to the dance with you and have you as my boyfriend out in the open."

His nod rubbed against my head and I nuzzled deeper into his neck.

"I know," he whispered. "I'll find out who's doing this shit and once I can prove that it isn't me, we'll take on your brother and his irrational need to claim territory, then let the whole world know we're together with one big jump out of the closet." He craned his neck to look at my face with a cheesy grin plastered across his. "So to speak."

"Okay."

I guess I didn't sound too convinced.

"I mean it, Manu." He stroked a hand down my back. "Soon we won't have to hide anymore. I promise."

Seventeen

"I didn't see you in class this morning," I remarked to Liv as she took the seat I offered her beside me in Art.

She stared at me for the longest time and then shook her head. "Nope. You sure didn't."

Her attitude got old fast. She was supposed to be my best friend and she was avoiding me like I had the plague. "Look, I think this is dragging on a bit long. I told you I was sorry for not telling you about my crush on Haze and that I'm a horrible friend, but blowing me off isn't helping things."

She turned her full body to face me then. "Yeah? What about not telling me that Romeo over there," she nodded her head toward where Haze sat talking with Mrs. Peris, "climbed up the tower to your window last Friday?"

"Who tol—"

"Your insane brother called me Sunday, demanding to know why I didn't tell him things between you and Haze were so serious! And I told him that I didn't know what he was talking about. You know what he said to me then?"

I shook my head, pretty sure I didn't want to know what he said to her then.

"He said, 'What kind of friend are you?' And you know what? I didn't have an answer because I thought we were the best kind, but apparently we're not."

Yeah, I was right about the not wanting to know that bit.

I took a deep breath, accepting the handout as Haze walked around the classroom and gave us each one. Liv looked like she wanted to hurl hers back at him.

"I thought we were through, Haze and me. We'd barely begun anything when the Cathy incident happened, and he came to my room to explain his actions and give me a verbal smackdown for mine. The rest of the weekend went by in a blur, and it isn't as if you called me to hang out or anything."

"I tried to call you, but you didn't answer your cell."

"I'm not exactly sure where it is half the time. I think the battery went dead because I tried to call it and—"

"You have a house phone," she countered.

"Yeah, but I don't know your number by heart."

She scoffed. "Don't you think you should know your own best friend's number?"

"Oh, right. And you know mine?"

"Yes," she hissed, complete with hair flip of indignation.

"Then what is it?"

"It's...two."

"What?"

Liv lifted a shoulder, trying to pretend she was being completely rational. "It's number two on my speed dial."

"Listen up!" Mrs. Peris called out to the class. "We're going to do a little landscaping of the mind today. I want you all to close your eyes, and for the next five minutes, I don't want to hear a peep out of any of you. I want you to visualize a landscape that brings out your emotions, happy, sad...silly, whatever. I want you to look at the negative space of that landscape, notice every detail. I want you to place yourself in the middle of this created image. And when the five minutes are over, I want you to open your eyes and draw what you saw."

"I see my best friend pouring toxic waste all over my landscape," Liv said.

I shook my head and closed my eyes as the teacher passed. If Liv wanted to be mad at me, I had no right to stop her. I couldn't say I blamed her either, but I wasn't going to respond to her snarky comments.

"You're frowning, Ms. Harvey. Try to relax for this exercise," Mrs. Peris reminded me.

"Yes, Ma'am."

A picture of the city popped into my head. A city I both loved and hated. I was proud to live in what the majority of the USA would label "the ghetto" and equally as proud of surviving in it. My city; worse than many but better than some. Homicides were a problem every other day instead of daily and most of them involved gangsters and not innocents, so we were ahead of the curve.

I zoomed in on the cityscape in my head, thinking about my favorite trick areas for parkour. The library statues, the pizza joint, and the place we call The Tops, where all of the roofs were within one story of each other and easy to jump across. I also thought about the gym across town where I practiced gymnastics during the summer.

But none of my favorite places remained in my head for long. Soon, I zeroed in on a wall. A particular one, relatively new to me.

The place where I met Haze.

Only this time, it was just him and me. He painted my mural on the wall, and I sat on the edge looking down at his serene face.

Yes. This was my landscape.

"Open your eyes and draw what you see."

The silence in the room felt strange. Everyone was actually focused on the project. I glanced up and looked around the room to see each student bent over their papers, furiously drawing. Even Haze took part in the project. Not that it surprised me. Any excuse to draw or paint and he'd jump on it. If I knew anything about him, I knew that.

"Quit mooning over your boyfriend and get to work before you get in trouble," Liv whispered.

I sighed and let her have her PMS moment before turning my attention to the wall scene in my head.

To say that I'm an artist is to insult all the artists who came before me, beginning with the cavemen finger-painting wall art. But for me, this exercise brought out an unknown gift. Inspiration must've beat me over the head because my drawing was actually good. I couldn't draw hands well, or people, so I sketched myself and Haze without much detail. The wall and the graffiti art, though, came out looking sweet.

I smiled down at the finished product when the bell rang.

"Is that all you think about?" Liv asked, practically spewing acid.

"Come on, Liv. I said I was sorry and I'll try to make it up to you if you'll let me, but now you're being a spoiled bitch."

She blinked at me and slammed a hand down on her drawing, crinkling it in her fist. A real shame, since from the glimpse I'd seen, it might've been the best thing she'd ever done. Without even glancing at me, she threw her drawing at the trash can.

"Whatever, Ellie! You're the one being a selfish bitch." I saw the hurt in her eyes, magnified by tears before she shoved her way past everyone and out of the room.

Ugh! I felt like a horrible person. The last week I'd been the one blowing Liv off. I'd been the one going out with her only when I had nothing else to do. And I hadn't told her anything about Haze and me.

I met my boyfriend's gaze over the throng of students shuffling out of class. The encouraging smile he gave me helped some, but I couldn't feel good about myself. Not yet.

I walked nearer to him under the pretense of saving Liv's discarded drawing. Picking up on my need to tell him something, he stalled on his way out.

"I don't think I'll make the park tonight," I whispered. "You cool with meeting up with Surge?"

"I'll go at it alone. I don't need Surge. He's taught me the techniques."

"You need him to call the ambulance."

Haze grinned at me. "Your confidence in me is amazing."

"Oh, come on." I laughed. "Even the veterans need 911."

"I'll take that," Mrs. Peris said, plucking the drawing out of my hand.

"Oh! Sorry, Mrs. Peris. I thought I'd give it back to her."

"I have a drawer labeled Artist Tantrums for a reason," she said, and I laughed. "At the end of the year, I hand them out so each artist can see what they almost lost."

Haze chuckled a little. "Everything Decay creates winds up in that drawer."

"Our Terrence is a bit of a volatile artist," Mrs. Peris admitted about Decay.

"Well, I think it's a cool idea," I said. "Guess I better get to my next class."

Mrs. Peris nodded while ironing out Liv's drawing. Haze took her distraction as a dismissal and walked me out of the room.

Once past the door, we pretended we weren't "in like."

“Emanuella, is it?” Liv’s mom, Mrs. Menesa, asked. Everything about her seemed severe. Her dark hair was pulled back facelift-tight and her clothes looked Amish or something. I didn’t see much resemblance between her and Liv.

Realizing I was gawking, I cleared my throat and thrust my hand out. “Yes, Ma’am.”

She smiled politely and shook my hand, but her eyes never quite lifted to meet mine. She didn’t seem the shy type. Instead, I was left to feel as though I were unworthy of notation. She backed away from the door and waved me inside.

The instant I stepped foot in Liv’s house, I felt cold down to my bones. Jesus. No wonder Liv complained about her home life so much. The place proved that money didn’t buy happiness, especially when you never stayed in one place long enough to put happiness in it.

The Menesas lived in the area of the hood called The Courts. Many of the middle-class could live like kings and queens here, and in Liv’s parents’ case, they did. They paid good money for their security system and chipped in with the rest of the small community who paid for men to patrol the four-block suburb.

I always wondered why those living in The Courts didn’t move to a better neighborhood, but Liv explained that no one could sell their homes and get what they were worth, and in better hoods, she and her family would be considered second-rate.

“Can’t have that,” she’d said snidely.

“Liv’s in her room, up the stairs and down the hall. Last door on the left.” Mrs. Menesa walked away and I had a feeling she forgot about me the second her back turned.

With every step I took, the polished floor sent echoes down the narrow corridor. The draft from the hall window went straight down my back. I half expected an axe murderer to jump out at me B-movie style, but I made it to Liv's room in one piece.

No wonder she always stayed at her nanny's place while her parents were gone. Rosahlia's pad might be smaller but it felt more like a home. Of course, she made great dinners every time I visited, so I might've been a little biased.

I couldn't be sure what made me so tense about *this* house, but something wasn't right. The decorations were bland, the halls a stark white with even whiter trim, and every piece of corridor furniture looked abused. Not in the normal wear-and-tear sense, but antique tables were scraped of their former paint, their natural wood forcefully exposed. Other pieces were painted white to match, though clearly they hadn't been made that way.

Furniture torture.

I knocked on Liv's door and rushed inside the moment she opened it.

Unfortunately, her room wasn't much better.

"Something the matter?"

"I don't know. Your house is kinda giving me the heebies."

"My parents are home. Enough said."

I felt a little guilty telling her I didn't like her house. "I guess I'm just used to Rosahlia's."

"No, it's really this place. It used to be cool but my mom redecorated everything, even my room. She didn't like my choices."

Ahh. That explained a lot.

"I think I woulda liked it better the way you had it."

She smiled begrudgingly. "How come you're here?"

"Because I'm a horrible friend."

"Go on," she said.

"I realized what you said in Art class is true. I've been so full of myself that I haven't bothered to ask how you're doing. I'm worried about a lot of things, but that's not a reason to ignore you and become self-involved. So, I'm here to offer myself to you."

Her brows furrowed. "What does that mean?"

"I'm here to listen, to pummel, to whine at—whatever you need, Liv. You've been there for me when I've let you, and now it's time to return the favor because I think there's something else going on with you other than me being selfish." I walked to her bed and sat on the edge. "And I'm not leaving here until you tell me why you were in such a foul mood in school."

She stared at me for a while and then lifted a shoulder with the same indifference she couldn't pull off earlier in Art. Parents often ignored this shrug thinking it was all part of teenage angst. But among ourselves, we all knew it was a way of saying "I hurt, and I don't know how to put it to words," so I dragged her down next to me and hugged her.

As I suspected, she cried and told me all about her horrible weekend with her coldhearted parents.

Once she calmed down, she spoke clearer and I could follow the conversation better. "I don't know what to say to them. They ask me questions and I'm terrified to say anything in case I get the answer wrong. And the questions aren't really the type normal kids worry about getting wrong."

"Like what?" I asked.

"This time, they asked me how school was and if I'd given any thought to what I might do when I'm old enough to move out. Pretty subtle, huh?"

I felt horrible for her. My mother had her moments of mood swings, but I never questioned that she loved me, even after she lost the battle with her depression. I couldn't imagine having a mother who thought of me as a burden. Though I knew firsthand, having a mother who thought of *herself* as a burden could be disastrous.

The air hung with the thickness of Liv's melancholy, so I wrapped her up in another hug, hoping my continuous affection would be enough to ward off the negativity. She sniffled.

I didn't want her to cry again. "Well, you could always tell her you hope to be a successful interior designer. Maybe then she won't attempt it herself, 'cause Jesus, Liv, this place is creepy."

"I know, right? I hope the 'rents leave soon so I can go back to Rosahlia's." She leaned away from me and eyed my pocket. "Is that your phone vibrating?"

"Huh?" At first I forgot I brought it. "Oh. Yeah. I'm trying to remember to have it on me all the time." I fished for my cell and eyed the display. A text message. "It's from Warp. That's weird."

WE NEED TO MEET NOW. SHOTGUN WALL.

I read the text message and frowned. "He wants to meet. You wanna come?"

Liv shrugged. "Sure. I'll have to meet you out front. I'm not sure why, but I'm grounded. As long as I don't leave in front of them, they'll never know I'm gone."

I smiled. "Okay, I'll meet you around the corner."

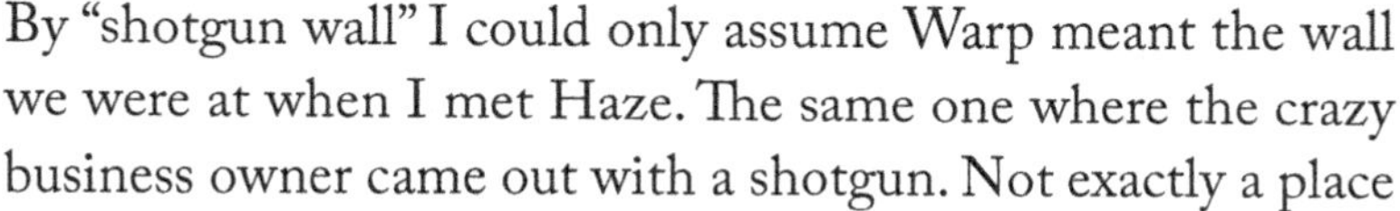

By "shotgun wall" I could only assume Warp meant the wall we were at when I met Haze. The same one where the crazy business owner came out with a shotgun. Not exactly a place

I wanted to revisit, but since Warp never texted me, I figured it was important.

Liv and I walked up, and though Warp stood there, I barely noticed him. All I could see was a big depiction of my face and beside me…Heather, both of us bathed in sunshine that stretched past the clouds. A halo hung over her head and her eyes were mockingly turned up to the sky. I looked pretty normal, though my eyes were slightly rounded, almost as if I were surprised by something.

"At least I'm not fat," I said, trying to downplay my anxiety.

"This is no time for jokes, Emanuella! This is a blatant threat. I told you hanging around that guy was trouble, and now look." Warp wore all black, looking a little like a Ninja warrior on a kill mission. I had an image of him running across rooftops anime-style wielding a large, sharpened, and unsheathed katana in search of Haze.

"He wouldn't do this."

"This is his signature style. No one else in this hood paints the way he does."

"You have no idea what you're talking about," I accused.

"I know exactly what I'm talking about. There is a particular style to every artist's work. And he is the only one with this thin to broad line style on the curves of these clouds, and that type of line is in every one of these pieces of you!"

"You don't know jack about graffiti, Warp. You think someone can't copy a style? People forge paintings all the time!"

"Yeah," he shot back. "For millions of dollars. Who would take the time for a no-name graffiti artist?"

I folded my arms across my chest, shaking my head at the ridiculousness of his accusations. "You're so against him you'll say anything."

"I don't know," Liv interjected, her voice low as if she didn't want to make me angry but wanted to give her opinion. "On a style so specific, it's hard to imagine someone copying it."

I studied the masterpiece more carefully. Other than the fact that I was situated beside a dead girl, I didn't see a reason to freak out. "Let's say you're both right and Haze is doing this. Why? It doesn't make any sense anymore."

"Since when does a psycho make sense?" Warp took out his phone and began texting.

"What are you doing?" I asked, afraid he was sending out a personal APB.

"I'm going to tell Surge. I want him to keep a close eye on you at all times."

"That's enough, Warp!" I walked over to him and slapped his cell out of his hand. It skittered a few feet away. "I know you're my brother and all, but you're not my father."

"Pops isn't at home and can't be, or I'd call him and tell him what's going on!"

"I don't know why you are making a big deal out of a stupid picture! It's just someone trying to bully me and get under your skin. You're falling for it!" But Haze's words came back to me, calling me a fool or some such for challenging the writer. Could someone really be trying to threaten me because I messed with their art? Could it be Haze?

"I'm going to tell Surge anyway." He bent and picked up his phone, rubbing it off on his pants.

"You'll be wasting his time."

Warp shook his head and palmed his phone. Digging around in his pocket with his other hand, he produced a folded piece of newspaper and with shaking hands, thrust it at me.

"You think I'm wasting my time?! Look at that, Emanuella, and tell me I'm being too cautious."

Liv moved next to me and rested her chin on my shoulder as I unfolded the paper. The color print of a graffiti wall was the first thing that came into view. The next was an outline of a body right below it traced with mourning flowers.

Liv gasped, and I scanned the parts of the article that had survived Warp's hasty ripping. I caught sight of Heather Craig's name and realized this was her murder scene photo as it had appeared in the *Tribune* two years ago…

I knew Warp felt this picture was proof of guilt, so my heart didn't want me to look too closely. My head, though, scanned the graffiti with a thirst to know the truth. The painted landscape was actually quite intricate and stunning. There were clouds that parted to reveal stylized rays of the sun, shining over the beginnings of a name over a swirling background. I could see the H and a few lines above the H that denoted there was more to the piece than I could see.

The graffiti proved Warp right about one thing, something bizarre was going on. I looked from the artwork in the photo and the newest painted on the shotgun wall in front of me. The article was damning, but I wanted more. I needed more. I needed something that didn't make Haze look guilty.

"The photo's caption says the graffiti is the last thing Heather ever painted. She worked on it seconds before she was murdered," I said out loud, but my brain was lost in the enigma.

"The fact that someone is spraying in the exact same style is proof the police were wrong, LL. Heather didn't paint that wall. Her murderer did. I think she knew whoever killed her and where he would be and she went there to confront him."

"You've already convicted Haze in your mind. You think he was there painting this piece and when she came to talk to him, he killed her?"

"The police suspected him," Warp pointed out.

"The police suspected everyone!"

I hadn't even felt Liv move away from me but I saw her now as she stood next to my brother, her face ghost white. "This is not good, Ellie," she said in a small voice.

I didn't want to agree with her but I did—only, not for the reason she would think if I voiced my agreement. Right now, all I knew was that Haze thought someone was biting his style. If he was right, and whoever was mocking his work killed his sister and was now painting me…shit was definitely not good. "I think I'm…"

"You're not thinking," my brother interrupted me with a yell. "The truth is staring you in the face! You broke up with him and now things are going to get worse unless I do something."

"Part of the article is missing," I mumbled. I stated a fact only, focusing on the one thing that didn't scare the pants off of me.

"I was in a bit of a hurry. They tend to frown when you rip stuff out of old newspapers in the library."

My head bobbed, acknowledging his words but unable to focus on any of them. "It wasn't Haze. He wouldn't kill his own sister."

Warp glared at me as if I was the stupidest woman alive.

Instead of being supportive, as I would have liked, Liv's face was contorted with concern. "Ellie, please."

"Like you said, we're not together anymore anyway. But even if we were, I know he wouldn't hurt me."

"You're being a moronic child," Warp came back at me. "This asshole is threatening you!"

"No, I'm being rational. There is someone else involved here, Warp. There has to be."

"Well I'm not taking the chance. Even if you're right and it isn't Haze, which I doubt, someone's obviously making a statement. And it's time to make one back."

In the background, I could hear Liv arguing that starting a war could make things worse. She begged him not to do it, to call the police. Warp argued that there wasn't enough evidence to hand over to the police and involving them might speed up my stalker's plan to kill me. I'd heard all I could take and drowned them out.

My entire body felt as though it were stretching in every direction, reaching toward every fear I'd ever experienced.

Who hated me so much? Who hated Haze so much?

Or was I really blind to the truth? Had Haze come up with an elaborate plot to find someone who reminded him of his sister, drag her through hell, pretend he liked her, harass her secretly while openly championing her, only to kill her in the end? Was he doing that to me?

Either way I looked at the situation, whether my boyfriend was at fault or not, one thing was straight-up: A murderer was targeting me.

Eighteen

UR not n class

I looked down at the message on my cell and sighed, half expecting the text to be from Haze. He'd been trying to get ahold of me since last night, but I couldn't bring myself to talk to him. Not yet.

Monday night, Surge had waited in the park for him like I asked, and the two of them were in the middle of discussing callus treatments when Warp's text telling Surge he thought Haze was after me went through.

According to Surge, Haze looked at the picture Warp sent of the graffiti on Surge's phone with a horrified expression, apologized and took off.

Nothing made sense. If Haze was some sister-murdering freak, why would he look so horrified? I knew my judgment might be clouded, but the way Surge explained Haze's shock-face in such detail, I think even he was a little doubtful of my boyfriend's guilt. Not that he would admit it to me.

"Aren't you supposed to shut those things off in here?" Surge asked, interrupting my thoughts—and the thoughts of everyone else in the library.

"Keep your voice down," I said and looked from the newspaper I'd been scouring to my phone on the table beside me. "I have it on vibrate. If Warp tries to text me and I don't answer he'll go apeshit."

"No, he'll call me and then go apeshit."

Poor Surge, he didn't dare leave my side. He claimed it was because my brother hounded him, but we both knew he was terrified something would happen to me the instant his back was turned.

"Is it Haze?"

"No. This time it's Liv. I told her I had something to check out but I had you with me."

He nodded. "Everyone is a little weirded out. I dunno what I want to wish for. That it isn't your boyfriend or that it is. I'd rather know who to strangle to keep you safe, but I know you don't want him to be guilty."

"You know as well as I do that things aren't adding up. Everything points to Haze but..."

"Yeah, I know, LL. I would've taken a beating last night if he were the type to kill. If I believed otherwise, I woulda knifed his ass."

I gagged on a sudden whoosh of breath. "Tell me you're not carrying a weapon around with you! You get caught with that, the cops really will bust you."

"It ain't metal. No alarms are gonna go off. My cousins told me how to keep myself armed for protection but fool the pat downs and metal detectors. I can't really protect you if I don't have a weapon, LL."

I blinked. The situation was getting beyond serious. The words death and murder were being thrown around a lot more in my inner circle than ever before, and Surge was taking to carrying a shiv. Maybe it was time to call Pops and the police.

"You're thinking kinda loud," Surge said.

"I'm thinking this is next-level shit, Surge. We're not cold case detectives. What are we doing?"

"We are being cautious. Someone with the exact graffiti style suspected in a murder two years ago is painting faces of you. It's too weak to go to the cops with some 'I-think-someone-might-be-threatening-me' complaint. They might call your dad, but I don't think they're going to spring for round-the-clock watch of a troubled teenager in the hood who has no evidence that anyone actually is threatening her."

"Well, there is my picture painted on the wall…."

"You mean the wall that was erased last night?"

I blinked. "Damn. You think Haze erased it?"

"I don't know who did, but anything that linked Heather's murder to a threat against you is gone."

This couldn't be good. I stared down at the newspaper in front of me, trembling. "This is all so fucked-up."

"Hey, I think I found the paper," Surge practically yelled, only to be shushed by the librarian. "Yeah, yeah lady, I'll zip it. Just give a brutha a break all right. Been in here three hours."

The librarian shook her head at Surge, but like almost everyone else in the city, she was instantly mollified by Surge's persona.

Making room on the table by pushing the other papers aside, I slid Surge's newspaper in front of me. Now that I didn't have my brother breathing down my neck, I took the time to read the whole article and shivered. The report said the attacker chased Heather up the fire escape, only to throw her over the edge when he'd caught up to her. What a horrible way to go out; no one deserved to die like that. I glanced up at the captured picture and frowned.

"Wait." I took out the torn piece Warp had given to me last night and placed it beside the article. "I don't get it. This newspaper is intact. Warp said he ripped it out of the library's copy."

I looked up in time to see Surge frown at me. "I don't get it, either."

The picture in the paper was easier to see than Warp's torn version, including a look at the crowd gathered for the vigil, and the outline of Heather's body traced end-to-end with flowers. In the background I could see Liv, as well as Heather's family. Haze stood there, the camera capturing his expression.

Grief was written all over his face. I recognized it well, as it mirrored my own feelings when my mother had passed.

I remembered my mother's funeral then and the sparse number of people who stood beside her casket to pay their respects. She had so few friends and even fewer family members. No wonder no one had seen her death coming. There was no one there to see the outcry, and my brothers and I had been too young to read the signs.

My brothers—oh my God, my brother!

I squinted down at the edge of the photo to the blur at the corner and felt my heart stop an instant before kicking into overdrive. "Oh my God, Surge. Look!"

I turned the paper toward him and pointed to the corner.

"So?"

"So," I repeated. "That hoodie look familiar to you?"

Surge peered down at the newspaper photo much like I had, before his shocked face jerked up to stare back at me.

"Next-level."

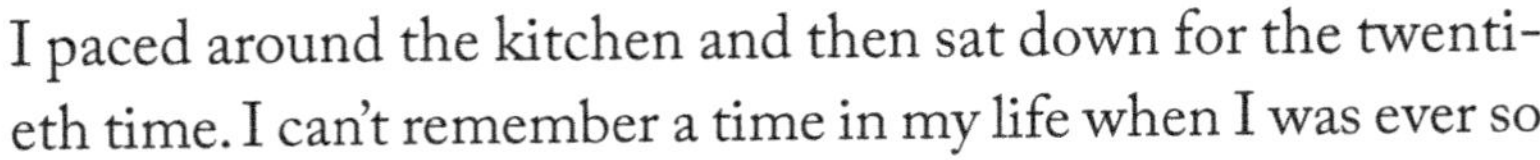

I paced around the kitchen and then sat down for the twentieth time. I can't remember a time in my life when I was ever so anxious about a run-in with my brother. Of course, I'd never suspected him of murder before.

A million thoughts went through my head, a million outcomes of confronting Warp with the full newspaper clipping, and none of them turned out with a hug of forgiveness in the end. What could he possibly say to make everything better?

Two years ago my brother started acting different. He had what Pops called a chip on his shoulder, whatever that meant. I'd always thought my mom's death had taken a little while to get to him and the realization finally sank in around that time. After all, it took a few years for me to understand the full impact of my mom's absence. But I guess I felt it before either of my brothers, because when my mom took her own life, I became the only female in the house, without anyone to confide in.

Ander's moment of anguish came shortly after mine. Warp's? Well, I'd assumed that our mother's death finally caused him to have his own downward spiral two years ago. But now I suspected a different reason for his personality change.

"What are you doing in here?" Warp asked, walking toward the fruit bowl. Most everything in the bowl was overripe but the apples were okay. He picked one up and took a bite, staring at me expectantly.

I reached into my pocket and withdrew the torn newspaper he gave me the night before.

He looked from it, to me and shrugged. "And?"

"You didn't get that from the library."

He stopped chewing and talked around the apple bits in his mouth. "What?"

"I went to the library to read the full story. I was hoping I'd see something that would clear Haze's name or at least give me insight as to why he might want to murder his sister and then me."

Warp swallowed hard. "So?"

"So…I found out some very interesting things. One, that you never went to the library to get this article, and two, the reason you tore it the way you did is because you didn't want to take a chance I might recognize you standing in the top left corner!"

I reached into my pocket again and withdrew the photocopied version of the newspaper with his silhouette circled in red pen.

"I don't know what you're talking about. You can't pick out a random guy and pretend it's me to clear your boyfriend's name. A boyfriend, by the way, that you told me you broke up with but now I'm thinking you never did!"

"Don't try to change the subject, Warp! That," I pointed to the hooded figure, "is you."

He shook his head and I wanted to scream in frustration. He obviously thought I was an idiot with the memory of a goldfish.

"The last hoodie Mom ever bought for you. You slept in it, you wore it every day, even to school. You fluffed it in the dryer when the stench became too strong, afraid to wash it or it might fall apart."

He looked away from me and set the apple down on the counter.

"We were beginning to learn parkour from Ander and you fell off Mr. Zegger's fence and tore open the right sleeve. You got up, looked at Ander and me, and you tried so hard not to cry. Blood was everywhere and you panicked, not wanting to do any more damage to the hoodie, so you ran home so fast that Ander said you were at—"

"Warp speed," he finished.

I nodded and tapped my finger against the picture. "There's a huge scar on that sleeve, in bright white thread so thick it looks like yarn. You started a fashion trend without intending to after you patched it up. But I remember the truth behind it. I bet after this showed up in the newspaper, you never wore it again so no one would know what you did."

His head snapped up and his eyes blazed with fury. "You think you got it all figured out, little sister? You think I killed Heather? You're a genius! This is exactly what you need to clear your boy of everything and see that your brother is behind bars. As long as *you're* happy, right?"

"What are you talking about? I wouldn't—"

"You think I don't know what this looks like? Why do you think I've been hiding it these last few years? I look guilty! If the cops find out I was involved with Heather, what do you think they'd do to me?"

"Johnny." I hadn't called him by his given name, in anything other than a joking manner, in a long time. He lifted his bloodshot eyes to mine when I whispered it. "I'm here to listen if you'll explain to me. Around the time of her death you changed. You became darker."

"Dark enough to want my own sister dead?"

"No, I don't think you want to kill me. I wouldn't confront you at our house alone if I thought you were capable of murdering me. But something isn't adding up and you need to tell me what is going on. Are you painting pictures of me so you can frame Haze?"

I watched his jaw tighten and his fists clench, and for the first time, I was afraid I'd been wrong about him, but I did my best to pretend I was calm on the inside.

"No. I need you to tell me what you think you know. You think seeing me at Heather's memorial somehow makes me guilty of killing her and makes Haze innocent?"

"No. But you lied to me, Johnny. I don't think you murdered her in cold blood. Maybe it was an accident, maybe you're protecting someone. I don't know. I only know you hid the fact you even knew Heather."

He leaned against the counter and pinched the bridge of his nose, the strain of his memories obviously weighing on his mind. He was quiet so long I thought he was just going to ignore me.

"Like you and Haze," he started, "Heather and me hid our relationship from everyone. There wasn't much of a rivalry back then, but there was definitely some tension. The city grouped parkour and graffiti artists in the hoodlum category together and practically dared us to take each other out. People were starting to choose sides.

"So when we started dating, we kept it quiet. I tried to show her some moves and she took to them immediately. She was resilient and graceful." The way Warp talked about her, I could tell he'd loved her. It reminded me of how I felt about Haze. He and his sister were so much alike, I could sympathize with the pain I saw shimmering in the corners or Warp's eyes. How would I feel if Haze was dead? Oh, God.

The grief he felt was palpable. His body shook with his attempt to hold back sobs he'd probably only dared let loose in private, if he ever had at all.

"She took care of me. I'd bust skin on a move and she'd be there, grinning, with gauze in her hands and med tape. She'd always use too much." He choked out the last, disguising his emotional hiccup with a cough.

My eyes started to water, and though I didn't need Warp to prove his innocence any longer, I didn't dare interrupt him. "She was nearing the point of telling her brother and his crew about us in hopes of bringing us all together. We talked about it the night she died. 'Freerunners and graffiti artists complement each other,' she said."

Swallowing repeatedly wasn't helping him. Loss laced every word he spoke.

"You don't have to say any more," I said, my voice unstable.

"No. You have to hear."

I nodded and he continued. "We met on a rooftop that night for her first-ever training session outside of a park. We made a few jumps and then we—" He shook his head, the details of the night haunting his face. "I had...presidential relations with her, yanno?"

"Yeah, I know."

"It was the first time for both of us. We could see the whole city from where we were and everything felt right. But she couldn't stay long. She told me she had made plans, and after what we'd just done, she wanted to tell everyone she knew how much she loved me." His gaze grew distant. "She still glowed. I waved at her and could see her face and...she glowed."

He broke down. Turning away from me, he put his elbows on the counter and his head in his hands and he actually wept.

I sat at the kitchen table and frowned, my eyes streaming with pity but my mind numb with shock. I'd never seen my brother react to anything so strongly. It was as if everything he'd been trying to hide behind his anger in the last few years came out in heart-wrenching grief.

In an unfamiliar place, I got up from the chair and walked over to him. I pressed against his back and wrapped my arms around his shoulders, feeling every shudder of his anguish as I hugged him.

"You shoulda told me."

"You were...too young to understand." He sniffed and stood straight, righting himself as abruptly as he shattered. He faced me and I was forced to let him go. His eyes were puffy but guarded once more. "Besides, I was too scared to even whisper her name. I thought for sure the cops would figure out through DNA who she'd been with and come knocking on the door any second. When they didn't, I knew she hadn't had the chance to tell anyone we were together, and since I haven't broken any laws, my DNA isn't on record. All I had to do was keep my mouth shut."

"You must've been terrified."

He did the macho shoulder lift, as if a severed heart was nothing more than a flesh wound. "I hated pretending she was some girl I'd heard of when I really wanted to confront her brother and his friends and beat the truth out of them. I know they had something to do with it. I feel it in my bones."

"You think she told Haze? Because of the graffiti bit?"

"Heather used to show me his stuff. I know what his style is like, little sister. I know you don't want to hear it but I wouldn't lie about something like that."

"And if someone is biting off his work to make it look like Haze?"

"Who would do that?"

I sighed and took a few steps back to reseat myself at the table. "I don't know. But I can't accuse Haze because of the graffiti. After what you just told me, it's clear not everything is what it looks like."

He folded his arms over his chest. "And sometimes it is."

"Why are you so sure it's Haze?"

"Because Heather was afraid of disappointing her little brother and she worried about his bouts of anger. She said her parents *had* to put him in karate to keep him from hurting others."

"A violent streak in young men is hardly rare. The dojos are filled with them. With as many times as you've provoked him, I think if Haze still had a problem with anger management, you would be the first to know."

"He showed it the other night."

"You practically made him hit you, Warp. You accused him of killing his sister."

He widened his eyes, accentuating each word. "Truth hurts."

My emotional roller coaster took another turn. I was trying very hard to understand where my brother was coming from, but I stopped feeling sorry for his loss when confronted with his stubbornness.

"I never knew Heather, but as a sister of a hotheaded brother I think I can safely say she'd be disappointed in you going after Haze because you think all the pieces fit. Well, they don't. If Heather told Haze about your affair, one word from him would bring the cops here, and your DNA would have matched what they found on her and you'd look like the guilty one, even though you're innocent, right?"

I saw him flinch, which meant he finally saw a tiny bit of truth in my words. It was a start.

"I think if you really loved Heather, you would help her by proving her brother innocent."

Warp's eye twitched. "How do you propose I do that?"

"Help me find out who's painting my face on these walls."

"And if it ends up I was right, and it is Haze?"

I was confident in Haze's innocence, and yet when Warp posed the question I stalled for a second. "If Haze is the man harassing me?" He nodded and I shifted my feet. "Then I'll help you bring him down for Heather's murder."

Nineteen

Liv stared at me, walking to school on autopilot Wednesday morning, eerily missing every bump in the sidewalk and overgrown limb without shifting her gaze. Then she snapped her gum. "Wow. You're living in a soap opera. Your boyfriend… oh, I mean ex-boyfriend…and your brother are both thinking the other is guilty of murder and threatening you. Meanwhile, your brother had a secret affair with the deceased sister of your ex-boyfriend, and Bren snuck in moments of young passionate love in a supply closet at school with you."

"Yeah," I said lamely.

"Wow," Liv said again and focused her gaze straight ahead. "Suddenly my life with my defunct 'rentables doesn't seem so bad."

"I know, right?" I grinned over at her but stopped when I noticed her frown. "What's up?"

"Heather had a secret relationship with Warp. You had a secret relationship with Haze. Neither one of you told me. I'm starting to think I'm not a very good friend."

"Oh, hey, Liv, seriously. You shouldn't think that. I can't speak for Heather but I can tell you that my fear of what would happen if my relationship with Haze got out made it hard to whisper it to myself, let alone tell you."

She shrugged. "I know I can be bossy sometimes too, Ellie, but I promise you, no more. I'm going to relax and make sure I'm much easier to talk to. I can't help but feel that if I listened to Heather more instead of always trying to grill her for the latest gossip in her life and school, maybe she would've told me something that could've brought her killer to justice."

I wanted to ask her if she suspected my brother, but I wasn't sure I'd like her answer. "We've both been a little off this year. It's to be expected with the added violence and tension, right?"

"Right," she answered, not sounding very sure.

"We'll both work on being better friends, all right?"

She nodded, and several seconds passed as we started walking again. True to form, the silence became too much for Liv. "So what are you going to do next?"

"I don't know. I haven't talked to Haze since Art class on Monday, and I know he's going to be looking for me today."

She sighed. "About that, Ellie. I know you have a lot of confidence in him and all, but I think you should at least be cautious. Not all killers look like unwashed psychopaths."

"I know."

"See, that's what I been telling her all along. But does she listen to me?"

I jumped as Surge emerged with his words of wisdom, and as a reward for his efforts, I threw a playful swat at his beaming face. "Jesus, you scared the hell outta me."

"You didn't actually think I was going to allow you to walk to school with only the beautiful Liv Menesa beside you, right?"

Liv stopped and put her hands on her hips. "You saying I couldn't scare some freak away from her?"

"I'm saying I'm here to protect the freak from you, kind lady. I think the cops would want him alive." Surge displayed a fine row of pearly whites as he wrapped an arm around both our shoulders and got us moving again. "I'm the stallion of the stables."

"Please," Liv said with drawn out emphasis. "Like I need to get involved in a ménage. It's bad enough everyone thinks you two are dating, throw me in, and the school has a new scandal to obsess about."

I tripped on my own foot, forcing Surge's forearm to ride over the back of my head and mess up my hair. Not that I cared, I simply pushed it out of my face and gawked at Liv. She slowed her gait to a halt, pushing Surge's arm off her shoulder and lifting an eyebrow at me.

"What? Like you're surprised?" Liv looked from me to Surge. "You two spend tons of time together. Guys and girls can't be friends without rumors, especially not in high school."

My bro-friend didn't look at all put out by this revelation. In fact, I'd say he looked pleased. "Surge?"

He held up his hands. "A few guys have asked me what's up. I don't say nothing. Ain't no one's business and if they think we're going out that means I can protect you better." Was that it? Or was he using me to hide his own closet secrets? I couldn't help but be annoyed.

"But Haze...hello!"

Liv shook her head. "I thought you said you weren't with him anymore."

"I said that the other day to keep Warp from freaking out. I told you we meet in the closet."

"You said 'met' as in *used to meet*."

I threw up my hands in frustration. "Well..."

"Ellie, either way, it's better if everyone thinks you're with Surge and not with Haze. Right?"

"I don't know. It doesn't seem fair to Haze."

"Then tell everyone you're not with Surge," she said impatiently, and I knew she needed more time to get used to the idea of Haze and me. "Useless, if you ask me. No one is gonna believe you two are friends with as much time as you spend together."

"Who did you hear the rumor from?" Surge asked.

"One of Ellie's gymnastic buddies, Ramona, called me under the pretense of needing some homework. She wanted to know if the two of you went to the tardy party at Damien's. Apparently, she's got a crush on you, Surge."

He seemed to mull the info over. "Really?"

"Don't get too excited, I told her it's possible you and Ellie are an item. That Ellie and I don't really talk about guys much."

"Oh come on, Liv. That ain't cool."

She sighed. "To be honest, Ellie, I wasn't sure if I should say anything at all, so I denied knowledge. I'm worried about this graffiti stuff, and I feel like I can't trust anyone with any kind of information. Like, I tell Ramona, but I don't know who she tells, and I couldn't bear it if someone who is out to get you…got you because of something I said."

A legitimate concern, and very thoughtful, which made me feel unworthy of her friendship for the millionth time. "You're probably right. It's better not to say anything at this point until we can figure out who is playing games with me."

The rest of the walk to school, none of us said a word.

The last few times an incident with me had occurred, everyone in the school seemed to respond to it with looks or giggles or comments. I suspected I would get the same treatment over the Surge rumors. I'm not sure why, since me dating Surge wouldn't actually be noteworthy. But I was pleasantly surprised by the lack of attention on the walk to my locker.

"Incoming," Liv whispered. I glanced up to see Haze and his friend, Decay, plowing their way through the crowded hall toward Liv, Surge, and me.

If pissed could be accurately defined in a look, Haze had it.

"This can't be good," I said under my breath. An understatement on my part. "Hey," I said to Haze, once he was close enough.

He glanced at Liv and then Surge before bringing his heated stare back to me. "Can I talk to you privately?"

"I don't think that's a good idea, bro," Surge started, surveying the interested students who suddenly walked much slower and gawked harder.

"No one asked you, little man," Decay responded, pushing his chest up higher with an inhale.

Surge balked. "Little man? You got what? An inch or two on me? That don't mean nothing."

Like a skunk spraying defensively, the smell of trouble misted and tainted the air.

"Okay, okay." I reached out and squeezed Surge's arm, trying to call him off the hunt. When I looked over at Haze, I was surprised to see he didn't bother to leash Decay this time around. Liv, however, poked the big guy in the chest a few times as she dressed him down right there in the hallway.

I couldn't hear what she said since my attention was firmly planted on Haze and his bizarre behavior. After all our sneaking around, he made a pretty bold statement coming up to me in the hallway. Why would he risk the declaration of war?

"Yeah. We can talk privately," I said.

Surge's face burst into a vast array of disapproving scowls, but I shook my head. I didn't need to hear anything from him right now.

"Ellie," I heard Liv call for me from somewhere behind my shoulder.

"It'll be fine. Go to class before we draw serious attention. Surge, you know I'll be okay," I quickly added when it looked like Surge might argue. "Please, it'll be quick. I'll see you next period break, okay?"

Surge's jaw worked as he stared down Haze. The two were not exactly friends, and not exactly enemies, I'd seen to that by asking Surge to help train Haze, but now with all the mystery surrounding my graffiti'd face, the walls of distrust were up. The fact my boy best friend and my boyfriend might come to blows was a very real, very upsetting possibility.

Though I could tell he didn't want to, Surge nodded and motioned for Liv to come with him. She and Decay finished a heated-whisper argument that Liv ended abruptly with a slap to Decay's face.

I winced, expecting a backlash, but he only stared after Liv when she walked away.

"You better be at your locker between periods, Ellie," she called over her shoulder. Surge walked beside her, uncertain, and I nodded to let him know everything would be all right.

That is, until Haze grabbed my hand and held it. Held my hand! Right there in the middle of the hallway for everyone to see.

I snatched it back. "Haze!"

"Take my hand, LL."

"But..." With a quick scan I confirmed what I suspected. A good majority of the hall's occupants were already whispering.

"LL!"

"Okay, okay. Jesus, when did you get so cranky?"

A moment later we were in the alcove to the pool room, and the locked metal door was at my back. Haze's hazel eyes were greener under fluorescent lights, boring into me with emotions I couldn't sift through to get to the heart of his issue.

"When did I get so cranky? When my girlfriend is rumored to be with someone other than me! It's like a bomb went off and everyone is talking about you and Surge hooking up at one of Damien's skip parties."

"What?" I laughed. If he only knew. "I don't even go to parties, Haze. You can't possibly believe that."

"Of course, I don't," he said, but I wasn't sure if he believed his own words. "Even though you've been avoiding me..."

"I had to get my head straight. With all this graffiti business, I wasn't feeling like being visible."

"I went by your house and you weren't there."

"When?"

"Tuesday, when you called out sick."

I bit my lip, recalling each day of the weekend. "Oh. I wasn't home Tuesday. I skipped with Surge."

Haze stared at me. *Oh!*

I couldn't help but grin. The rumors did seem to coincide with my absence from Haze, but really, it was all a big misunderstanding, which made his jealousy and irrational need to lay claim to me, beyond cute. I was flattered.

"Brennen." I sighed, and brought my hands up to his face. Pulling him into me, I slid my mouth against his and felt the tension ease in him. His arms swept around my back in that familiar way and he squeezed me against his chest.

His lips took instant possession of mine, as if he could define our relationship in this one kiss, and damn the world if they discovered he wanted me and I belonged to him.

He had the last part right!

Returning each lap of his tongue, I put every ounce of my adoration for him in my reaction. *Please believe in me.*

The brief soft press of lips he used to end his kiss was sweeter than I ever remembered. Like an apology without words. Panting, connected by our foreheads, we stared down at each other's swollen lips until he lifted his gaze to mine.

"I can't do this."

Okay, that threw me for a bit of a loop. My gut welcomed my heart. "I don't—What do you mean?"

"I can't have the entire school believe you belong to someone else when you belong with me." He reached down and clasped both of my hands.

I squeezed. *Phew!* "I know it isn't an ideal situation. But what choice do we have?"

"We have choices. So what if people find out? Your brother suspects we're together still, I'm sure, and if we can just talk some sense into him he can calm his troops down with a word. And if he won't help, we'll go to your older brother like you suggested. My side won't be as much of a problem. I told Decay that night at the theatre I was digging you, so he can help me with the rest of my crew to smooth things over. This can be done."

I frowned. "You were so certain it couldn't be…"

"No," he interrupted me. "I wasn't sure it would be worth getting into trouble with our crews for or starting shit with your brother. Now I know it is."

"And if violence ensues?"

"Right now, your brother is the issue. I'm not going to start any violence. If anyone from your crew and mine are willing, we could band together and figure out who is throwing a character of you up all over the place and why. Then your brother wouldn't have any reason to stand in our way."

"My brother still believes it's you."

One side of his mouth twisted in a smirk. "I bet he does."

"He showed me an old newspaper article with the wall your sister was painting before she was killed and the style matches yours."

"I told you," he snapped. "Whoever helped my sister paint my birthday present, took my style. Same as here and now."

"I believe you, Haze. But others might need more convincing."

"So, your brother shows you an article and you ignore me, is that what happened? You thought maybe I could be doing this?"

"I didn't know. Surge and I went to the library to see for ourselves, but I don't care about what looks guilty. Brennen, I believe in you. I think you're being set up."

He worried his bottom lip and leaned against the door beside me. "I know. There's a connection between it all I just can't figure out what. Maybe it goes beyond Heather's hormones. Maybe she was in some trouble, maybe drugs or something. I don't know. They say people do crazy stuff when they're on them and she was definitely stepping into some crazy behavior."

"Maybe she didn't change because of drugs. Maybe she changed because of a guy—or something."

"A secret crush? Maybe. Then whoever she was with is probably the guy I'm looking for."

"Well," I stalled. I didn't know if I should tell Haze what I'd found out about his sister and my brother. But I wasn't sure which was worse, having Haze discover it and draw the wrong conclusions, or hearing it from me and listening to my explanation. "It wasn't the guy she was secretly dating."

Haze practically lurched from the door as if it were boiling his palms. He stared me down, the anger of his youth I'd heard so much about, glinting in his eyes. "What did you find out?"

He shook with tension and I reached out to ease him only to feel him jerk away.

"What did you find out?" he repeated more forcefully.

I couldn't tell him.

Already he looked ready to kill someone, and I wanted to swallow my tongue or better yet, sleep for the next ten years so I wouldn't have to face the outcome of the storm I mistakenly created.

"Tell me! It was Surge, wasn't it?"

Oh, God. "No! Jesus, Brennen, stop."

"You have to tell me…you have to—" His voice cut off around an audible swallow. I could imagine how long he'd waited for a break in his sister's case, and I was flashing him an answer without following through.

"Brennen, listen to me very carefully. You have to get the complete story before you go off on a vengeance spree. You're emotional right now," I paused as he laughed bitterly. "Yes, I know how that sounds, but please, give me a chance."

He did. I explained about my brother and his sister and I left nothing out, not even the intimacy Warp and Heather shared. I knew if he could relate to what my brother felt, he would know, as well as I, that Warp hadn't murdered his sister.

When the entire tale was told, I held my breath and waited for his response.

"You should've told me right away," he whispered.

"I recently found out myself! I was investigating all day and night yesterday, trying to keep an open mind. Both you and my brother have the best motives for your sister's murder. You have an alibi. My brother doesn't."

"And because of his bullshit story, you believe him? He's playing you, LL!"

Panic gagged me. I had to fight to keep myself from fainting. "W-what?"

"Your brother was with my sister right before she died, and he said nothing!"

"He would have been pinned for the murder and you know it. Oh, God, Brennen, please. You know I wouldn't have told you this if I thought for a second you would think my brother was guilty. As I have asked him to believe in your innocence, I'm begging you to believe in his! Trust me. Please."

Haze backed away from me, his eyes narrowed, body shaking, and without another word, he ran.

Twenty

"Here, breathe into this."

Liv held a paper lunch bag to my mouth, but I pushed it away. When I'd texted her that I was having a panic attack in the pool hallway, I didn't expect her to show up with an arsenal of stolen first aid items.

"I'm not hyperventilating, Liv. I'm freaking out."

Surge rounded the corner, his look of panic melting away when he saw me alive.

"What'd he do? I'll kill him."

I shook my head, looking at her. "You texted Surge?"

"I figured he'd want to know you were okay," she said defensively. I nodded, annoyed that I didn't think of it first.

"So?" Surge held his arms straight out to his sides. "Tell me where he is."

"He didn't do anything, Surge." I closed my eyes and all I could see was the burning hate in Haze's eyes. "I'm screwed. I messed up bad. Oh God. Oh shit!" My chest was so tight with pressure…I banged my head back against the pool doors just to move the pain elsewhere so I could breathe again—so I could think.

Surge squatted down beside me. "I know it probably feels that way," he started.

"I told Haze that Heather and Warp were dating, and that Warp was with her right before she died."

He winced, not able to hide the reaction. "You're right. You're proper fucked. I'm going to text your bro, give him the duck warning."

I nodded, leaning my head back to stare at the ceiling, tears streaming across my cheeks and into my ears. I refused to wipe them away. They deserved to stain my face for all time.

"I thought I could keep problems from happening if I told Brennen the truth about Heather and Warp's affair. Warp loved her. He really did, and if I could make Haze see that, the two of them could piece together what they know and find out who killed Heather. I feel it!"

Liv wadded up the paper bag with jerky motions. "I think Haze is right to be mad. Maybe your brother is lying to you. Either way, he should've come forward with his relationship with Heather and faced the music."

I frowned. "Liv. I don't think you realize what that would've meant for Warp."

"I don't care. You told me they were dating today, but you failed to mention he was with her the night she died. Maybe something he might have said about that night could've been helpful to the police."

"I know she was your best friend, but you should try to understand how he was feeling."

"And I think you should try and imagine your brother when he's angry. Maybe he didn't go to the police because he was guilty. Ever think of that, Ellie?"

I couldn't believe Liv was taking a side against Warp. She seemed to like him. I thought she might even date him eventually. She often came around the house unannounced and talked to him quite a bit. Sometimes I saw her feeble reasons for coming to see me as an excuse to chat up my brother, even though at school she pretended to hate him.

"You really think my brother is capable of murder?"

"No way," Surge piped in, but Liv didn't answer right away.

"He's hidden himself from police," she finally said. "And as you've often said, he hasn't been acting himself the last few years. Maybe he killed her accidentally and is living with the guilt, or maybe he acquired a taste for violence. All I'm saying is, watch your back."

Haze wasn't in the closet waiting for me. He stood *me* up this time. We didn't actually say we'd meet up, but our time behind doors was a daily thing. His absence told me a lot about his frame of mind.

I searched the school for him but didn't find him. According to rumors, he stormed out the front door with the principal yelling after him shortly after he and I paraded down the hallway hand-in-hand.

On the heels of that rumor was the buzz about my brother scouring the halls in search of me. Yay.

I didn't know if Surge told my brother the full story about how I outted his relationship with Heather to Haze or if he'd just heard about the scene Haze made at my locker. Either way, I knew I didn't want to deal with his hysterical reprimand.

So I skipped again. Sneaking out the window the way Liv taught me wasn't an exit that made a statement, but it worked. Of course, she'd yell at me for abusing her technique when she found out I was cutting class without her.

I'd apologize for my friendship ineptitude later, but right then, I needed to at least try to find Haze before he confronted my brother. Warp was safe at school, but Haze was out on the streets somewhere, I just knew it. Whenever I become overwhelmed, I always turn to my passions, parkour and gymnastics—so I guessed he'd turned to his. I was sure I'd find him throwing up an awesome masterpiece of an avenging angel or some such.

I spent the next few hours freerunning around Three Rivers Academy territory, climbing buildings, jumping walls, and indulging in the occasional handspring, twist, or twirl all while keeping my eyes open for Haze.

In the middle of a Speed Vault, my phone vibrated in my pocket. Maybe Haze had finally responded to one of my texts! But in the alleys of the city, I knew my reception would be crap. The sun had gone down, but the neon lights of the fast food joint across the street illuminated the area just enough for me to see. I climbed up the rungs of the nearest fire escape ladder to the tops.

I unzipped my pocket and took out my cell, only to see it was yelling at me to plug it in right before the screen went blank. Well, crap. I'd seen that I had at least one message. Was it my brother looking for me? My boyfriend finally answering me? Was he my boyfriend after today?

While my brain worked, my body went through the motions heading toward my house—the long way of course. Circumstances kept me from enjoying my night out on the town, but I could at least release some stress on the road home.

I balanced on the lip of the rooftop as if it were a beam at the gym. I did my winning routine at Regionals until I ran out of space, and without pause, I jumped down to the neighboring roof, landing with a roll.

Ta *fucking* da!

No applause today.

Only birds flying into the last vestiges of light before the sun retired behind the growing storm clouds. I could smell the rain in the sky an instant before the first few droplets splattered my hoodie.

Time to stop screwing around and take the direct route in, I figured. I stuffed my hair into my hood and peered through the growing downpour over at the roof adjacent to mine.

I froze.

Someone stood there, with what might have been a can of paint in hand, arms down to their sides with their back to me. The rain poured down on them as well as on the portrait they'd painted—a portrait of my decayed face underneath a gnarled tree. Beneath it the bubbled words: Death Comes.

My heart choked me. My sudden wheezing stole my breath. I tried to scream at whoever it was to get them to turn around, but the rain fell so hard it obstructed my view and drowned my words.

Frustration eventually cinched my throat to near closing.

I took a step forward, and another. I wanted to get over there, but I resisted the temptation to make the jump from the roof I stood on to the one across from me. As eager as I was to find out who it was, I wasn't eager to end up like the curious cat.

I squinted, only able to make out the shape of a human and no more. Size, dimensions...all out of my visual ability to interpret.

"Who—who are you?" I choked out.

Whoever it was couldn't hear me.

"Please," I sobbed, more to myself than to my would-be killer. "Why did you do this?"

The next few seconds passed as hours while I waited for rational ideas to form in my brain. I couldn't call the cops because my phone was dead. I couldn't confront the person, or I'd be dead.

The person snapped their head to the side, hearing a noise I couldn't, and darted away from the wall.

I could see the graffiti clearer now. My painted face dripped a little, the red simulating fresh blood ominously as it oozed over the gray flesh of death. The hypnotic swirl in the background looked like it was going to suck my corpse-like face into hell, rotted tree, rain cloud, flailing blue strand of hair and all. Death and decay. This wasn't harassment anymore. This was a threat. I felt death sitting on my shoulder, giggling in my ear.

And I got angry.

How dare this person ruin my whole life so casually, throwing mortality in my face? They wielded a power against me and I was allowing it to go on! The culprit was right there, and I stood motionless like a dumbass.

Well, not anymore.

I ran to the fire escape full steam, fueled by my rage. The bottom of my Tribal shoe gripped the topmost rung of the ladder and I pushed off, launching myself to the opposite emergency stairwell. In hindsight, I knew I was a fool to try the jump in wet conditions, but I successfully landed on the opposite balcony only one floor down from the top sans broken bones, though my face scraped against the bricks as I slid into it. The bizarre road rash would negate the "I entered the wrong building" alibi I was working on in the event of cop interference, but the fact I hadn't killed myself eased the loss.

Taking a deep breath, I began the stealthy climb up the ladder to the roof where I'd seen my harasser. Hopefully, I wouldn't run into them as soon as my head crested the rim and give them a pimp target.

To be safe, I stopped and listened. I could hear the rain dripping into recently created puddles but nothing more. The atmosphere turned eerie. Each step I took I imagined the entire apartment complex could hear it.

Though it took me a little while, I finally made it over the roof's rail and onto the tar.

The rain made it nearly impossible to see my surroundings, lending me a heaping helping of vulnerability. Awesome.

I crouched down and looked around.

There were two small shed-like structures on the top of the building, one housing the electrical outlets and stuff and the other the emergency exit for the stairs. Two very good places where someone could hide and jump out at me with weapons of various sorts.

Chicken pens, or coops or whatever the hell they were called, were sitting in the center of the rooftop. A sign of the times I supposed, where breeding chickens was cheaper than buying them from stores, but someone musta been damned broke, 'cause there were no chickens left.

The tarp lying over the tops of the cages would give me a little cover but not much, so I avoided the bird pens and made my way to the emergency stairs.

A pair of hands grabbed my arms and slung me into the shadow of the emergency exit opposite of where my newest graffiti picture was painted. I drew in a breath to scream but the wet body gnashed into me so hard I lost all diaphragm possibilities. The attacker's fingers dug into my throat, holding my voice box hostage while his other hand yanked my hoodie away from my face.

Not to be outdone, I grabbed my assailant's hood to get a good look at…

…my boyfriend.

"LL! Jesus, you scared the shit out of me," he whispered and removed his hand from my neck.

"Me?!" I choked, partly due to his nerve. "Haze…"

"Where did you come from?"

"I was on the roof searching for you when I saw—Haze! How could you? I believed you when you said it wasn't you!"

"We gotta get out of here."

He clasped my hand and pulled me down to a crouch. We took a few steps toward the edge before I yanked back to reality and out of his grip. "I'm not going anywhere with you until you explain to me why you are painting my zombified face on the side of this exit shed!"

"I wasn't!" He turned to face me, looking over my shoulder. "Manu, please. Someone is up here with some hardware neither one of us has an answer to. Okay? We'll talk as soon as we're down."

"H-hardware? Like a gun?" I hoped I was whispering.

"Shit. Run!"

I looked behind me but I didn't see anything. There was a loud crack of thunder, and I couldn't hear much of anything, let alone Haze's next command. He regained possession of my hand and ran me toward the roof's edge.

I didn't know if it was my adrenaline having a rock'n'roll concert in my ears, or the thunder, but I thought I heard… gunshots. In front of me, I could see the rim coming closer. "Don't stop," Haze yelled, and I found myself briefly wondering if he was ready for this level. We'd never trained building jumps.

"Focus on the jump," I instructed a second before I flattened out my body and made the distance. I landed correctly, but Haze's feet slid on a wet patch and he hit hard.

I helped him to his feet but he pushed me ahead. "Next... roof," he wheezed.

I sized the building up...and up. It was a good three stories higher than the building we were on which meant we'd have to perform a successful Cat Leap. Not good.

In theory I was good at going from the ground to a wall top, but this was different. This was from the roof to a window ledge, fingers making the difference between success and death, and that was only if I was lucky enough to make a solid grab. If I didn't, there was only the option of death.

"Haze. With the rain..." I slowed but he urged me ahead of him again.

"Focus, Manu. I'm right behind you."

I nodded but I doubted he saw it in the downpour. I heard him grunt in pain and I figured he injured himself with the first leap. We neared the next building and I realized we faced the fire-escape side. Less of a jump than I thought, but the landing might be a little rougher.

We didn't need to run balls-out, though. I doubted the person chasing us would've made the jump behind us, and they certainly couldn't see us by now.

We could do a simple leap that would carry us to the other building. I paused to see if he was feeling okay to—

I felt his hands at my back shove me forward. I let out a bizarre squeak—a mixture of shock and terror—and flew forward over the edge.

I heard a bellow, or another crack of thunder maybe. It sounded like the reaper calling my name, but I wasn't ready to go just yet! All the nights of training came down to the moment of instinct where I had just enough brain juice to tell myself to push out. I didn't get much power behind it, but I arched and extended my arms. There might've been a quick prayer involved as well, wrapped in curse words.

The ground came closer, my fingers barely grazed the balcony on floor four. Floor three slapped the center of my hand but my grip couldn't hold the wet metal. The second floor was all mine, and I held on as my torso jerked downward putting my upper-body strength to the test.

If I hadn't used the Cat Leap technique by tucking my legs up, the jolt would have pulled my arms out of my sockets. Though saved from permanent damage, I couldn't hold on for long, and I dropped to the alley.

Any trained parkour athlete knows how to absorb a decent fall with proper leg-bendage, but my foot slipped on a bit of garbage saturated by rain, and I landed hard on my back. The instinct to keep my head up kept the contact with the concrete down to a tap, but I had to lie still to collect myself.

I'd...almost died. Was I alive or only thinking I was?

The small of my back throbbed a bit. Yeah, I was still alive, but my head felt a bit light.

Five seconds ago, I'd been cursing the rain, but now I welcomed it. The cold drops splattered across my face, keeping me alert.

I felt nauseous and I wanted to keep my eyes closed for a little while longer, except the survival part of my brain wouldn't stop screaming. *Get up.*

Get up.

I heard someone screaming my name, or maybe it was the lady who came out onto her balcony to let me know she called the cops and was glad I fell. I lifted a hand to shield my eyes from the rain to look up at her. I caught a glimpse of

Haze leaning over the rooftop looking down for a brief second before he disappeared.

Shit. Had he seen me move?

An image of him readying his cans of paint to spray my face until I choked to death got me to my feet faster than was probably good for me. The woman above me continued to berate me, telling me she got a good look at me, and proceeded to call me "young man" over and over. Yeah, she got a real good look.

I stumbled a bit and grabbed the side of the wall for support.

No time to stop. Haze would be down any second and the sirens in the distance were growing louder.

"See? They coming for you, young man," the woman reminded me.

I was a big believer in respecting one's elders, but this woman was dying for a bird, so I gave her one, right before I turned the corner and did my best to jog-stumble home.

Twenty-one

Call the police.

My inner voice screamed at me to preserve my life status by calling in the troops, yet I stood in my dark, empty house staring at the phone, poised to do something but unsure of what. The living room felt larger, less homey than I remembered. Probably because no one was in it. No one except me, dripping on the carpet.

Call the police.

And tell them what exactly? My boyfriend is putting up horribly graphic cartoonish pictures of me on walls all over the city? That he tried to kill me by pushing me off a building?

I remembered the article I read about Heather and how her killer had scuffled a bit with her on the ground. Then it was speculated that he followed her up the fire escape, dragged her to the edge, and threw her over.

Was Haze trying to reenact what had happened with his sister?

The thought of him—my Brennen—viciously attacking his sister, and me, was beyond my comprehension, and yet, my sore ass and head made a valid argument for his guilt.

I sighed, going over every second since picking myself up off the unsanitary ground. Haze encouraged me to run. I heard him grunting behind me, and then I felt a push. Maybe he hadn't meant to push me so hard. He'd nudged me several times before the pivotal shove, convinced someone was on our heels. Perhaps he got carried away.

Or perhaps I was deeply in love with a killer and needed saving from myself. I needed to call the police.

I reached for the house phone and jumped when it rang. I took a calming breath, trying to staunch the fear of who was on the other line. Was it Haze calling to talk me into listening to his excuses? Was it one of my brothers looking for an explanation or worse...was it my father?

No one was home, which meant Warp was probably out on the streets looking for me, buried in panic with no way of knowing my phone died.

I picked up the house phone on the fifth ring. "Hello?"

"Jesus fucking Christ!"

"Hey, Warp," I said, trying to pretend nothing was amiss.

"Don't 'hey Warp' me, Emanuella! I've been trying to call you!"

"My phone died. Sorry. I didn't mean to worry you."

"Just get to the hospital."

"The hospital? Why?" I felt my rapid heartbeat in my earlobes and held my breath. "What happened? Is it Pops?"

I never understood why people took forever to tell you bad news. Finding the right words could possibly explain their pause, but in their fumbling, they gave off a 'something awful happened' vibe that's like...torturous to people waiting on the other end of the conversation. "Jesus! Tell me," I snapped.

"Someone ran Surge down."

I fought to define every word in that one simple sentence, and what I came up with was absurd.

"No." Nothing was allowed to happen to Surge.

"No? Dammit, Emanuella, get your head off your boyfriend troubles for five seconds and hear what I'm saying to you! Someone ran down…"

"No! No. He's fine. You're lying."

Warp got quiet on the other end of the line, probably realizing by the sound of my voice I was on the verge of hysterics. The razor's edge of his tone dulled. "Just come down here."

"I don't understand. When? What happened? Is he going to be all right?"

He said nothing.

"Johnny," I yelled into the phone, wishing I could reach through and pummel the answers out of him. "Is he going to be all right?" Of course he was. Surge was in my intimate circle and things like that weren't possible.

"I don't know," he said gently. "Come down here."

The phone receiver hung from my hand and all I could see was those fucking red paper hearts.

"Ellie, get in!" Liv saw me jogging through the rain a couple of blocks away from my house toward the hospital and pulled up near the curb.

I climbed into the passenger seat, barely noticing I soaked the upholstery. "Thanks."

"I heard about what happened. I guess it was only a matter of time before the war."

I blinked out of thoughts about Surge dying on some hospital bed and pushed them back long enough to grill for details. "What did you hear?"

Liv shrugged. "So far, only that Decay and Surge were supposed to continue their fight at Tucker Park an hour after school. Decay didn't show on time, but he came screaming up with his car, driving through the fence and running down Surge. Haze was in the passenger seat—laughing."

She snorted and shook her head, believing the rumor true without facts. I knew better.

"What? No. That's impossible."

"God, Ellie! When are you going to stop sticking up for that bastard and realize that he's the villain here?"

Liv's fingers were white-knuckled as they gripped the steering wheel, and her entire body shook with emotion. She thought I was being irrational, but in reality, I had proof in the form of a bruise on my butt that Haze hadn't been in the car. I didn't see how it was possible for him to run down Surge at Tucker Park with Decay and then paint a new sadistic mural of me downtown all before pushing me off a rooftop. He'd be one hell of a multitasker.

"Liv, you said Decay and Surge were going to continue their fight after school? What fight?"

She seemed pissed at me and for a moment, I wasn't sure she'd answer. "Yeah. After you left, Decay tried to pick a fight with your brother. Surge walked up and challenged him with a punch to the face before a teacher broke them up and suspended them for a few days. The two agreed to meet to finish it."

I didn't have to ask why Decay would be after my brother. All the graffiti crew would be since I opened my big mouth. "This is all my fault for telling Haze about Warp's relationship with Heather."

From the corner of my eye I watched Liv wring her hands around the wheel as she drove. I knew she hated that Warp didn't come forward when Heather died. She even suspected him of killing her best friend. "I told you before, Liv. Warp didn't kill Heather. I know it."

"Yeah, maybe. The evidence is piling up against Haze. Warp seems the victim of circumstance."

I should have agreed with her. After all, I knew the truth about what Haze had done to me, but I couldn't help but compare notes by playing devil's advocate. "There's nothing that points at Haze if you believe someone's been ripping off his style."

"You're a fool, Ellie. Not only is the graffiti style hard to duplicate, there's no one around these parts with the talent to do it. And he is trying to distract away from his guilt by running down Surge to start a war between the traceurs and writers."

I pounced. "See, that's where you're wrong. I ran into another masterpiece, and I saw Haze. There's no way he could be downtown throwing up a piece while running down Surge at Tucker Park."

The light overhead of us turned yellow and Liv uncharacteristically stopped for it, having to slam on her brakes to do so.

She turned to face me, her eyes narrowing. "You were with Haze?"

"Well, not with him. But I saw him standing next to the new piece on the roof of an apartment complex." I decided not to mention he held a can of spray paint in his hand.

"That's great." Liv's eyes turned on the high beams. "You witnessed him painting your face, which could link him to…"

"I didn't actually see him paint it."

"Come on, Ellie. You're grasping at straws here. I told you he was the villain."

Yeah—the villain. Then why couldn't I stop thinking of him as a victim?

"He couldn't have been with Decay."

"Maybe he was. Maybe he painted it earlier, hooked up with Decay to run down Surge and then had Decay drop him back off downtown to finish his morbid artwork."

That seemed pretty unlikely.

"Or maybe," she continued, "he wasn't with Decay at all. Maybe he orchestrated it."

The one thing that bothered me about Liv was her ability to jump on the picket line against whoever looked the guiltiest at that particular moment. It didn't say much for her sense of loyalty. Of course, the rational part of me realized I was probably angrier at her for first accusing my brother, and then my boyfriend, of a hideous crime. But after what Haze had done that evening, I couldn't exactly say she was wrong.

We pulled into the emergency entrance of the hospital, and I had the car door open before Liv could come to a complete stop.

"I'll just park," she yelled behind me. I gave her the classic "Whatever" wave.

I knew she was only concerned for me and was trying to find out who wanted to hurt me, but I couldn't help but be annoyed by her air of superiority, like she was Sherlock what's-his-face and I was—that other guy.

"Surg—" I started, and then corrected myself. "Lawrence Whitney?" I asked at the admittance desk, only to feel a hand at my shoulder.

Warp stood there, frowning as always, but this time not at me. He opened his arms and I rushed into them, sobbing openly as he patted my back.

"I don't understand what's going on."

"I've heard a lot of different things." He ran a hand over my wet hair. "All kinda jumbled, really, but I guess Decay decided to declare war against us. I've called our crew and they're out looking for him now. Retaliation has to be swift."

Bodies. That's all I could see at the end of this story. "I don't want to know. I don't want to talk about this, Johnny. I want to know how Surge is."

"They'll let us know when he's out of surgery. Come and sit down. We've got a bit of a party going on in the waiting room, much to this hospital's 'tude. But we're keeping it low so we don't get kicked out."

When Warp led me around the corner, I was shocked by how many people were there. Our crew was out scouring the streets for Decay, but, unlike me, Surge had a lot of friends outside of our little group.

I saw Bonnie and a couple of other gymnasts in the corner.

"Hey!" Bonnie stood and frantically waved me over, a smile on her face despite the dark tidings. I broke off from Warp, who left to collect Liv, and walked over to Bonnie and friends.

"Hey, LL," Ramona said, forcing a smile to her face.

I returned it halfheartedly but with equal amounts of plastic. "Hey. How long have you all been here?"

"About an hour. Sorry to hear about Surge. I really like him," Bonnie said, offering me the seat next to her.

"Who doesn't? I think half the school has a crush on him," Ramona piped in, looking at me with a weird expression on her face. Hatred? Envy? I resisted the urge to smack it off.

Bonnie giggled and nudged Ramona with the toe of her shoe. "You're practically in love with him. Everyone knows it."

Wow, that's right. I remembered Liv mentioning something about Ramona's crush. Envy, then. I always thought she didn't like me because of gymnastics. Now I knew she disliked my relationship with Surge.

"You should ask him out, yanno…if—" I started to tear and all the girls in the circle stared at me. I didn't care. Maybe offering dating advice was bad form with Surge on his deathbed, but I needed to pretend everything was normal.

"Dramatic much?" Ramona scoffed.

I couldn't believe how callous she was being. I nearly jumped out of my chair at her but Bonnie grabbed my arm, her eyes bulging like one of those tree frogs I'd seen on Animal Planet. "Excuse me? My friend was run down by a car and is being put together like Humpty Dumpty on some operating table, and you're going to talk to me like that?"

"Um, Emanuella?" Bonnie started cautiously, putting more pressure on my arm to keep me from rising up and performing an old-fashioned ground-stomping. "Ramona and I were there to see Surge's fight. The car came up over the curb, through the fence and toward him."

"Surge was pretty quick, running his sexy ass left and right, all zigzagging around. Would have been funny if…"

"Yeah, he tried to make it to that big tree by the swings but the car was on him," Bonnie continued, "so he jumped and did this weird flip thing and landed on the hood of the car, rolling up and over."

"Then the car took off," Ramona said. "It was gross as hell! Surge's head was all bloodied up and he was cussing a road to hell."

"So, he's not like—dying?"

"Nope. He's going to be fine but they have to do something to his shoulder," Bonnie smiled, obviously glad she could let go of me.

I sagged back in my chair and let the tears flow freely. "Warp made it sound like he was dying!"

"Your brother's kinda mean to do that," Bonnie said and gave my arm a reassuring pat.

"So you really think I've got a shot with Surge?" Ramona asked, failing miserably at casual.

"Sure," I said, absently thinking about Surge's sexual uncertainty. I shrugged, thinking she had a fifty-fifty shot.

Warp paced into view, his head bent toward his phone. I rose from my chair and made my way toward him.

"What's—" Warp started. But I didn't let him finish.

I slapped his cheek so hard I put the sting in my teeth. "How could you let me think Surge could die?"

"I don't know his condition."

"But you probably heard the same as I did. That he was cussing and lucid when the ambulance took him away! How could you puppet me like that?"

"I tried to call you and you weren't answering your phone. You've been blowing everything off to hang out with that idiot boyfriend of yours. I couldn't be sure you'd come down here, and I needed to be sure you were safe."

"You're such an asshole! Like anything would keep me from Surge's side when he's in the hospital? I have morals and priorities that escape you, but you're going to stand there on some high horse, doing pony-tricks for the audience, pretending you have to keep *me* in line? To make sure that *I* do the right thing? Oh, you're triple thick!"

Warp and I faced each other down until Liv positioned herself between us. "Okay, calm down before you both give the staff excuses to throw us all out," she scolded.

My brother didn't even look her way, which was surprising for him. "I know you, Emanuella. You don't think rationally where Haze is concerned. You'd walk right up to him and let him kill you, realizing too late what he is."

I flinched. Warp had no idea the amount of truth behind his words.

"I did what I had to do to make sure you were where I could see you. I ain't gonna let someone take you like they did Heather."

I wanted to be mad at him, but in his eyes I could see worry and fear. He thought I was going to be killed.

He wasn't the only one.

Twenty-two

"You look like you were run over by a truck." Surge grinned at me as I sat down in the visitor's chair.

"That's my line." I grinned back.

Shimmying out of my coat, I winced. Once the adrenaline of my adventurous day faded, the soreness was setting in. I was tempted to steal Surge's IV filled with pain-killers.

"I have an excuse to look like this. What's yours?"

"My boyfriend tried to kill me and his best friend tried to run down one of my best friends. I guess I really don't have an excuse." I tried to smile but there was no hiding the tears clouding my vision.

"Hey, LL. I'm good here. I'll be back to practicing with the crew in no time a'ight? No reason to get all emo and blame-tastic."

I leaned against the side of his bed and grabbed his hand, kissing the back of it. "I thought you were dying. Warp went all drama on me to get me down here. I felt so—lost."

"Well, we both know your brother's an attention whore these days. I'm sorry you got so scared, girl. But I'm good. I'm serious. I get to keep all my parts and the number of girls my dad said are out in the waiting room—keeps them from thinking I'm gay for a while longer."

I smiled and squeezed his hand. My backside hurt too much to remain in the sulking position, so I sat back in the chair with a little groan of pain and closed my eyes. This was one crazy day.

"What happened?" he asked.

I opened my eyes to see Surge's face back to serious mode and tried to brush it off. "I did a lot of parkour after school. Guess I spent too much time out there. Maybe if I hadn't, I could've been around to make sure you didn't do anything crazy, like challenge a guy bigger than you to a fight."

"Hey, I would've had him and he knew it. Why you think he ran me over instead of getting out to fight me? He knew he couldn't win."

"Or he wanted to make sure you were out of the way because of how protective you've been over me."

He frowned. "You're saying Decay ran me over to make sure you were accessible?"

"I don't know, but Liv told me a lot of people heard Decay cackling and Haze laughing in the passenger seat. That seems like a good explanation as to why you were run over and why Decay challenged you to a fight in the first place, don't you think?"

"Sounds like a good theory, girl. I wish I could help you prove it, but I didn't see or hear anything cuz I was busy gettin' run over and all."

I sighed and rubbed my hand down the front of my face. "You know what's horrible? All the clues point to Haze and friends and I still can't bring myself to believe it. Even with some of the proof stamped on my ass."

Surge sat up quick, gasping as the pain of the movement caught up with his impulse. "Ow! Shit!" He swallowed and worked his mouth, trying hard not to squeal like a girl, I was betting. After a couple of minutes, he came back to the track. "What's stamped on your ass?"

The look on his face told me he wouldn't budge on the subject until he had all the details. And in truth I wanted to tell him everything, from the moment I left the school to the moment his parents allowed me to come in and visit him.

I felt a little bit selfish. Like I was taking advantage of Surge's moment. Here he was, sitting in a hospital bed with his glossy eyes trying to focus on every word I said, and me telling him about all *I* had been through. Liv was right. I truly was a selfish bitch.

When I finished telling him everything, I shook my head. "I'm so sorry to bug you with all this but—you're like, my best friend. The only person I've been honest with from the beginning and the only one I trust to tell about this."

"I'm not sure you should trust me with this, LL. All I wanna do right now is reach for the phone and call the police. The only reason I haven't is that I can't reach the phone."

I pressed my lips together, trying to fight off another wave of tears. "I know. I know I should've called the cops, and I feel like a newb for not doing it, but Surge, something doesn't add up here. And maybe he accidentally pushed me too hard, yanno? He was sure someone was after us. He even called me Manu, which he only does when he's concerned about me or being kinda…"

"Mushy?"

"Yeah."

"So, he pushed you hard and you went over the edge nearly to your death. And it would've been end-game if you weren't a freerunner."

"Which he knows," I interjected.

"Granted," he acknowledged. "And you saw him standing near a dripping piece of you painted all dead-like with a can in his hand."

"Yeah. I think it was him, I don't know. Maybe."

"Okay. Despite the condensed indecision, that's pretty incriminating. And the only thing telling you that he might be innocent is—?" He let the question hang for my fill-in-the-blank.

"My gut."

"Your gut?"

"Also, if he ran you down with Decay he would've had to drive downtown, climb to the roof and paint a wicked-sized piece of zombie-me in very little time. He couldn't do all of that. I dunno. The truth is, I didn't see him painting. I couldn't see much of anything in the rain from a distance with just the storage shed security light on. Liv thinks maybe he did run you down and came to finish something he started earlier. If that's the case, I think he would've painted the piece of me and just had his buddy run you down, less gas money." I sighed. All the speculating giving me a headache.

Surge's head lay back on his pillow, and I could tell he was fighting to stay awake. I felt selfish again.

"I'm sorry, Surge. We shouldn't talk about this now. You get some rest and I'm going to come back tomorrow."

"No!" he practically sonic-boomed. "You're going to stay here with me."

"What? I need to go home and get my phone charger. I'm not going to—"

"Argue with me? You're damned right you're not. Right now, hospital security is all I've got to protect you with, LL. Anyone you need to be talking to right now is here or knows you're here and can call my room. And Ander would have my ass if I didn't keep you safe. Promise me. Promise me you won't go anywhere."

I stood up and kissed his forehead, grinning down at him as his eyes lost the fight. "I won't go anywhere," I promised. And for Surge's sake, I had to keep it.

After his nap, Surge visited with a good portion of the friends who had come to make sure he wasn't dead or dying. The nursing staff and hospital security lost their cool after the third group of schoolmates, making everyone but Warp, Liv, and me leave.

Warp visited with Surge while Liv and I went down to the cafeteria to get some dinner. I chased the food around my plastic plate with my broken spork for a few minutes before Liv sat down across from me with half the cafeteria's food on her tray.

"Hungry?" I mused and took a bite of my expensive and bland beef stew.

"Starving." she smiled. "It's been a weird day."

The silence stretched between us, the remnants of our conversation in her car. "Look, Ellie, about earlier..."

"I really don't wanna talk about it."

"I know. But it is important to me that you realize I say the things I do because I care about you. I'm worried you're not thinking straight on this. Your boyfriend is trying to kill you and you're just—"

"Jesus, Liv. Didn't I say I didn't wanna talk about it?"

She blinked at me and pushed her tray into the middle of the table as if the fifty bucks she spent on mediocre food would go to waste because of my outburst.

I sighed. "I have a long night ahead of me in this damned hospital and I don't feel like talking about Haze or anything else emotionally draining."

Pouting, she reached for the orange on her tray and began to peel it one tiny circle at a time. "I doubt your brother is going to stay long. He seemed eager to join in the search for Decay. When he comes down we can get the hell out of here."

"Not me. I promised Surge I'd stay."

She set the orange aside, and I had the feeling I made her lose her appetite again. "What?"

Telling her why Surge wanted me to stay was out of the question, so I simply lifted a shoulder in a pseudo shrug. "Yeah, I won't have a phone, but I'm pretty tired. I'll probably just nap anyway."

"I think it's selfish of him to want you to stay here with him all night so that *he* feels more comfortable, especially when you're going to be bored as hell without your phone."

"I'm not really up to hearing from anyone right now anyway, so it's probably a good thing." Would Haze try to contact me? Was he already trying and leaving a million voice messages? I was okay not dealing with it just then.

"Not even me? Fine. Whatever. I still say it's selfish of Surge to guilt you into staying here." Liv was going to have another of her spaz-rants. Yippee.

"He was run over by a car, Liv."

"He's fine." She huffed.

"I think he's entitled to make a small request to his best friend."

She sat up straighter. "And what about me? I'm not your best friend, too? My opinion doesn't count?"

"I didn't say that," I sighed. I was going about this all wrong. Between my inability to confide in her and her bullheadedness, we were doomed to end this conversation, and our friendship, badly. I didn't want that. When Liv was being normal and funny, I really dug hanging around her. But I'd never seen how she'd react not being the center of attention before.

"Of course your opinion counts. We'll hang out tomorrow and do whatever you like, but tonight, I'm staying here with Surge. What's the big deal?"

"People will talk. Your reputation won't thank you for it."

I had to laugh. "And we're what? In the Renaissance era? What do I care what people think? If everyone in school wants to think I'm with Surge…" I paused, thinking about Haze and how it would hurt him to hear the rumors. I sighed. "My friendship isn't sold out because I fear what people might say. You should know better than that by now."

"You know, Ellie, sometimes a little selfishness is necessary."

I couldn't argue that point. I agreed, usually. But Surge wouldn't be able to rest—not to mention he would open his big mouth and bring down the wrath of Ander on me—if I even thought about reneging on my promise.

"Yeah," I said, "but not in this case. I don't get why you're making such a big deal out of it."

The chair scraped as she stood from it abruptly. "Enjoy your night."

"Come on, Liv. Don't get all pissy because I agreed to stay here."

"I'm not," she said unconvincingly. "Your brother should be down any second and I'm going to meet him in the lobby."

"Don't go. Sit."

I was surprised when she did, but unsurprised by the pouting. "What?" she practically barked at me.

"Things are weird between us. It feels like you don't want

to be friends anymore. And I want to let you know that's okay with me if that's what you want."

"That's not what I want, Ellie. What I want is for you to watch out for yourself. For you to stop acting like a lovestruck sap and see the evidence that is right in front of you! I'm not looking forward to losing another best friend, all right!"

Ah! Her attitude finally made a little bit of sense. She was worried history was repeating itself.

A few other hospital visitors looked over at us when Liv raised her voice and I shushed her. Grabbing the back of her chair I pulled mine closer to her to keep my voice down.

"I understand this is hard for you. But I'm going to figure it out. I might even need your help to do it, which means I need you to be a little more open-minded. I can't point a finger without solid proof."

She stared straight into my eyes and shook her head. "Ellie, you're never going to find the proof you're looking for. Your heart will make sure of it."

With that she rose and walked out of the cafeteria.

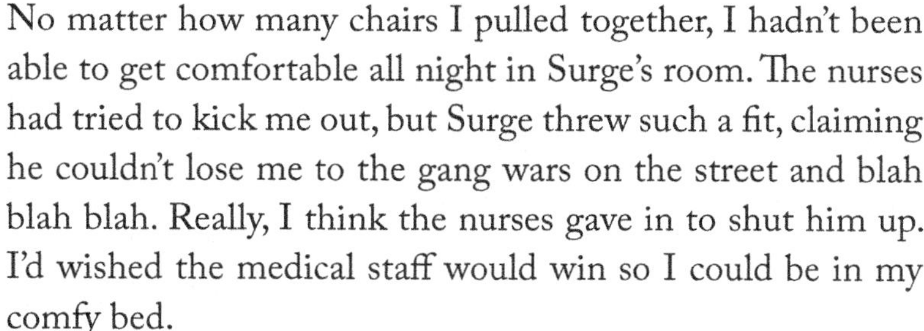

No matter how many chairs I pulled together, I hadn't been able to get comfortable all night in Surge's room. The nurses had tried to kick me out, but Surge threw such a fit, claiming he couldn't lose me to the gang wars on the street and blah blah blah. Really, I think the nurses gave in to shut him up. I'd wished the medical staff would win so I could be in my comfy bed.

I wasn't that lucky.

Now Surge's parents officially thought we were an item, and in one of his lucid moments, he made me promise to keep up the ruse.

"It's easier than the truth. Just pretend you love me."

That part was easy enough. I did love Surge. Right now he was one of my bestest friends in the world. Soon to be my only when Liv's frustration or mine got the better of us. Or maybe he'd always been the only friend, but I wanted so badly to have a *girl* friend, that I couldn't see it until now.

What did Liv and I even have in common any more other than stubbornness?

Lately, I'd begun to see why I'd never be the popular chick on campus. I didn't have the judgmental gene apparently needed to be in the Homecoming Court crowd, and that was fine with me. Not to say that Liv and I couldn't be friends. Her heart was in the right place. I just couldn't give her the vapid responses she obviously deemed important in a friendship, and in the last few days, we'd disagreed more than agreed. A clear sign of a dwindling friendship. Last time I experienced it was in grade school and I wasn't looking forward to the awkward "moving on" speech, especially when I knew she still suffered from losing Haze's sister.

There wouldn't be a happy ending to the situation, so I did my best to focus on solving the mystery of why my boyfriend just tried to kill me.

By the following afternoon, Surge's doctors were talking release with pain-killers, and my body wanted me to ask for one. Falling several stories to the ground, coupled with a night in the hospital made me almost wish I'd died on the landing.

Okay, not true.

All the pain made me wanna take a bat to Haze—or to whoever had killed Heather and wanted me dead.

"So, you're still eager to prove Haze didn't kill his sister?" Surge asked as we waited for his parents to bring the car around.

"I just need definitive proof. I've noticed how messy it gets when accusations are thrown around without it."

"He pushed you from a building, LL. You don't get much guiltier than that."

I sighed. "I can't help but remember the grunt behind me before he shoved me over...." A light bulb lit in my heart, traveling to my head as a glimmer of hope. "Yes! That's it, Surge. What if someone shoved him into me? What if the grunt I heard was Haze fighting someone off or someone attacking him before pushing me over and that's why I thought he pushed me! And who else would be on the roof but the true guilty bastard?"

Surge lifted a brow, leaning heavily on me as he tried to look at me without an awkward closeness. "I don't know. But if you really think he didn't do it, start at the beginning, girl. Go over everything again and find the proof before something else happens. You've got until tonight before I start calling around, starting with the police and your big brother."

"Surge..."

He held up his hand, his eyes pleading with me to understand. "I don't feel comfortable with this. What if something were to happen to you and I had told no one what I knew?"

I tried to put myself in his shoes and had to nod. "I get it. Maybe I'd feel the same way, I guess. If I only have until tonight, I better go."

"Wait," he called me back when I took a step away.

Whoops. I'd forgotten he was drugged. I helped him to the decorative brick tree platform and grimaced. "I'm a dork."

"Uh huh," he agreed. "You're also on some serious drugs if you think I'm going to let you outta here without taking my phone so I can call you every few minutes."

"Don't you need it?"

"Nah. I've got my landline, and I'm not feeling particularly chatty today. I'm too fuzzy to think straight. Last thing I need is to make a few drugged confessions."

I smiled and took the phone he held out to me. "All right, I'll only answer calls coming from your landline."

"Or your brother's phone. He's coming over later, so I'm guessing he's going to want to know I only let you go *with* a cell in your possession. Make sure you answer it this time. Cool?"

"Cool." I nodded and kissed his cheek, waving as his parents pulled up to collect him.

"Till tonight, LL. Once it gets dark—" he called after me.

I waved in acknowledgement as I ran toward downtown. I had a few hours to find out what really happened on the roof and identify the true culprit before Surge called down hell.

Twenty-three

Staring at a depiction of what you'd look like as a corpse is disturbing, no matter who you are. But for me, I didn't have the luxury of being grossed out or taking a moment to ride the wiggins. Nope, I had to look past the willies into the artwork itself. Each stroke of the spray can needed to be explored. This macabre masterpiece was all I had to go on to prove Haze innocent or to solidify his guilt.

I looked down at the color copy of the newspaper clipping in my hand, comparing the old to the new, and trying to remember the homage Haze painted to his sister on the wall where we met.

The style was exactly the same. Each artistic face, sunray, cloud, and bubbled letter seemed painted by the same writer.

The subtle swirling backgrounds of the newspaper photo, each of the pieces I'd seen, and the mural before me were similar too.

Even though the bloated piece of me was a little out of character—the consistency of style was undeniable. The same person who had killed Heather back then had made that obvious death threat against me now. And Haze had been on the roof when the mural had been painted.

"Dammit!"

Exasperated, I walked a few steps away and balled the piece of paper in my fist. I was being irrational to harbor any doubt. Haze and his crew wanted me dead, to bring on a war they'd been longing to start with my brother and the rest of the freerunners for dominance in the new school. All the clues pointed to the neat little guilt package—and I didn't want to accept it because of my heart.

I'd die at a young age because I lacked the ability to call the cops on someone who had pushed me over the edge of a building and kissed like a champ.

With a heavy sigh, I decided to stop being the Queen of the Clueless and admit defeat. I'd call Surge and agree to call the cops.

Commotion behind me stole my attention away from my pity party. "What the hell?" I rushed to the rail edge and peered over at the buildings nearby. I saw my brother and a few others in our crew, running the cityscape. Were they looking for me? Great, nothing would top my day off like a bleeding-ear lecture by Warp in front of the crew.

"Gah!" I pressed a hand to my throat as Haze leapt over the fire ladder and landed beside me. Too shocked to scream, I stared at him in amazement. "W-what?"

The emotion on his face halted the rest of the words in my throat. He looked so—sad.

"Your brother's—" he started and then shook his head, changing his mind. "I've been looking all over for you. I called you all last night. I saw you walk away but I didn't know if you were badly hurt or not. I went to the hospital today to see if you were there but ran into your brother and crew. He said they'd all kill me for pushing you off the roof. Why would you tell him I pushed you?"

"I...didn't." It was true. I didn't tell my brother, but apparently someone had.

Dammit, Surge. I knew it had been too easy to convince him to let me go out on my own and investigate. I wonder if he waited more than five seconds before calling Warp.

"I don't understand, Manu."

He reached for me and the fear of him grabbing my hand and hurling me to my death made me shrink back. If possible, the pain on his face intensified and I felt guilty for my reaction for some reason.

"How could you think I'd hurt you?"

"Are you kidding? You pushed me! I almost died."

The dumbstruck stare he gave me made me feel hope again. "I didn't push you. Jesus, LL! I was flat on my face. It was the other guy!"

"I didn't see anyone else. We were running and I felt you push me from behind, Bren."

"No! We were running and somebody jumped out from behind the A/C shed and tripped me up. I saw him push you and screamed. I thought you were dead. I got to my feet and I...I could've caught him, but instead...I was so scared.... I ran to the edge and I looked down—I've never been so relieved in my life. When I turned around, the guy was gone."

I wanted to believe him. It sounded possible. I had heard him grunt, though at the time I chalked it up to the rough landing a few seconds before. Then I was pushed.

"I wish I could believe what you're saying."

He looked behind me to the wall with my deranged portrait and walked toward it. "I get it," he whispered. "You thought you saw me standing there and concluded I did this."

"Why wouldn't I? It looked like you had paint in your hand. And the mural is the same style as all the others. Including the one at your sister's murder scene. Including the one I saw you painting when we met, Haze."

"I know! I know you can see me in all the pieces of you, but I need you to see what isn't me, LL! I can paint faces and clouds and the like, but that?" He pointed at the right-most side of the piece.

I stared at the gnarled mess of branches reaching across the swirly background, framing my decaying visage. Oh, God! What an idiot. The proof stared me straight in the face. Whoever wanted me dead would have to be great with all types of nature art, not just clouds. Haze couldn't draw trees.

"Come on, Manu. I need you to believe me."

My brother and crew grew closer. I could hear them sound the alarm that they saw Haze on the rooftop with me. We were out of time.

"Go! They'll be here any second."

"I've been able to keep a step ahead. All that traceur training." His downtrodden smile melted my heart. "I'm not running. Now that I've found you and know you're okay, I'm staying right here."

"Don't be stupid."

"I don't seem able to help myself." He laughed a little.

Every step he took back to me was cautionary, as though I were a wild stallion about to bolt. That wasn't the case anymore. My steps swallowed the rest of the distance between us.

We had less than half a minute but he didn't seem to care. He tugged me into him and kissed me like he had many times before but with a desperation that made my eyes tear. I didn't want this to be the last kiss, the one that would have to last the rest of my lifetime, but that was exactly what it could turn out to be if he didn't run.

I broke away, reaching for his hand. "Go," I choked.

"No. Running makes it look like I tried to kill you."

"Trust in me to find something that proves you innocent."

He shook his head, but I squeezed his hand and nudged him toward the ledge. "Please. I believe in you, Brennen. Now I need you to survive, and believe in me."

Reluctantly he let my fingers fall from his grip. "I love you, Manu," He whispered.

I felt the tingle of his words down to my toes. His admission sounded beautiful and ominous. Besides the kisses in and out of the closet and his few outbursts of jealousy, he'd never confessed his feelings before. Now, he threw his emotions out there as if he didn't expect to live past the day.

I wanted to tell him not to give up, not to say such things since they only wigged me out, but like him, I knew that our chances of averting some serious violence was slim. "I love you, Brennen."

"Emanuella!" Warp bellowed as he and three others landed on the rooftop. I looked to them and then back to where Haze stood, but he was already gone.

"Warp, listen to me."

"I'm done listening to you, little sister," he said as he approached me. Stopping a foot away, he pointed a finger and the rest of the crew continued on to follow Haze. "You shoulda told me the second you walked into the hospital that this asshole tried to off you."

"He didn't, Warp! I know it. I know how to prove it!"

Warp's lip curled toward his nose in disgust. "I can't believe you. You'd lie for him even now? Go home, Emanuella. Surge is there waiting for us to come back."

"No. I'm not going anywhere, and neither are you." I kept him with me, grabbing his arm out of desperation. "Call them off, Warp, I mean it!"

He shook off my hand and took off at a run for the roof's edge.

I followed closely on his heels.

We both dove across the expanse between buildings, but, typically, Warp's leg strength on his push-off doubled mine. He landed in a perfect drop, able to keep the flow, but I was more of a Level to Level Cat. My fingers grabbed hold of the roof rim while my legs folded in toward my body, catching my momentum against the wall before I climbed up and vaulted over the ledge. The difference was a mere ten seconds, but ten seconds could mean the death of Brennen "Haze" Craig.

In my mind, I could already see his obit.

My legs pumped, hurriedly trying to gain ground not only on my brother, but on the rest of our crew. They were like mindless monkeys sometimes, following Warp because of Ander's well-known reputation. Their blind loyalty was normally a tribute to them, but for once, I wouldn't mind seeing a little dissension in the ranks.

Ander was my brother, too! But I guess my relationship with "the enemy" ruined my credibility.

The guys from our crew, Zone and Epic, stood on the ledge of the next roof looking down, and as always, my heart skipped a beat. Usually people only stopped a run for a wicked fall.

Warp and I caught up with the rest and I thought I might vomit when I saw Spry, a guy from our crew, sprawled on a metal fire escape balcony. One floor below him, Haze stalled in a Crane Moonstep with one foot planted firmly on a metal rail, his other leg dangling. I saw him glance up at me and my crew before eyeing Spry, as though he were weighing his options of climbing up a flight and pulse checking.

I breathed a sigh of relief as Spry, clearly a misnomer, groaned and sat up. He shook his head like he was trying to get the fuzz outta his brain and gave Warp a wave, signaling he was all right.

The chase was on again.

Epic, Zone, and Warp all Cat Leapt to the balcony where Spry nursed his bruises and continued on their way down to Haze, who'd wisely started his own descent. Three-to-one was better odds but not great.

Although Haze's training had been good, he didn't have the same experience as the rest, and I knew Warp would eventually take him.

I lowered into a Cat, hanging off the wall, and did a few One-Eighty Cats, descending by bouncing from wall to opposite wall. The moves swallowed the distance between me and the boys in seconds.

I reached for Warp's jacket and yanked him backwards.

Haze hit the ground feet-first and darted to the mouth of the alley. Epic and Zone were on him, but Warp was the one who needed a bigger handicap.

"Dammit, LL. Stop being a fucking nuisance!" He shoved me back and took off toward the chase.

Though I had to stumble a few steps in reverse, I wasn't too far behind him. From my distant vantage point, I watched as Haze ran straight at a wall. Like me, Epic and Zone expected him to wall-run up and over, but instead Haze planted his palms on the bricks at the last second. He ran his legs up the wall in an arc and dropped his right hand. Anchoring his left, he propelled the rest of his body over and did a successful turn, leaving Epic and Zone hanging from the wall by their fingers in stunned silence.

A perfect wall-spin. I never taught him that.

Warp paused next to me, as shocked as I. "Someone's been YouTube-ing."

Someone's been Surge-ing, I thought.

Since we were a little behind the chase, Warp and I were able to run a line of interference, avoiding the more complicated jumps to gain ground. That also meant we were going to collide with Haze.

Pedestrians complained loudly, a few of the guys we passed made threats they knew we probably wouldn't stop long enough to take up.

If we made it to the el, Haze could have a good shot at surviving the day by jumping on a railcar. But if he took the main entrance, Warp would overtake him. And with a couple of buddies at his back, all the karate in the world wouldn't keep my boyfriend breathing.

"Brennen, to the right!" I yelled, and he glanced back at me before veering in that direction. I felt relieved he trusted me enough to listen.

"LL," Warp chastised beside me, shaking his head and picking up speed.

I knew that if I weren't his sister, he probably woulda elbowed me in the face.

Haze disappeared up the steps to the city transit station and around the corner. He would've probably missed the entrance, tucked back into an alcove as it was, if I hadn't told him to turn. Everyone always went for the main entrance straight ahead instead of the emergency stairs. Except the freerunners.

I chose his escape based on the knowledge that Haze had mean vault skills.

Warp ran up the steps ahead of me, cursing my name, and by the time I hit the top, I saw the blur that was Haze run to the turnstiles and Speed Vault to the opposite side. Pride welled inside of me.

Epic caught the toe of his shoe and fell forward on his knees, his face following suit soon after.

Zone managed to follow Haze onto the platform, though, where both cat and mouse disappeared.

Warp vaulted lazily over to the opposite side and offered an arm up to Epic as security ran up yelling and carrying on.

I grinned and casually walked toward the cashier to pay for Haze and Zone. The woman behind the Plexiglas glared at me, but she didn't dent the happiness I felt in knowing that Haze would get away. Zone was the king of the obstacle course, but his improvisational skills sucked as bad as his endurance.

Warp and Epic were in a heated discussion with transit police, trying to keep themselves from getting a ticket.

"LL, tell them," Warp yelled at me over the turnstile.

"Tell them what?"

"We were trying to protect you from that murdering bastard!"

The security guards looked dubious. Far be it for me to disappoint them. "This has gotta stop, Warp." He cursed at me again, but I turned my attention to the transit police. "I paid for the two boys that made it to the platform, but now I'm broke so these two," I nodded to Epic and my dear brother. "They're on their own."

Twenty-four

"Emanuella," my Pops growled into the phone. "What the hell is going on over there? I get a clipped phone call from your brother about getting detained by the transit police."

"Let's face it, Pops. It isn't the first time one of us has been detained by the transit police, now is it?" Despite my flippant tone, I feared I was about to pee my pants.

I'd returned home to find Surge standing at the open front door. Before I could tear him a new one, he had thrust the phone at me mouthing *Pops* as a warning. But nothing coulda prepared me for the wrath in my father's voice. Quite honestly, I was scared.

"I've told both you and your brother time and again that you are not to do anything troublesome while I'm away on a trip. I'm contracted out, Emanuella. I own the rig, but I don't own my time and I am NOT going to break the contract for anything less than death. If I have to come home and bail someone out of jail, I am not going to be happy. Do you understand me?"

I tried to make my gulp as silent as possible. "Yeah, I understand. But they're not going to arrest him. They're going to make him sweat it out and give him a ticket."

"John told me you coulda helped him out, but you left him there."

"I only had enough money for a few fares, Pops. Warp was dumb and got himself caught."

"And now I'm going to have to pay a hefty price for it." He sighed. I knew he stressed over money all the time, and I did feel guilty, but I needed Warp to be detained so I could get to the school and do what I needed to.

"I know, Pops. I'm sorry. We'll keep clear of the dramatics okay? I won't ruin this for you. I promise." I hoped I didn't do anything "troublesome" to break my promise—like die.

Again, my father sighed heavily and I could hear the wind whipping into his rig through a cracked window and the low murmur of country music. He wanted to say more but obviously wasn't sure what.

"I love you, Daddy. Just drive safe, okay?"

I heard him swallow. I rarely called him Daddy. He was always Pops, but in case I did get killed, I wanted the last thing I said to him to be tender.

Of course that was probably the worst thing I coulda done.

"Emanuella? What's really going on?"

"What?" My feigned surprise sounded lame even to me. "Nothing! I want you to know I love you and that I will try to do better, that's all. I'll keep out of trouble, as well as hold Warp down when he decides to do something idiotic."

"You sure that's where you stand on the issue? We got cut off so John's gonna call me when he can. Is his story going to be the same as yours? That nothing's going on?"

No.

"Yup! No worries, Pops. I'll call you every night when I get home so you know I'm safe and sound and right on curfew."

"Uh huh." He sounded doubtful.

"And I'm surrounded by boys who look out for me. Surge even answered the phone, so you know I'm not lying."

My dad was quiet for so long, I knew he was mulling things over. Did he think there was something between Surge and me, too? Seemed to be the theme lately. "I expect a phone call later."

"Of course. When do you rest?"

"Probably soon. I want to be on the road again by nine tonight."

I nodded to the phone. "Okay. I'll call you around ten or eleven."

"Ten. It's a school night."

"Right, right. Ten, it is."

"Good. I love you, too, darling. Tell Surge I said hi and stay outta my beer. He sounded drunk as hell, babbling on about graffiti."

Oh, hell. "Uh…sure will." I was glad to hang up. I could finally breathe—and shake.

Surge came over, took the phone out of my hands, and hung it back on its receiver.

I stared at him for a minute and guided him to the couch. "What are you doing here? You should be at home resting. I can't believe your parents let you out of the house."

"They don't exactly know I'm here. They gave me my pills and went to work and I felt AWESOME." He grinned at me all goofy-like, and for the first time since I walked into my house I really looked at him.

"Oh my God. You're beyond stoned."

He tried to look casual in his shrug but his ear-to-ear grin was all the confirmation I needed. "Surge! You shouldn't be out walking around and definitely not answering my house phone. Yanno, once those drugs wear off, you're going to be bumming big-time."

"I'll take more. That's what pills are for."

"No. Pills are to take away the pain in between rest and only to be taken every few hours, you jackass. Ugh!" I gently pushed him back until he lay down on the couch. I covered him with an afghan and pushed a pillow beneath his head. "I so don't have time for this right now."

Pursing his lips together, he tilted his head at me. "I'm sensing some pissy coming off of you."

"Good to know your sensors aren't broken."

"What did I do?"

"You mean besides putting your recovery in jeopardy, talking to my Pops about graffiti, and telling my brother what I confided in you about Haze? Nothing much," I finished with sarcastic flourish.

His face looked genuinely horrified. "Oh, LL. I'm sorry. I remember now. I woke up from a weird dream."

"A drug-infused dream filled with paranoia, no doubt."

He frowned. "Well, yeah I guess. I called Liv and had her drive me over here to stop you from going out tonight and Warp was here."

"Lucky me," I interjected.

"He asked me what could be so important to have Liv chauffer me over."

"And being the awesome friend you are—you gave him the whole story."

I took a little bit of pleasure in Surge's wince.

"Well, not the whole story but, I did spill a little. Chemical persuasion aside, you know I wouldn't hand you over unless I was really worried about you dyin', right?"

I did know that. But letting him off the hook early wouldn't do me any good. I stayed quiet, going for the emotional torture.

"Aw, come on, baby girl. You know better."

"Right now, the only thing I know is that there will be a huge brawl tonight, and someone will get hurt unless I make it to the school and get some of Decay's artwork to prove Haze didn't kill his sister. Where's Liv?"

"Said she needed to apologize or something. So she went to see if she could catch up with you, and oh, to keep you from doing anything stupid."

"Doing stupid things are what I do best."

"Wait, I skipped a step. You think Decay's the guy? Warp swears the style of your stalker is the same he's seen of Haze in the past."

I sighed. "Who better to bite off Haze than his best friend?"

"If it *is* Decay, that's messed up. But what's outing him gonna do to stop the shit going down tonight?"

"I dunno, but I have to try something. All I can think about is paper hearts and it's tearing at me. I think about Warp and Haze trying to really hurt each other and I can't deal with it, Surge. I can't let anything happen. I have to believe deep down that Warp doesn't want this war. That it isn't power making him act like such an ass but the pain of losing first Mom, and then Heather." My eyes moistened, and I had to swallow several times to keep from choking.

"Hey, hey." Surge tried to sit up, but I pushed him back down and sat in the alcove his stomach created. "LL, we'll get this sorted, a'ight? I'll come with you. We'll storm the school and steal whatever we need...."

"No. You're going to stay here and when Warp gets home, you're going to keep him from calling Pops. Liv and I are going to the school to get what I need."

"What do I tell Warp when he gets home?"

"Well, I'm hoping the transit police will keep him for questioning for a little while to mess with his head. That's why I have to head there now. The sun's going down, so I can get in and out without anyone seeing me."

"I don't think you and Liv should be out running around without me."

"Please. Zone ran off Haze and no one's seen Decay since he rubbed down his Camaro with your face. He's probably hiding from the police. Right now everyone else is recovering from the run, and Spry is probably at Mercy General getting an X-ray."

"Why would Spry need an X-ray?"

"He missed a Level to Level."

"Oh, man. He sucks at those."

"Mmhm. This is further proof of his epic fail. My point is, I can get to the school and back without involving anyone."

"Pfft. Except Liv, and of course, me. You don't seem to mind involving me in this."

"You asked for it by opening your mouth."

He gave me the fish-lip. "A'ight, that might be true."

I called Liv, and within minutes I heard her pull up outside.

I stood and Surge grabbed my hand. "You still got my cell?" When I nodded, he added, "Call me when you're on your way back. Call me if you run into trouble. Call if you need anything."

"I'm sensing you want me to…call?"

He glared at me and I laughed some of my tension away.

"Yes, dear. I promise. Tell Liv what's going on, I'm going to go change."

I smiled and ran up the steps to my room, threw on my lucky black hoodie and equally dark Ima-break-n-enter-something jeans, and stuffed the news clipping photocopy in my back pocket. My shoe collection was a little out of sorts but I found a pair of cheap black shoes that barely had a sole. I liked them the best for freerunning because I could feel the contours of whatever course I was on, like I was barefoot but without the bleeding calluses. In case I got caught tonight, I might have to use my skills to do a little escaping.

I tromped back down the stairs snagging one of Pops' mini flashlights and frowned at Surge, who stood pacing my living room in front of a reserved Liv.

"Promise me you'll be okay?" Surge asked. "That dream—"

"—was just a dream," I finished. "Surge, Liv's driving, we'll be there and back before you know it."

He nodded and I hoped, once again, I'd be able to keep my promise.

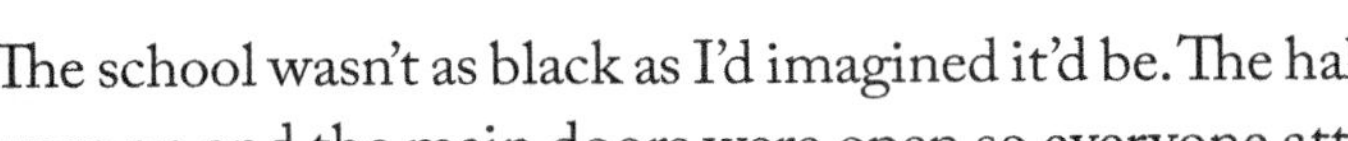

The school wasn't as black as I'd imagined it'd be. The hall lights were on and the main doors were open so everyone attending the football game had access to the bathrooms.

I hadn't accounted for high traffic. The night lights illuminated everything, including sneaky-me as I crept along the brick wall toward the Art classroom windows.

"Yeah, this is a real covert operation, Ellie."

"Shh! At least try not to draw attention to us. You're supposed to be pretending to wait around for your boyfriend."

"Yeah, cuz what our little saga needs is an *invented* troublesome penis to go with all the other ones."

I grunted but I didn't commit fully to Liv's man-hating snark.

"Wouldn't it be easier to just go through the main entrance and pick the lock of the Art Room door?"

"No. Haze leaves this window open. Besides, there are cameras everywhere inside and a lot more lighting. Out here I'm just going to look like a dark blob with a blond blob."

In the background, I could hear the cheers of the crowd, probably for the visitors, as our football team had the motto "The team with the most unnecessary roughness calls, wins the game."

"Hurry up. I feel like I've slammed a few hundred energy drinks."

"Okay, okay. Try to relax and look casual. I'll be right back."

Pushing the blue lock of hair behind my ear beneath the cowl of my hoodie, I moved in between the row of waist-high bushes and the building until I stood outside the Art Room.

I curled my fingers under the lip of the slightly cracked window and tugged. My eyes crinkled, half-expecting Haze to have forgotten to leave it open and some dramatic alarms to sound.

Nothing.

Phew. Good to know I was just paranoid.

I climbed through the tiny opening and over the radiator, which I remembered this time, trying to be as quiet as possible even while fighting with the thick curtain for freedom. Once it spit me out, the curtain settled and the hemmed sides gaped enough to let the field lights peek through, but the small stream of illumination wasn't enough to navigate by. If I tried I'd probably fall and bash my head open. A nice little present for Mrs. Peris when she opened her door in the morning.

I patted down my clothes until I felt my small flashlight and pulled it out. I'd seen too many movies to go around waving it like a light sword, so when I flicked it on, I kept it pointed to the floor as I walked to the students' art drawers.

Shining the light over the names of the students, I was surprised by how many drawers there were. Even Warp had one.

Hm. I'd assumed Warp had no interest in graffiti, but he'd dated Heather for a while and I'd been clueless about that. Even though I was certain Decay was my target, I had to look. I opened his drawer and my heart fluttered. What if going through Warp's drawer turned up proof of his guilt?

A second later I was disabused of that notion. An artist my brother was not. Giggling, I flipped through his portraits, his objects, his shadings and, on the top, his most recent landscapes. He actually drew a tree with cloud-shaped canopies like he was five. Poor Warp. How embarrassing.

I shut his drawer and reached for Decay's, my fingers trembling in anticipation for the big reveal.

The drawer came open—but nothing was inside it.

Damn! Who cleaned out Decay's drawer? Did he? He more than likely knew about Haze leaving this place open.

My phone vibrated. Well, Surge's phone vibrated, but I could barely feel it. I slammed the drawer shut, ready to give up, when I remembered Mrs. Peris' favorite collection.

Steering the flashlight to the last cabinet on my right, I zeroed in on the Artists'Tantrums drawer. Haze had made the comment that all Decay's projects ended up in there.

The phone incessantly buzzed.

I knew if I didn't answer, Surge would probably call the cops just to make sure I wasn't dead somewhere. I pulled the phone out of my belly pocket.

"What?" I whispered, annoyed at being interrupted when I was so close to proving Haze innocent I could taste the victory.

"Your brother was here. Said he was done with the games and then took the other guys with him to Haze's."

"Oh, no."

"Sorry, LL. I tried to talk sense into him but I can't argue with psycho logic. He's determined to kill your boy."

Damn. Damn. Damn. "Surge, call Haze, tell him to get out of the house. Liv and I will be on our way to him and we'll meet up at the Pizza Pie Pagoda."

"You find what you need?"

"I hope so! Go. Call Haze."

I tucked the cell in my pocket, jerked open the Artists' Tantrum drawer and grabbed every piece of paper in it.

A second later I was falling out of the window and yelling for Liv to get in the car. "We gotta get to the Pizza Pie Pagoda now-ish, Liv. Drive like it's your mom's favorite Mercedes."

"What are you looking for?" Liv asked me as we sped down the road.

I sat in the passenger seat sifting through paintings and drawings, trying not to drop anything on the floor. "Anything with Decay's name on it."

"Oh. Is that who you're looking to blame it on now?"

"Just drive, Liv. We can claw each other's eyes out later, but right now I need to try to keep people from dying."

I found a couple of landscapes, but nothing that matched the tree in the masterpiece of me. I shuffled through the artwork one by one till I felt my phone vibe in my pocket.

"Did you get hold of Haze?" I asked, shifting a watercolor still life to the bottom of the stack of papers.

"Yeah, girl. I did. I don't think he's going to listen. He's pretty upset."

"Getting chased around the city will do that to a person." I glanced down and there, on top of the stack of papers, was the break I'd been looking for. A perfect likeness of the tree next to my bloodied face in all its gnarled branch-y goodness. Jackpot. "But it doesn't matter now, because I got it, Surge, I—"

"No, LL. There won't be peace now. They found Decay."

"Wait. Who found him? I don't understand."

"Haze called to tell your brother that the war is on. They found Decay's body behind a dumpster on Harper and Laine."

My stomach turned and I thought for sure I was going to revisit my blueberry PopTart. "Haze thinks—"

"Your brother and our crew killed Decay, yeah."

"No."

"Everyone knows after I was run down, Warp and the crew were looking for some vengeance on Decay. Needless to say, the cops are gonna come calling sooner or later looking for answers, too."

A funny feeling quivered in my chest. "Did they say how long he'd been dead?"

"Who's dead?" Liv slammed on the brakes, catching a red light. I shushed her with a quick glare.

"I didn't ask. Haze wasn't exactly chatty."

"Dammit, Surge, we need to know how—Liv, what are you doing?"

Liv grabbed the drawing on the top of my stack out of my hand and rolled down her window. "I'm getting your head back where it should be! Stop looking at pictures and let go of—"

The phone fell to my lap as I made a quick grab for the drawing before Liv could let it sail down the street. Her grip held tight as I pulled, ripping it in half.

"LL?" Surge called to me, but I couldn't move.

There, scrawled across the bottom of the torn art paper in my hand was the name, Livia Menesa. My heart slithered down into my stomach.

Oh, shit.

"LL, what's wrong? Talk to me girl."

"Holy. Shit." I couldn't process what the proof was telling me.

Liv. I didn't want to believe it, but my mind was telling me: My deathly-afraid-of-heights best friend, was not only a liar, but a murderer.

Headlights of the passing cars poured over our faces. Her gaze and mine met and held, gauging each other's reaction. Her left eye twitched and I knew she knew I knew.

A stalemate kept us both locked in the moment. Surge was yelling from my lap, demanding I talk to him, but I didn't want to make any sudden movements.

We might have sat there for a century if the horn of the car behind us didn't break the spell. The contours of her face changed from shocked to sad to panicked, and she slammed her foot on the accelerator.

Surge was screaming now. I tucked the phone, along with the torn drawing in my belly pocket.

"Liv, stop the car."

"No, I have to make you understand."

I'd seen enough psycho-thrillers on TV to know that was a phrase I didn't want to hear.

Liv jerked the steering wheel sharply to the left, and I knew I had to make my move. If I waited until we were in the cramped space of the alley, I'd be forced to stay in the car or risk bouncing off the wall and getting churned to burger beneath her back tires. I yanked the door handle.

Locked.

My fingers worked against Liv's incessant pushing of the lock button, but the door wouldn't open.

With a scream of fury I threw the other art papers at her face and yanked the door open when she instinctively raised her hands.

Like in freerunning, I didn't have time to plan, only react. I flung myself out the door, whacking my ankle on the frame. I cried out in pain, but maintained my roll, keeping my shoulder tucked tight to absorb the momentum. I bowled over a cache of rubber trash cans, landing in an awkward sprawl. For a nanosecond I lay there, mentally checking myself for signs of life.

Good, I wasn't dead—though when I heard Liv's car squeal to a halt I added—yet.

I fished in my pocket and pulled out Surge's phone. "Surge?" I managed between panicked breaths.

"LL! Don't think I won't hang up on you. You tell me now what's going on? You're turning me white, girl."

"It's—Liv. She's gonna kill—me. Call cops," I couldn't catch my breath. "m'at office place."

"Wait, what? That don't make any sense."

Liv got out of her car, clutching something that looked like a short pipe.

There were tears shiny on her cheeks as the neon light pollution played on her face. I was the one in pain, why was she the one crying?

"She's—coming." I stumbled to my feet.

"Hang in there, girl. The cops'll be on their way. LL, listen to me. Don't be afraid to take a bitch out, you feel me?"

"How could you do this to me, Ellie?" Liv cried. With a jerk, the rod she held in her hand extended to a full on bat-sized life-beater. An ASP baton!

This was probably going to hurt a lot. "Oh God, Surge, I'm scared." I took a step, and my eyes teared up. The best I could do was hobble away, but there wasn't a chance in hell I was going to turn my back on Liv now.

"I don't want to let you go, baby girl, but I gotta call the cops. I gotta save you, I gotta…Dammit, Emanuella, you survive. Please, baby."

Surge's voice was so strained with worry I felt I had to fight to save him from a lifetime of if-onlys. "Okay. Okay."

Liv growled and lunged, lashing out. I raised my fist to ward off the blow and cried out as the baton smashed through the cell into my palm. The hot rush of blood filled my hand and it began to swell. The bits of phone fell from my numb fingertips. I was gonna owe Surge a phone—if I lived.

Grabbing a nearby trash-can lid with my good hand, I blocked her wild swings like I carried a medieval buckler. "Liv, stop!"

She swung the baton down on me. The soft rubber girth took the blow, but I knew Liv would simply readjust and try again and again until she hit pay dirt.

"I thought you would come to me," she pleaded between strikes. "I thought you were special. We were special!"

"And I thought you weren't mentally deranged. I guess we were both wrong."

She came at me with a shriek of rage, wielding her weapon over her head.

Twenty-six

Using her anger against her, I let her take another swing and miss. Once she teetered off balance, I drove a shoulder into her side and sent her flailing into the garbage cans.

I ran.

I knew she wouldn't be far behind me, but I liked my chances. I had a bit of distance to offset the handicap of a screwed-up ankle and throbbing hand.

I couldn't wait for the cops to come, but if I could make it to Haze's subdivision, I'd have the backing of my crew. I needed to scale the first building and take the chase to the rooftops where I'd be at an advantage.

With my survival instincts pumping me full of fuel, I made the leap to the bottom rung of the fire escape of the office building. I pulled my knees up to my chest and was looking for purchase when Liv's ASP slammed against the foot of the injured ankle. I yelled, but managed to get my feet on the bottom rung without putting too much pressure on my injured foot, and began ascending the ladder. I chanced a glance over my shoulder but immediately wished I hadn't.

In one swift motion, Liv closed the ASP with a tap against

the wall, and backed up a few feet. She let her arms dangle at her sides, her eyes focused on the emergency ladder.

Oh my God, she was going to make the jump. I realized if she was the killer she probably wasn't as fearful of heights as she claimed, but parkour-dabbling? It was too much.

I turned my head back to the wall and ran up the rungs three at a time. The moment I set foot on the tar and paper roof, I knew I wouldn't make the run.

Pain, pain, pain. My foot felt as though it were on fire and five times its normal size.

Keep running. Don't stop.

I felt the panic rise in my throat as I hobbled over to the opposite side of the roof and peered over. The distance looked daunting. In my condition, I'd most likely fall and break some bones on the landing, leaving me easy prey for my deranged ex-best friend.

"You won't make it," Liv stated behind me.

I turned to face her, trembling with anger. Anger at myself for stalling out, anger at Liv for deceiving me, and most importantly, anger at her for trying to kill me.

Why was she trying to kill me? What did I do? I was about to expose that she killed Heather, but that was only a recent development.

"I told Surge and he'll tell everyone. Killing me isn't going to cover this up. It's over," I said.

She came closer to me, slicing the air with practice swings of the baton like she was a professional fencer warming up or something. Nothing would surprise me anymore.

"I mean it, Liv. Surge is calling the cops right now! Your best bet is to run."

"I panicked and left too soon," Liv said, sighing as if she were annoyed with herself. "I was so afraid someone would see me because Decay's window tint wasn't dark enough that I didn't finish the job. I should've backed up and ran Surge over again and again until that thug-wanna-be had to be toothpicked out of the tire tread. I'd have shot him but I couldn't risk having the gun on me after shooting Decay."

All the air was sucked out of my brain, leaving me lightheaded. I didn't care anymore why she wanted me dead. She sounded so casual about something so evil that I wanted to kill *her*.

I reached down to the roof, grasping whatever I could wrap my fingers around and hurled stones and chipped pieces of tar at her. "You bitch! Why? Surge never did anything to you."

The debris bounced off her chest, only one stone scraped across her cheek. She barely reacted, merely flinched and brushed a hand down the front of her shirt to get rid of the dirt like some fucking android.

"How could I get to you with him sniffing his way up your ass all the time, Ellie? Warp's little lap dog on a mission to save you."

Warp. He was the thing that Heather and I had in common.

Liv didn't receive attention from my brother like she used to. Wrapped up in the school merger and protecting me, he didn't have time for Liv anymore...and after she'd killed Heather and everything...

My laugh sounded dry and empty when it echoed back to me. "You stupid whore! You think my brother will have you after this? He'll know the truth."

"You think I want your brother?" She pursed her lips together and looked off to the side as though she were replaying the last week or so over in her head. "I guess I could see where you'd come up with that."

I took a step back, but the rough tip of her ASP pointed into my neck. I froze, waiting for next move while my mind scrambled around for the best way to block her next attack from each conceivable angle.

"I did kill Heather because she was with your brother. You're right-on, there. She stood me up that night. We'd painted a beautiful masterpiece together. We were supposed to finish it and show it to her little brother. Homage to his talent for his birthday, complete with the tree he could never paint quite right. Heather wasn't there, so I started without her and waited. And waited. And waited," she choked. "I was going to ruin the piece on purpose. Fuck her and her brother, I don't allow anyone to stand me up! And I was going to tell her so when she arrived."

Liv's face changed from fury to hurt, swinging from mood to mood like an overactive monkey swings from branch to branch. "But when she finally showed up, she looked so beautiful I was ready to forgive her anything. Then she said she had to tell me something, but I had to promise not to tell a single soul until she did. She wanted to tell her brother and her family that she discovered love."

She stepped around me, keeping the baton pressed against my neck, her voice laced with heartbreak. "I thought I'd already shown it to her."

Oh! I shivered as the pieces fell into place. "She loved my brother—and not you. You killed her because you came in second? That's so stupid, Liv!"

"Like you'd know anything about coming in second, or third or...last, Heather!" I could hear her momentary lapse of control in the vibration of her voice. She'd called me Heather, but I didn't want to point out her mistake. Whether she noticed or not, I couldn't say. She took a little breath and the silence scared me.

"She was your friend, your best friend. You shouldn't have felt so threatened just because she liked Warp."

"You don't get it. For months she wanted to practice parkour and begged me to learn with her. I did whatever she wanted because I thought it was something she wanted to do together for fun, as a break from graffiti. But she was training to impress HIM, to become HIS! She gave herself to that asshole when she belonged to me."

And there was her motive. I'd heard all I needed. Maybe too much. Didn't villains usually kill someone after they revealed their secrets? Just in case it was true, I picked that moment to throw my elbow back into her gut. She stumbled back, giving me precious seconds to throw myself on the mercy of fate.

Two steps to the ledge and I pushed off.

I arched my back and held my arms straight out from my head, focusing my gaze on my ideal landing site, but I wouldn't make it. Already, my momentum reeled me in short.

Mid flight I realized I wouldn't land on the roof but if I reached out, I could grab the edge. The fingers on my right hand had a solid grip but my left hand was too numb with pain to clamp down. I couldn't be sure how strong my hold was.

My feet planted against the side of another office building, catching the rest of my body and taking the hit, but I could feel the gravel dig and tear at my fingertips. I wouldn't last long in the hang.

I struggled to haul myself over the rim, hefting my weight up until I dragged my elbows under my chest to support my balance.

I had to stop and rest with my legs still dangling, waiting for the pain to subside long enough to pull myself over. But time wasn't mine to use.

Looking over my shoulder, I saw Liv backstepping to make a run and knew I had to vault myself onto the roof or she'd kill me. All it would take was a single kick to the face or a stomp on my good hand and I'd fall to my death—like Heather.

"Oh, God. Someone help!" Screaming for my life wasn't something I ever imagined I'd do, but I didn't imagine someone wanting to murder me either.

The blur of Liv as she sailed past me and landed on the roof gave me the adrenaline rush I needed to pull myself over the edge. I fell heavily on the rooftop, at least, but I could barely move.

"You were supposed to make it all better," Liv said, panting with exertion. "But then you were hiding shit from me too. You were seeing Heather's brother, fucking him in some closet like a dirty skank!"

Even breathing hurt. I was done. My only weapon was my voice. "No. I never!"

"I don't believe you." She came closer and took the ASP out of her back pocket, flicking it open to its full lethal potential.

The blunt object slammed into my side and I screamed again, hating the sound of my pain as it bounced off the cityscape and came right back at me.

"I don't believe you, Ellie," she repeated, looking so sad. "I put myself out there for you, taking out that mutinous gymnast bitch."

Holy hell. She shot Wenda, too? I didn't want to hear any more. "Liv, stop."

"You disappointed me! We had a moment, didn't we? You held me in my room and made me think everything would be okay. Things were over between you and Haze and we could be together."

Tears of pain spilled down my face, and I hated that I wasn't strong enough to stop them. Maybe I could at least make use of them. "I never…meant to hurt you. I'm sorry, Livia."

"I'm sorry, Livia," she mocked, sniffling as she wiped her free hand across her nose. "The same thing Heather said!" She sobbed. "But she wasn't sorry. Just like you're not sorry! You kept lying to me and lying to me. Do you have any idea how much it hurt knowing I'd have to kill you, too?"

"What's the point? Everyone will know what you've done."

"Funny how a gang war cleans up a lot of messes. With Decay dead, Haze is going to come running with his crew to meet your brother and friends—how likely do you think it is they're going to start talking things out when they see each other?"

It was like she hit me in the gut, but this time it wasn't with her weapon.

She'd killed Decay, and tried to kill Surge, all to start a war. She'd arranged everything…all to silence me and to keep her murder of Heather a secret forever.

The worst part was that I wouldn't be the only person to die. Warp and Haze would kill each other, their boys striking out until none who knew the truth were left standing.

Well, one would be.

Liv.

The death toll would make national headlines and the story would be used for public service announcements but no one would ever know the truth.

"Somebody help me!" But I knew even if someone heard me they wouldn't be able to pinpoint where the yelling was coming from. They'd only arrive in time for the cleanup.

"LL?"

I heard his voice and experienced a fleeting moment of relief. Even though I couldn't see him, I knew he was there.

Liv's head snapped up and she tightened her grip on the baton, as if anticipating killing him, too. Okay I wanted someone to help me, but not him. I couldn't bear the thought of him dying trying to save me.

"Haze! Run. G-get help," I yelled and threw a feeble kick at Liv's ankle. She hopped backwards, easily evading my pathetic attempt.

My battered foot and tired legs no longer able to hold me up without serious effort, I rolled to my knees and lifted myself to see over the parapet of the roof. Sure enough, Haze stood on the roof of the office supply building beside ours, the one I'd told Surge about. Also the one I'd just leapt from.

Figures.

My head lolled back, revolting against the effort it took to keep it upright, but I wanted to see him until my eyes shut down forever.

I tightened my hold on the rim of the parapet with one hand and reached for him with the other. Haze. My Brennen Craig.

I saw him turn his head to the side for a moment as though he were trying to collect himself. I could only imagine how much of a mess I looked. My fingers were bleeding all over the place, and I was sure I was smeared with blood too.

"Manu..."

"It's okay." My voice hiccupped on a sob. "It'll be okay."

"No," he said, shaking his head.

Liv coiled a hand in the back of my hoodie and hauled me up to my feet, bracing my weight between the roof edge and her body. "This is your fault, Brennen! If you'd just stayed away from her—"

I could barely stand, so I had no delusions about how easy it'd be for her to shove me to my death. I also knew I didn't have anything left in the tank to work a little traceur magic and save my ass this time.

"Emanuella!" I heard my brother yell my name and glanced over my shoulder.

Liv spun us to face him and cussed.

"Liv," Warp yelled, "what the hell are you doing? Let my sister go."

"You," she screeched, "you took Heather from me, once, but this one stays with me."

My body jerked as she pulled me toward the roof's edge.

"No!" My brother yelled. "Liv, wait, let me explain. Heather and I, that was just a phase for her. She cared about you much more than she did me. There was this time she told me all about—"

I stopped listening.

From the corner of my eye I spotted Haze taking a few steps back from the ledge like he was going to try to make the jump. Risky for someone new to parkour and I doubted he'd be able to land faster than Liv could throw me.

The fact he wanted to rescue me did make me smile. So did my brother's lies to Liv and my crew's words of encouragement murmured in the background. Actually, everything made me smile. I guess facing my death made the last few moments of my life seem glorious.

"Not this time," Liv was saying. I tried to focus.

"LL, stay with us, girl." The crew shouted. Like they all knew I was visiting fairyland.

My backside rested on the top of the parapet as Liv jumped on top of it and pushed until I hung over the edge. Oh God, oh God. Would it hurt?

I could see an upside-down Haze, his face scowling with determination, and in the jumble of screams, I heard his command. "Don't go without her!"

It took a second for his words to catch, but I got the message in time.

She dropped her hold on my hoodie and I began the descent, but damn if I was going alone. My gift to my brother and to Haze. I'd kill the girl who killed Heather—and me. I grabbed onto her boot and held tight, closing my eyes as I surrendered to the death fall.

Twenty-seven

Something hard nailed my side, and my fingers lost their grip. I should have been falling to my death, but instead an arm coiled around my waist and painfully snatched me out of midair. My spine bent awkwardly, snapped out of motion and I knew I'd have whiplash from hell, but the pain only meant I was alive and safe in Haze's trembling arms—well arm.

"Brennen," I whispered. "How'd you—?"

"Kong-to-Cat, baby," he said through gnashed teeth.

Taking a flying leap over the ledge, he'd snagged me midair before he landed with one hand on the windowpane and the other around me. His legs bore the brunt of the impact and because we were really, really lucky, we lived.

He blinked several times, fighting to keep the smile on his face through the strain of holding me, or maybe he fought back the emotions of the moment.

"Jesus Christ, Emanuella."

I peered up at the roof to see my brother and crew staring back at me, their eyes rounded with panic. "We thought she—"

"A little help here, fellas?" Haze grunted.

Warp and the others scrambled over the parapet, climbing down to where Haze and I hung precariously on a window ledge.

Once my brother helped me to the fire escape, I looked down at the alley floor.

Liv lay on the ground, bathed in street light and an expanding pool of blood. Her arms and legs were twisted awkwardly.

I knew I shouldn't stare, that I needed to look away instead of searing the image into my brain for life, but I couldn't force myself to close my eyes. The reality of the situation was far from locked in, and I suspected it would take me a long while to come to terms with how close I'd come to dying.

Sirens wailed and people came out of the municipal building, some to make sure we were okay, others to threaten us if we didn't leave, but we barely heard.

Haze threw his arms around me and kissed all over my face once we were both on solid ground. Warp nudged him aside, but only to get his own hugs in.

"Ow, shit! Gently, Warp."

"I thought you were dead," Warp said, his voice thick with emotion. "Surge kept calling us all. Haze was closest but even he wasn't near enough…we all thought…we didn't know if we'd make it."

"I know. I'm all right, though. It's all over." I'd tell him anything if it meant he'd let go.

My brother kept an arm around me while he issued orders to the rest of the guys. "Go wave down the cops, they're on the wrong side of the block."

When the crew scattered, an awkward silence stretched between Haze, Warp, and me. The two of them had been close to violence just a little while ago. How could they start a conversation after threatening to kill each other?

I eased out of Warp's hold and limped to Haze, burying my head beneath his chin. I stared at my brother, proclaiming with actions what I was too tired to do with words.

Warp looked between my boyfriend and me, and then reluctantly nodded his head. "You saved my sister's life tonight, man," he said, his voice hesitant but free of venom.

"I wouldn't have been able to deal if she'd—" Haze obviously didn't want to think about what could've happened. I didn't blame him. I didn't want to think about it either.

He kissed the top of my head repeatedly, as if reassuring himself that he didn't dream my rescue.

"I'm okay," I whispered and met my brother's eyes to let him know, too.

"Liv." Warp mused. He looked over the edge, probably staring at Liv's mangled body just as I had. I knew thinking of my ex-best friend as a murderer was hard to process. "She killed Heather."

"She shot Wenda, killed Decay, then used his car to run down Surge."

"Shit's messed." Warp ran a hand over his face, trying to downplay wiping the wetness in his eyes. I reached out and squeezed his hand and he held mine. For several minutes, we all just stood there, too crazed in the head to think or even speak.

Once the cops arrived on scene and the crew returned, Warp cleared his throat and dropped my hold. "A lot of rumors to set straight to retract the war."

"Won't be easy," Haze agreed, his words vibrating against my skull as he rested his chin on my head. It felt good to have him so close.

"Starts here, I guess." Warp held out his hand and urged Haze to take it with an up-nod.

I moved to Haze's side, so he and my brother could make peace face-to-face.

"Gotta start somewhere," Haze said with a weak smile as he shook my brother's hand.

"How grounded am I for this one?" I whispered as Pops rolled me down the hospital corridor toward the exit.

"You gotta tell me what you mean by 'this one,' Emanuella. If by 'this one' you mean breaking into the high school, I'd say at least a week. If you're talking about you lying to me about everything being okay at home, then you're grounded until you graduate. But I suppose, factoring in your involvement for solving a two-year-old murder and helping a nice family get closure, I guess we'll call it fair with two weeks."

I pursed my lips and thought about that. Two weeks was more generous than I'd expected Pops to be. I imagined the fact that I'd lived through a murder attempt was swaying him a little. "Sounds fair." I smiled.

My smile twitched when I noticed who stood beside my dad's rig. "You didn't tell me."

"He wanted it to be a surprise."

"So, is he gonna play good cop or bad cop?"

My Pops leaned around the side of my wheelchair until I could see his mischievous grin. "You figure it out. Either way, a couple of lectures all week from Ander will keep you in line until your graduation."

I groaned, but in my heart I was extremely glad to see my elder brother, no matter the scowl. I couldn't tell if it was a scowl of worry, or a sign of one of the impending lectures my Pops referred to.

We neared the rig and Ander helped me out of the chair. Lucky for me, he didn't chime right in to the "should have told me" rant. Instead, he wrapped me up in his six-foot-two frame and hugged me tight.

After a moment he stepped back and looked into my eyes,

tucking my blue lock of hair behind my ear with a smile. "Way to run the course, baby Sis."

His praise meant the world to me. I threw myself back into his arms and cried.

We drove up to the circus that was my house. A few news vans were parked outside, ready to swoop down with a ton of uncomfortable questions, on the girl who solved a chilly case.

Bad enough the media had nearly run my dad's rig off the road trying to get a personal interview, but now they were going to stalk me at home.

"It looks like your release from the hospital got passed around the horn."

I nodded to my dad and snuggled deeper in the crook of Ander's arm as we pulled into the driveway.

Microphones and flashes assaulted me and I was glad for Ander's support. He pushed and pulled until we were through the throng and safely behind the front door.

"We're good. Pops will run them off."

"Our appearance here probably doesn't help. Sorry, Manu."

I peeked out from Ander's chest and saw Haze standing there with his parents. "Brennen," I cried and flung myself at him.

When he laughed, I could feel it while he held me. "Hey, there."

"I missed you," I said and backed up a little to peer up at his handsome face. I knew I should probably act more proper in front of his family but I couldn't help it.

"And I you. I'm sorry I couldn't visit you sooner. We've been a little press-harassed, and we were afraid they'd follow us to the hospital."

I nodded. "It doesn't matter. You're here now."

He smiled and swept a hand toward the couple beside him. "Mom, Dad, this is M—Emanuella."

I broke away from Haze long enough to shake the hands of both his parents. "Mr. and Mrs. Craig, it's very nice to meet you."

"We won't stay long. We understand you're still recovering," Mr. Craig said.

"We wanted to—" Mrs. Craig swallowed and looked up at her husband for moral support. He nodded and she turned to face me again. "All this time we've wondered about Heather and who would do such a thing. You're such a brave girl and we can't begin to—"

Her tears brought on my own, and I went to her. "It's okay. It's okay. I know." I didn't want to hear her struggle for words anymore, it was easier to just stand there and grieve together.

"I told myself I wasn't gonna have to fill one of these out, ever," Surge said and shook his head as he crumpled up a red paper heart and tossed it in the trash. Obviously he was having problems expressing himself.

I poked him. "Don't make me cry again. Just focus on the positive, like me. I'm filling this out for one instead of many."

"Yeah, I know. I'm just glad I signed your cast and not your funeral home visitor's log."

I winced at Surge's ever-blunt speak and looked down at the cast on my foot. It was broken, but I'd heal and be back on the beam by next season. "Yeah. Thank goodness for that."

I signed Decay's paper heart, blinking back tears. Surge wrapped an arm around me and walked with me to where Haze and Warp stood talking next to the memorial wall.

In the weeks since the incident, the two of them had become good friends. Haze wanted to be accepted as my boyfriend and Warp felt permanently indebted to Haze for saving my life.

Whatever kept them from killing each other was fine by me.

Maybe the violence of the school would ebb, now that two of the biggest groups stood back-to-back in friendship instead of face-to-face in challenge. I sighed and taped my heart to the office window, trying not to notice how little space was left.

I truly hoped the wars were over because I was pretty damned sick of drama.

"Hey, hands off," Haze said to Surge with a grin. His arm replaced that of my best friend's, and we all walked down the hall to our lockers.

"Hey Emaneulla," a student I didn't recognize called to me.

His friend said hello to me as well. And another student, and another, until I finally stopped in my tracks. "What the hell is going on?"

"Popularity comes with heroics." Haze grinned at me.

"Yeah, the way I bled all over the place was real heroic."

Warp laughed. "No one falls off a building like you do, LL."

"Yeah, yeah," I said and rolled my eyes.

"It's true," Surge insisted. "You're a living legend…like a comic book hero or something."

"Oh God, make him stop," I pleaded.

Warp laughed at me and Haze kissed the top of my head.

"Lady of the Ledge," Surge said, putting his love-master voice behind the title. "I came up with that, yanno."

"Guess that makes you cool by association," Warp quipped.

"Naw, man. I'm just cool."

We all laughed, glad to have something to laugh about, and walked down the hall leaving the red paper hearts behind us.

Author's Note

Parkour, and/or freerunning, is near and dear to my heart. I've followed the expression soon after it first hit the Internet and researched as much as I could about it for several years. I confess that I am not a professional traceur, just an avid fan. I haven't jumped head-first into forum and blog debates over what it means to be a freerunner. I wouldn't dare to presume. With this book, I'm not looking to make any declarations; I'm simply using my love of something real, and making a fictional story from it. Though freerunner tribes in this book are treated as gangs, it is important to me to stress this is a manipulation that gives the finger to truth for purposes of entertainment. It is my hope that within these pages my respect for freedom of movement is clearly stated

To receive a free catalog of Poisoned Pen Press titles, please provide your name, address, and email address in one of the following ways:

Phone: 1-800-421-3976
Facsimile: 1-480-949-1707
Email: info@poisonedpenpress.com
Website: www.poisonedpenpress.com

Poisoned Pen Press
6962 E. First Ave. Ste 103
Scottsdale, AZ 85251